What the Pauper Did

A BODY SWAP MYSTERY ROMANCE

MARINA PACHECO

MARINA PACHECO

Get all my short stories for FREE!

Building a relationship with my readers is one of the great things about being a writer. That is why I continue to upload a wide collection of short stories for free on my website. These currently include a collection of short stories, and some individual longer short stories including a Galen spin off, a quirky tale about a rabbit in Lisbon and a couple of Christmas romances.

Sign up for my no-spam newsletter that only goes out when there is a new book or freebie available, at: www.marinapacheco.me

Contents

Historical background   VII

1. Chapter 1   1

2. Chapter 2   15

3. Chapter 3   23

4. Chapter 4   39

5. Chapter 5   58

6. Chapter 6   67

7. Chapter 7   83

8. Chapter 8   94

9. Chapter 9   112

10. Chapter 10   126

11. Chapter 11   144

12. Chapter 12   158

13. Chapter 13   182

14. Chapter 14   204

15. Chapter 15   214

16. Chapter 16   228

17. Chapter 17   236

18. Chapter 18   244

19. Chapter 19   264

20. Chapter 20   271

21. Chapter 21   285

Also By   290

About Author   294

Acknowledgments   295

Historical background

I have been a frequent visitor to Portugal for the last 30 years and relocated here nearly four years ago. It is a beautiful, relaxed, sunny country, and I have been inspired to write a series of novels based in and around Lisbon. Lisbon is apparently one of the oldest capital cities in Europe, with a fascinating history, but unless you're a local, or a fan of Portuguese history, it's unlikely that you'll know much about it. I set this novel during a formative moment in Lisbon's history: the rebuilding of the city after a devastating natural disaster.

In 1755, on the morning of All Saints' Day, a massive earthquake struck Lisbon. Forty minutes later, the city was swamped by a succession of tidal waves. Finally, the remaining ruins were reduced to ashes by a fire that raged for five days. The quake was so huge that its effects were felt in North Africa, Brazil, the Caribbean and southern England. Around 40,000 of the original 200,000 inhabitants of Lisbon were killed and 85% of the city's buildings were destroyed.

News of the destruction of Lisbon was carried to every corner of Europe. The fact that the earthquake struck on a Holy Day when most of the residents were in church and that the churches collapsed, killing the occupants, profoundly shook religious establishments and strongly influenced the intelligentsia of the European Age of Enlightenment.

While I set this book in the historical context of Lisbon and the earthquake, I have created entirely different characters for this novel. As far as I am aware, not a single one of the people I describe existed. I did model the duque on the Marques de Pombal. He was the man responsible for holding the kingdom together after the quake and rebuilding the city as a modern model of the Enlightenment. By all accounts, he was a cruel and vengeful man, but he also created a city so beautiful that tourists continue flocking to it to this day.

A note on language

To preserve some of the flavour of the Portuguese context of the novel, I have opted for the Portuguese spelling of duke, so you will see it written as duque.

Portuguese people are still quite formal and even now will address letters to Your Excellency or even Your Exulted Excellency. So you will see characters with no official standing addressed as Your Excellency in the novel.

The unit of currency at the time was the real, which, translated into English, would be 'royal'. The plural for real in Portuguese is reais, which I have used in the novel because writing it as reals just looked weird to me.

1

The man was certain someone had cleaved his skull open with an axe and left it there, and he feared what he would see if he opened his eyes. That was if he *could* open his eyes. It would take a monumental effort. Even breathing was so painful he wished he could stop the rise and fall of his chest for the moment of relief it might give him.

He forced an eyelid open a crack – one would have to do. Through this gap, he could see an ornate ceiling. Someone had built the dark, crisscrossing wooden beams up in layers to achieve a three-dimensional effect of squares and had painted hunting scenes inside each square.

The throbbing in his head made the squares advance and retreat, leaving him woozy. He closed his eye and tried to gather his forces. What in God's name had happened?

The sound of somebody clearing their throat penetrated through the drumming in his ears and he forced his eyes open again.

'Who the devil are you?' he muttered at the man looming over him.

He was dressed in black, which didn't augur well.

'You made quite the night of it, didn't you, master?' the man said in a thick, phlegmy, far-too-loud voice.

The man feared his eardrums might burst but the words did permeate into his befuddled brain. They didn't ring true.

'I'm hungover?'

'Can't say I've ever seen you in a worse state,' the man said in an inappropriately cheerful voice. 'It took four lads to carry you up to your bed.'

'My bed?'

He tried to turn his head to get a view of what he could only make out as a vague outline with four tall posts. There was definitely something wrong; no hangover caused you to lose your ability to recognise people and familiar places.

'I feared you'd be feeling under the weather, so I brought you this, master,' the man said, holding a mug up to his lips. 'It's a fine, reviving cordial.'

'It will have to be a bloody miracle cure to be of any use.'

'That it is, sir, that it is,' the mysterious man in black said, and lifted his head up only enough to sip the cordial.

He feared he might black out, but the drink that was tipped into his mouth distracted him. It was either swallow or choke. So he gulped it down.

'That's better, master. You'll be feeling right as rain in no time at all.'

'I very much doubt that,' he said and slipped back into oblivion.

∼∞∼

'You look perfect,' Lady Odete said as she added the last pin to young Lady Mafalda's piled high hairdo, with rosebuds artfully dotted amongst the curls.

It was the best Odete could do and she hoped it would keep the young lady happy.

Lady Mafalda examined herself in the gilt-framed mirror and her eyes narrowed.

'I don't like it.' Then she turned to the other ladies-in-waiting. 'Maria da Luz, Pia, what do you think?'

The two women gazed thoughtfully at the fifteen-year-old. They and Odete had been her ladies-in-waiting for three years now, and they knew how temperamental she could be. Sometimes Mafalda was charming, and sometimes she was a spoiled brat. She was an extremely powerful brat, the only remaining child of the Duque de Louredo, so Odete, Maria and Pia always weighed their words carefully before speaking.

'It is the height of fashion,' Maria da Luz said with an envious sigh as she patted her generous belly. 'I wish I could look half as pretty in anything. But even the weight loss charm I bought at great expense from the best witch in Lisbon has done nothing for me.'

'You don't need a charm you just need to eat less,' Mafalda said, staring meaningfully at Maria as she helped herself to a dainty almond tart from a silver salver on the dressing table that was topped to overflowing with sugary treats, and bit it in half.

'Your father will be very pleased,' she added with a puff of icing sugar as she held the remains of the tart just in front of her mouth.

Maria's strength, Odete had always thought, was her ability to ignore anything she didn't want to hear.

'It really is lovely. The prince will like it too.'

Pia always stepped in to try and prevent arguments. She was the youngest of the three ladies-in-waiting and with her staring blue eyes and flyaway fair hair, she always looked frazzled.

'The prince?' Mafalda said. 'I don't give a snap of my fingers for the prince and what he would or would not like.'

'No, no, of course not, I'm sure. I didn't mean to imply–'

'You just look very pretty,' Odete said. 'None will outshine you today.'

'They'd better not,' Mafalda said, as she looked Odete up and down.

It was Odete's misfortune to be considered the prettiest of the three ladies-in-waiting. She thought she looked rather dull, with her dark brown hair and dark brown eyes, but she had to admit to a pretty pair of bow-shaped lips and gracefully arching dark eyebrows, not to mention thick, dark lashes that accentuated her pale skin.

The fashion was for fair ladies now. If they couldn't achieve that through nature, they applied copious amounts of powder and paste for the required effect. For that reason, Mafalda's hair had a light dusting of white powder that made her look at once fair and older than a fifteen-year-old should.

'Anyway, now that I am dressed, let's go for a walk.'

Mafalda shook out her sky-blue skirt and examined the pink rosebuds embroidered along the edge of her matching blue gown. An inverted triangular stomacher of blue, heavily ornamented with pink ribbons, pressed flat against her chest and gave her face a pinkish hue of reflected light.

'Where would you like to go?' Odete asked.

They had a limited choice for their walks. They were not allowed to leave the royal palace. It was an enormous building but, after three years of living there, Odete knew every nook and cranny and wished every day that she could leave.

Their only respite was when they left the heat of the city in the summer and headed for the royal palace in Sintra. That palace was perched on the edge of a mountain beside a small town surrounded by lush and pleasantly cool forests.

'Let's promenade down the south walk,' Mafalda said. 'It's boiling and I fancy we have the best chance of a cool breeze coming up the river from there.'

'As well as the reek of fish,' Maria da Luz said cheerfully.

'Oh dear, yes, the smell of fish is always so intense there,' Pia murmured.

'It shouldn't be so bad after last night's storm,' Odete said. 'That's sure to have washed away the worst of the smell.'

'But the rain has made everything so humid. It's exhausting. I hope we'll relocate to Sintra soon.'

'That is up to my father,' Mafalda said.

Which was true, Odete thought, but not right. The Duque de Louredo, uncle to the prince, had acted as regent since the king and queen were killed in the great earthquake fifteen years ago. He'd held the kingdom together and overseen the rebuilding of Lisbon while the prince had lain at death's door. Over the following years the duque had cemented his power and now hung on, even though the prince had long since reached his majority.

Odete wondered whether the prince would ever be able to wrest the kingdom away from his uncle's cruel grip. There were whispers at court about the battle between the prince and the duque, but so far no change in who was in charge.

True, the duque had rebuilt a shattered and shocked capital city that earned him the people's gratitude. Too much gratitude, for he'd appropriated land and swept much away to rebuild the city in the classical ideal he had for it. People complained, but the duque didn't care.

The city was his masterpiece. Odete got the impression that he was more interested in the perfect straight roads and classical buildings he was putting up than in the city's people. They were still suffering.

She followed Mafalda, Pia and Maria da Luz as they stepped out into the wide corridor that linked all the rooms on this upper level of the palace. It was as wide as a main road and immaculately decorated. Yet more of the duque's influence. He'd insisted that the palace had to reflect the glory of the kingdom.

The fact that the kingdom had suffered a severe financial blow because of the earthquake didn't concern him at all. So the four ladies drifted along an avenue of blue and white tiled walls with swirling yellow frames that depicted idealised courtly pursuits. Life-sized ladies and gentlemen cavorted through a landscape of forests, swung from the branches of billowing trees or hunted a rich variety of game. Their life looked more idyllic than her own.

It was a quiet day in the palace and, aside from a couple of servants, it didn't look like they would run into anybody. This suited Odete. She preferred to avoid the hangers-on, nobility, businessmen and every other person who found a reason to see the duque.

She was just thinking they might reach the south balcony without having to stop and make small talk when the duque himself stepped out of the music room, followed by Prince Juliano. Odete froze. Both men always had that effect upon her. The duque because she was afraid of him. He had genuine power and was ruthless with it. Power he'd used when he'd visited her mother to request that Odete become a lady-in-waiting to his daughter.

Odete had objected and he'd turned round and said, 'My dear, what makes you think you have a choice? Your future holds nothing greater than what I have to offer. Your father is dead. Your family is impoverished. You have no chance of finding a husband under these circumstances. The only advantage you have is that your family has royal blood. It comes from an ancient and defunct line, admittedly, but it is royal and makes you a suitable companion. The best you can do is to become a lady-in-waiting.'

She'd been crushed, and her mother, very flustered, had accepted the duque's offer without further discussion. The duque gave Odete twenty minutes to pack and then took her to the palace, although, thankfully, not in the same coach as him.

His complete indifference to her and her plight hurt her then and continued to do so.

Prince Juliano was another matter. Her heart had given an unfamiliar flutter the first time she saw him and she felt foolish and tongue-tied whenever she saw him thereafter. But when she found the courage to look up into his face for the first time, she discovered he was smiling at her.

That had annoyed her and she'd stared defiantly back, which had made him laugh. From then onwards, he always gave her a smile when they passed each other in the palace. Occasionally, he'd even stop and exchange a few pleasantries. Usually it was about the weather, or some activity at court. It could never be more than that because the prince had to marry someone of rank and influence. If the duque had his way, it would be marriage to his daughter.

Odete wished with all her heart that it could be otherwise. However, much as she hated the duque, he was right. She was the impoverished daughter of a minor noble; a posthumous child, the last of a large family left in dire straits by her father's death. She had to accept that she would never marry.

Still, she watched Prince Juliano as he and the duque approached. Despite the fact that the duque had married into the royal family, the two men shared an uncanny similarity. Both men were tall and slim, with narrow shoulders and narrow hips. But while the duque was grey and his face was craggy and lined with age, the prince had jet-black hair tied at the base of his neck with a black ribbon, and a handsome face with firm lips and wide grey eyes. He was the definition of princely perfection.

'Ah, I see you are out for a walk,' the duque said to his daughter.

'It's getting too hot and stuffy to stay in my room, and I'm bored,' Mafalda said, pointedly not looking at the prince.

He looked different today, Odete thought. He wasn't wearing his usual black, but had opted for a dark blue suit, spangled with silver stars. He also looked pale, and a frown creased his perfect brow.

What was infinitely worse was that he appeared not to notice her. He always gave the ladies a bow and bestowed a smile upon them that ended at Odete. Today it was as if they didn't exist.

'If I am to find Tiago, I have to go,' Prince Juliano said in what Odete could only describe as a petulant tone.

It surprised her; she'd never heard him speak this way before. His uncle often infuriated him to the point where they'd both be shouting at each other, but he'd never whined.

'Are you going to greet your betrothed at least?' the duque said.

Prince Juliano looked for a moment like he was unsure which of the women was his betrothed. Then he apparently decided it was the tall, skinny girl standing right in front of him. He took her hand and gave it a perfunctory kiss as he murmured a distracted greeting.

'Now, I must be off,' he said, as he bowed to the duke and hurried away.

He didn't notice the stir his behaviour created but it left the ladies bereft of speech.

'Well!' Mafalda gasped.

'Juliano is not himself today,' the duque said. He gave the ladies a nod and wandered away.

'Prince Juliano isn't himself?' Pia said. 'He has never, ever, kissed your hand.'

'He always repudiates your father's claim of betrothal and keeps his distance,' Maria da Luz said. 'What has got into him today?'

It was an excellent question, Odete thought, because the man walking so briskly away from them wasn't even walking in the way he used to. Something was wrong and she was willing to bet it either had something to do with the duque or the grand alchemist, Dr Zuniga. Who knew what kind of mysterious magic the alchemist could cast? Her only consolation was that Dr Zuniga was an ally to Prince Juliano so if magic was involved it was more likely to be cast in the prince's favour.

The ladies had started walking again when Mafalda came to a sudden stop.

'What did he mean that he had to find Tiago?'

Odete had been so distracted by the prince's behaviour that his words hadn't registered. While Mafalda had no interest in the prince, they had all seen her increasing infatuation with Lord Tiago Andrade, bosom companion of the prince.

'I dare say he's running an errand or something like that,' Odete said, making sure to sound untroubled.

'Do you think so?' Mafalda said, and she looked genuinely worried.

'How could she be sure?' Maria da Luz said. 'But Lord Andrade is the prince's best friend. He is surely in no danger.'

'He'd better not be.'

Odete decided silence was the safest option and started walking to the south balcony where the view might distract Mafalda.

The palace was aligned east to west along the Commercial Square, so the south balcony ran along one of the short ends of the building. It was a deep balcony and the roof above was finished in a chocolate brown wood, topped with terracotta tiles.

The balcony's edge was a solid bright white wall. Set at right angles to the wall was a row of facing stone benches. They were only wide enough for a single person, and the arrangement made them perfect for a tête-à-tête.

Since the benches were in the sun, the ladies headed for a collection of wicker chairs pulled against the inner wall of the balcony in the deepest shade.

Odete watched as everyone settled, unfurled their fans and set to cooling themselves. She felt too restless to sit, so knelt on the bench and leaned over the wall for a better view of the harbour below.

Most of the fishing fleet was out and only a couple of men remained on the quayside darning their nets. On the sparkling blue water beyond were the galleons, some filled with cannon and used to protect the city, some used for trade. Beside them were the massive floating castles called carracks. These were the ships that brought the spices, cloth, gold and dye back to Lisbon from the four corners of the world.

Odete looked past the ships to the distant shore where she could make out a small village, little more than a collection of houses clustered in a valley. Pine tree-covered hills rose around the village and flanked the river.

It was the same for Lisbon. Aside from the relatively flat land at the edge of the mighty Tagus river, the rest of the city was built on hills.

On a hot summer's day like today, it felt like the city was inside a bowl that was being baked by the merciless sun. There wasn't even a breeze to cool them.

Odete climbed down from the bench and glanced back at Lady Mafalda and the dozing ladies-in-waiting. How could they even be asleep, when they'd only just risen from their beds?

As it looked like Mafalda might not need her for a while, Odete took out her sketchbook and slipped back into the palace. She would go for a walk, do some drawing and listen for the latest gossip.

When the man woke, he felt numb and disembodied but, thankfully, the pain had subsided. He opened one cautious eye and then the other. A warm golden light filtered through slatted shutters and hinted at late morning.

He stared at the utterly unfamiliar ceiling. It was such a unique design he should have known if he'd seen it before. He looked down at the foot of the bed. Two dark wooden posts spiralled upwards at each corner but stirred no trace of recognition. Beyond the bed was a solid, dark wooden chest, also ornately carved, each twirling carved vine coated in gold leaf. Surely he should remember that.

The sound of snoring drew his gaze to the man in black sitting in a stiff-backed chair pulled up to the side of the bed. His chin was resting on his chest and his hands were folded in his lap. He had a simple grey wig with a couple of rows of curls along the bottom. He was portly, and his fat neck squeezed through a too-tight collar around which was tied a neat white neckcloth. His face was plain and ruddy and he had bushy grey eyebrows.

'You, wake up,' he said and prodded the man in black's ample paunch.

The man gave a snort and stared blearily at him.

'Ah, master, you've finally woken up.'

'I have. Now you'd better tell me who the devil you are.'

The man looked puzzled and said, 'You know me, sir, I'm Arriscado. Surely you can't still be so befuddled that you don't know who I am?'

'Arriscado?'

The name was as unfamiliar to him as the man's face.

'Master, are you feeling alright?' Arriscado asked as he eyed him with gathering concern.

'No, I'm not alright. I don't know who the devil you are and I don't know this room.'

'Oh dear! I fear you must have taken a blow to your head, sir. Surely you can remember me. I have looked after you, man and boy, in this very room. You can't have forgotten all of that.'

'Lies,' he muttered, and pushed himself upright.

He was wearing a white nightdress with lace ruffles around the throat and wrist that was also unfamiliar to him.

'Master, this isn't good. Something is wrong,' Arriscado said as he leaped to his feet, rubbing his hands together anxiously. 'How bad could this possibly be? At least tell me you know your own name.'

'Of course I do,' he snapped and then stopped, one foot just about to land on the floor.

What was his name? This was one thing he must surely know. But now, when asked, he couldn't recall it.

He rubbed his thumb over the base of his ring finger. There should have been a gold ring set with a crest engraved into the red gem. He felt nothing and, as he looked down at his hand, the memory of the ring evaporated. He tried to hold on to it, but it faded as he looked at his bare fingers.

'No,' he muttered, 'I don't know my name.'

'Oh no! You must have been set upon. Somebody must have given you a blow to your head. And there I thought you were drunk. Can you ever forgive me? I'll send for the doctor at once,' Arriscado said and rushed to the door.

'Wait, what is my name?' he shouted after the fast-vanishing servant.

'Herculano, Herculano Escovar,' Arriscado said as he slammed the door shut.

'Herculano Escovar?' he said to the now-empty room. 'Herculano Escovar?' No, that didn't sound familiar either.

He pushed himself upright and clung with one hand to the bedpost to steady himself. The fat valet was right about one thing: this was no ordinary hangover. He took another look around the room while he waited for the dizziness to subside. There was a shuttered French window to his right and a cupboard of dark wood, gold leaf and painted figures that took up the entire left wall. In the centre of this massive piece of furniture was a mirror.

He approached with caution but wasn't as shocked as he might have been to find himself staring at a stranger. Everything else was wrong about this place. He had no expectations about his looks.

It wasn't a bad face. It had a moderate nose, heavily lidded eyes and a generous mouth. A stubble of black hair covered his chin and he ran his fingers over it, feeling its prickly coarseness. The reflection also had darkish brown hair that fell to slightly below his shoulders. Closer examination revealed that it had been powdered and a greyish white dust clung to the roots and speckled the top of a slightly receding hairline.

The man was well built with broad shoulders and muscular arms. All in all, not someone to trifle with. He felt nothing like the man he was staring back at.

A shiver of distaste mingled with fear ran down his spine. This was all wrong, and yet, it had to be him. He had to be Herculano Escovar. How could it be otherwise?

A small portrait in a circular frame propped up against the end of the mirror caught his eye. It was of an elderly man. He looked like a prosperous merchant, with ruddy cheeks and a bit of a paunch. He was dressed in a black suit and his deep brown eyes stared out at the world with a melancholic air. Herculano assumed he had some importance, although he had no idea who he was.

He put down the painting and made his way to the French doors. They stood open, allowing air through the slatted shutters. He paused only for a moment before he pushed them open.

It was brighter outside than he'd expected and the sun dazzled him for a moment. He stepped out onto the small balcony and looked down into a street that he must have seen a thousand times before. Nothing looked familiar here either.

He faced a steep, cobbled street that headed uphill to his left and downhill to his right. It was a wide road with a drain down the middle. It must have rained heavily during the night because the drain was still running with water and accumulated debris.

A well-dressed man and woman walked hand in hand down the street, avoiding the beggars that reached out to them. A gilded sedan chair, carved with images of elephants, was carried up the road by two black men. A fisherwoman and a bread seller shouted their wares, their baskets of produce hitched up against one hip.

Herculano leaned further over the balcony to examine the house he was in. It was by far the largest building on the street and was tiled in a blue and white patterned tile that went all the way to the roofline. A pale grey limestone, carved to resemble scalloped shells, surrounded the large windows. A generous door had the same shell-carved portico and surround.

To the left of the house was another fine building painted canary yellow, and to the right, a house painted a dusty pink. Opposite his house was a ruin, little more than a pile of light-coloured stone and mud. Everything else of use had already been stripped and carried away.

It was a relic from the great earthquake and had yet to be rebuilt. That was probably because the original owner had died in the quake and the state had yet to determine whom the property belonged to now. It was like many such buildings in Lisbon. The reconstruction was going slowly.

To his surprise, he remembered the quake. It was hard to forget the way the earth had turned into a rolling, thundering beast that tossed you about like a ball.

A building had collapsed on top of him. He was suffocating and filled with dread when the wave had swept in. The tar-black, churning wash lifted him from his rocky prison and hurled him along with the deluge, rolling him over with the stone blocks from the houses, pummelling and pushing till he blacked out again.

It was as if his memory stopped there, for, try as he might, he could remember only that. Nothing till the moment he'd opened his eyes in this room. It was as if the two events merged into one.

That couldn't be right. He was a boy during the earthquake, of no more than seven or eight. Now, he was a grown man.

2

D oes this hurt?' the doctor asked as he prodded his fingers over Herculano's skull.

'No, damn it, there are no injuries to my head.'

Herculano had already examined himself before the doctor arrived and told him so, but the man insisted on doing it again. Why couldn't people take somebody else's word for anything?

The doctor was a short, thin man dressed in a tight black suit with extravagant lacy cuffs. One kept flopping into Herculano's eyes, exacerbating his frayed temper.

'Enough!' Herculano said and pushed the doctor away. 'If you can't find anything wrong with me, I have no further use for you.'

'The fact that I can find nothing wrong may hide something far more serious,' the doctor said, but kept his distance as he rummaged through his big black valise, lifting out one glass bottle to examine it.

'If any other symptoms arise, I'll call you back,' Herculano said and tilted his head at Arriscado for him to show the doctor out.

He noticed that the maid who'd come in to clear away his bath was staring open-mouthed and now crossed herself three times in quick succession at the doctor's pronouncement.

'It isn't down to witchcraft either,' Herculano said. 'So you can be done with trying to ward off evil while you're at it.'

The maid whispered an apology as she hoisted the metal bathtub and fled. This behaviour irritated Herculano even more, but he turned his attention back to the doctor who was taking his time packing his bag.

'Why are you still here?'

The man closed the clasp of his valise with a snap and said, 'It would be unwise to discount magic as a cause for your lost memory, Your Excellency.'

'What nonsense! Who would put a spell on me?'

'How do you know whom you might have offended?'

'I can tell, even without my memory, that I'm not the kind of man who has anything to do with those who dabble in magic.'

It surprised him that an undefinable flicker crossed Arriscado's face as he spoke. He'd ask about that, but later. For now, he wanted the doctor gone. Arriscado held the bedroom door open and bowed the doctor out.

Then he turned back to Herculano and said, 'If you won't be needing me, sir, I have a few errands to run.'

'Go.'

Arriscado bothered Herculano profoundly. He was supposed to have raised him and yet it felt like he'd never met Arriscado before this morning.

There was also something off about him. Herculano felt he was being examined, but each time he looked up, Arriscado hastily looked away. He told himself that it would confuse any servant worth his salt to see his master in this state, but it felt like something more.

He needed to think, and he was heartily sick of this room. It felt constricted and stuffy. That was odd because it was a well-appointed room in a large house. Yet it left him feeling as though he didn't have room to breathe.

He grabbed the coat hanging on the bedpost and examined it with distaste. It was an olive green satin embroidered with a pattern of contrasting brown leaves. It was the least colourful garment he could find in his wardrobe. Why that annoyed him, he couldn't yet fathom.

He flung the coat on and headed downstairs. A pair of footmen converged on him and he wasn't sure if it was to stop him or to open the front door. He didn't give them a chance either way, just wrenched the door open himself and stepped out into the street.

'Chair, Your Excellency?' a scruffy man said, and waved at the sedan that he and his equally scruffy partner had rested on the cobbles.

'Good God, no!'

Herculano needed a walk. He had no idea what lay to the left or right of this street, but he could see the glint of the river over the tops of the houses and headed downhill towards it.

A black-cloaked figure darted from the kitchen door through the crowded street, also heading downhill. His behaviour struck Herculano as furtive and, if he wasn't very much mistaken, it was Arriscado. Herculano quickened his pace and followed the man.

Herculano hurried through the crowded streets after his valet and on down to the massive Commerce Square that faced onto the wide Tagus River. It was so recently rebuilt that the cobbles still shone white beneath his feet. In the centre of the square was a monument of epic proportions to the last king, astride a rearing horse, waves washing around its hooves. It had to be huge so as not to be dwarfed by the grand scale of the square and the equally imposing facade of the royal palace.

The palace took up one entire side of the square. The other two sides were filled with government buildings, predominantly those that dealt with trade from the kingdom's colonies.

The square lived up to its name and was packed with merchants standing by their stalls. They were all makeshift wood and canvas that could be broken down and carried away if needed, but they had a permanent air. It implied that most remained in the spots they'd paid for, day and night.

Herculano pushed his way through the dawdling shoppers who kept stopping to feel the quality of cloth or test the firmness of a peach. It infuriated him that he had to slow to their pace and, when possible, he'd dive through a gap and hurry on.

Herculano was flabbergasted when Arriscado stopped at a side entrance to the palace and waved a paper at the guard. It had to be impressive, judging by the way the guard went from slack-jawed imbecility to alert.

As Arriscado was walking in the midst of a crowd, Herculano rushed for the door and slipped in after Arriscado as if they were together. It worried him that he'd got too close to his valet, but it was unnecessary. The man had taken off into the palace at high speed. He was so focused on where he was going that Herculano guessed that he'd have to grab hold of him to be noticed. As it was, he matched his valet's pace so he wouldn't be heard walking along behind him.

It was sheer madness to have entered the palace, but he felt compelled. He prayed nobody would challenge him. So far, only a couple of liveried servants and a cluster of nobility had walked past. He assumed that, as he was in, people expected he was supposed to be there and left him alone.

He followed Arriscado up a wide, white marble staircase at the end of the long passageway. A massive window cast light through heavy steel bars, yet it felt gloomy and cool. The hubbub of traders outside sounded far away and part of another world.

Arriscado walked halfway down the second-floor corridor and stopped to knock at a door identical to all the others. Herculano froze and prayed that the valet didn't look his way. There was nowhere to hide. Fortunately, Arriscado was called inside almost immediately.

Since there was nobody else about, Herculano put his ear to the smooth, slightly warm wood of the door and concentrated. He could just make out an indistinct murmur of voices, perhaps of two men, but it was impossible to work out what they were saying.

'Who are you?' a woman's voice said right beside him.

Herculano jumped and swung round, reaching for words of explanation.

'I know you!' he gasped and he felt as if a bolt of magic had hit him as his gaze fell upon a dark-haired, fair-skinned young woman.

'Well, I don't know you. What is more, you haven't explained yourself. What are you doing listening at the door of the grand alchemist?'

'The grand alchemist? This is the grand alchemist's room?'

'As if you didn't know that.'

The woman's voice was filled with scorn, one hand on her hip, the other clutching a notebook and pen.

'Madam, I assure you, I don't.'

'A likely story, pretending you don't know the alchemist but you know me.'

Herculano shook his head. The shock of recognition was fading and now he wasn't so certain. But there was something about this woman. He felt a great warmth for her.

'What is your name?'

'I thought you said you knew me.'

'Perhaps I was mistaken. Please, tell me your name.'

'Why would I do that? Next you'll be using my name as evidence that you belong and I don't think you do.'

'How else could I be in the palace? It isn't like they'd let just anyone in.'

'Alright then, who are you here to visit?'

Herculano pointed his thumb at the door.

'If you're here to see the grand alchemist, then knock and go in,' the young woman said, folding her arms and glaring at him.

If it wasn't for the seriousness of his situation, Herculano might laugh.

As it was, he suppressed the desire to grab this woman in a bear hug, and said, 'The thing is, he has somebody else with him.'

'Who?'

'A scoundrel by the name of Arriscado. Perhaps you know him?'

Herculano wondered whether Arriscado was a regular visitor to the palace and this woman might know.

'Who?'

'An oldish man, dresses in black, wears a grey wig and has a very fat neck.'

Herculano shrugged. The description was inadequate.

'I've never heard of him.'

'Well, never mind. I can't see the grand alchemist while he's there, so I may as well leave and come back later.'

'I don't think so,' the woman said as she stepped out of reach and shouted, 'Guards! Guards!'

'No, please.'

Herculano leaped across the gap and slapped his hand over the woman's mouth.

'Let go of me,' she shrieked as she pushed him away and scrambled back. 'Guards, we have a spy!'

Her shout rang through the corridor, bouncing across the tiles. The bang of opening doors and the sound of running followed it.

'Damn!' Herculano muttered and turned to the stairs just as a couple of guards ran up. The doors opposite opened and a woman peered out of one while a man stepped out of the other.

'He's a spy!' the young woman shouted, pointing at Herculano.

'Damn it, you'll get me killed!'

Herculano ran away from the guards pounding down the corridor. He had no idea where he was going, nor how to get out, but he wouldn't give up without a fight. His feet slapped loudly on the floor as he gave his all and people erupted from the rooms on either side of him.

A gigantic man leaped out into the corridor ahead of him and Herculano jinked left, slipped on the smooth floor and careened into the wall. He pushed out as the big man lunged for him and somebody else grabbed him from behind and wrapped his arms around his waist, dragging him down. He fell to the floor. The tackling man went down with him and the big man dropped on top of the two of them.

'Get off!' Herculano shouted and heaved at them with all his might.

'Hold him!' somebody shouted, but Herculano hardly heard it, he was so smothered by bodies. 'Alright, let's take a look at him. Everybody off,' the same voice said.

It had an air of command and it didn't surprise Herculano to see a guard in palace livery looking down at him as the men got off and he could roll over.

'I am not a spy.'

'Ask him who he's here to see,' the young woman said.

It sent a spark of irritation through him. Who was this busybody? And why the devil was she being so damned persistent?

'Well?' the guard said. 'Who are you here to see?'

Herculano sighed and examined the woman again. Her face was flushed as she stared at him with her big brown eyes. The door he'd been listening at opened and Arriscado stepped out, followed by a tall, slim man.

Herculano's breath caught. The man looked sleek and cold and dangerous. How a person could look dangerous was a curious thought, but Herculano just knew it to be true.

'I came to see him,' he said with a sigh as he pointed at the man. 'The grand alchemist.'

'Your Excellency, Dr Zuniga,' the guard said and gave a deep bow. 'Do you know this man?'

Dr Zuniga stalked over to Herculano, leaned down till they were face to face, and gazed at him with an unblinking, lizard-like stare.

'Yes, I know him,' he said as he straightened up. 'Let him up, he will join me.'

'You do know him?' the young woman said with deep surprise.

She was no more astonished than Herculano himself.

'I do, Lady Odete,' Dr Zuniga said. 'Is there a reason you're here and not with Lady Mafalda?'

'She's resting,' the woman said, and flushed a deep red.

Her embarrassment made Herculano feel sorry for her and wish he could defend her against the alchemist. He was also interested to note that Arriscado had stepped back into the alchemist's room. Was he keeping himself out of sight?

3

Odete pulled her skirts up with both hands so she could run up the stairs. She felt foolish and her nerves were making her hands shake. What had possessed her to get involved? Why had she challenged that man?

He wasn't the first person she'd seen lurking about where he shouldn't. She had spent many intriguing hours herself, peeping from behind a tapestry or eavesdropping on conversations while pretending to be interested in whatever Lady Mafalda had to say.

Maybe it was because this man was so blatant. Or maybe it was because he was dressed like a merchant. Either way, he had no business spying on the grand alchemist.

Odete emerged from the stairs and smacked into somebody tall as her fingers sank into warm, dark blue silk. She pushed herself away and the man grabbed her arm and pulled her to an abrupt stop.

'Lady Odete?' Prince Juliano said and tilted his head to better see her face.

'Your Highness!' Odete gasped and dropped her gaze to the floor as she felt her already flushed face grow even hotter.

'You're in a hurry.'

'I'm sorry. I should have looked where I was going,' Odete said and realised that she could only see one pair of feet. 'Are you alone?'

'As you see,' Juliano said and waved his hand to encompass the empty corridor. 'I was tired of being followed around.'

'Were you? How odd.'

'Is it?' Juliano said and gave her a more measuring look.

'I don't think I've ever seen you on your own before.'

'That would imply that I have never seen you on your own before, either.'

Odete gasped at his words and rechecked the corridor to make sure they were alone. The way he'd spoken was odd, as if he was asking a question.

'No, we have never met like this before. We have never said more to each other than a polite greeting in passing.'

'That's a pity. I had a feeling there was something more between us.'

'You... you had a feeling?'

'Was I wrong?'

The blush that had subsided sprang back to life and Odete hastily looked away.

'How can I tell you that, Your Highness?'

'Well, somebody better had. I've had the most godforsaken day today. Everything feels wrong, but I can't say why.'

He was back to sounding uncertain. It was strange because usually he was full of bullish determination.

'Did anything out of the ordinary happen yesterday?' Prince Juliano asked.

Odete paused to consider.

'Aside from the storm last night?'

'That's hardly unusual.'

'I suppose not. It was very loud though, lots of thunder and lightning. Speaking of loud, you and the duque had a massive argument. We could hear the two of you roaring at each other all the way in Lady Mafalda's room.'

'Really? I don't suppose you know what it was about?'

'I assumed it's what your arguments are always about. You want to be king. Maybe you should ask His Excellency, Dr Zuniga, about your problem.'

'No, I thank you, but no. He was in my room this morning when I woke and that, believe me, is enough to give anyone nightmares.'

'I see.'

Odete couldn't stop herself from looking back up into the prince's face. He seemed genuinely repulsed by her suggestion.

'I sense I've just said the wrong thing,' Juliano said.

'It's just... I've always had the feeling that you trust Dr Zuniga with your life.'

'Do I? I wonder why?' Juliano said and scratched his head. It was also an unfamiliar gesture. 'So, I like him?'

'I didn't say that. I only said you trust him. At least, you trust him more than you trust the duque.'

'I don't trust the duque?'

'What?' Odete gasped. 'Are you playing a game with me? If you are, please stop. I don't understand, and it isn't funny. If anyone were to overhear us we'd be in so much trouble.'

'I apologise,' Juliano said and gave her a slight bow. 'I am out of sorts today. Perhaps I will go and see the grand alchemist after all.'

'I hope you do.' The prince made to head down the stairs when something else occurred to Odete. 'Oh, wait. May I ask you something?'

The prince paused and only half turned around.

'Ask. I will see whether I answer.'

That was more obtuse than usual as well.

'This morning you said you were going in search of Lord Andrade. Did you find him?'

The prince shook his head, and a deeply worried expression settled on his face.

'I have no idea where he has gone.'

'Oh!' Odete said, and his words filled her with dread. 'His father?'

'Has not heard from him either.'

'Well, I hope you find him soon.'

Odete gave the prince a curtsy and hurried back to the balcony and to Lady Mafalda and her ladies-in-waiting.

Thankfully, Lady Mafalda and the others were still enjoying their nap and hadn't noticed her absence. Relieved, she retired to the far end of the balcony and felt around in her skirt pocket for her only family heirloom. It was a tiny crystal perfume bottle carved into the shape of a seashell with a delicate gold lid. She popped it open, held the mouth against her pulse and tipped the bottle so that the golden liquid touched her skin. Then she brought the scent up to her nose. The aroma of roses wafted up to her and she felt herself relax.

She closed her eyes and took several more deep breaths. It was amazing how soothing a beautiful fragrance could be. Thank heavens she had it.

Once she'd calmed down, she leaned over the balcony and gazed at the bustling market, thinking. Maybe it was the disappearance of Tiago Andrade that had shaken the prince and made him seem so different. But would shock make him forget things? He appeared not to recognise her at all, and the feelings she thought they shared were absent.

Could something have happened to him? Maybe that was why he'd woken with the grand alchemist in his room. Although they were allies, Odete rarely saw them together. Something serious must have happened for Dr Zuniga to have been so blatant as to be in the prince's room.

How could she doubt that when Prince Juliano was behaving so strangely? Something was definitely going on. Should she do something about it?

Was it even necessary? If she'd noticed the change in him, then everybody else would have too. The duque had even said he was not himself that morning. Dr Zuniga must have thought the same.

What could she do anyway? What could any lady-in-waiting do? Watch, that was all.

She'd learned, early on, that the best way to keep herself safe in the palace was to mind her own business and keep her mouth shut. But what if something dreadful had happened to Prince Juliano? Could she really stand by and do nothing?

❧

'Do you know me?' Herculano said as he stepped into the grand alchemist's quarters and looked around.

He wasn't sure what he'd expected, but this tidy room filled with books wasn't it. Well, maybe the books, but there was nothing else in this place to suggest it belonged to an alchemist.

'I know you, in a manner of speaking,' Dr Zuniga said and waved one long-fingered hand at a wooden chair. 'Sit.'

The squashed cushion didn't make it look any more comfortable. It was the kind of chair you might make a recalcitrant student use.

'Do you know me or not?' Herculano said and tried to look as relaxed as one could, when only moments before he'd been suffocating under a pile of men.

'I met you a long time ago.' Dr Zuniga crossed to his big black desk and rummaged in the drawer. 'You were just a boy then.'

'I see, so that's why you were staring at me like I was some specimen of beetle earlier on. You were working out if you knew me.' Herculano glanced across at Arriscado, who was hovering nearby. 'But you know my valet.'

'I have known him for many more years, although it has been a while since we have spoken,' Dr Zuniga said and approached Herculano with a shining needle in one hand and a white porcelain saucer in the other. 'Hold out your finger, please.'

'Why? What are you doing?' Herculano asked and leaned back in his chair.

'I need a drop of your blood.'

'My blood? What in heaven's name for?'

'Because I need to check something.'

'Check something? Can you be more specific?'

Blood was used for all sorts of black magic, so Herculano was reluctant, but also didn't feel he could refuse and did as ordered.

Dr Zuniga stabbed the finger with a swift prick and twisted it around so that the blood dripped onto the saucer. The porcelain was a luminous white and the drops of blood glowed a brilliant red in contrast.

Dr Zuniga placed the saucer on his desk, returned the needle to its drawer, then waved his hand over the blood, muttering under his breath. It shimmered and turned purple.

'Mother of God,' Arriscado muttered and crossed himself.

'What is it?' Herculano asked. 'Why did my blood change colour?'

'Don't you know?' Dr Zuniga asked.

'Why would I know?'

'I cast a spell to reveal whether you have royal blood. It appears that you do.'

'I do?'

Herculano launched to his feet and took a closer look at the blood. It was a mix of red and blue that created a marbled effect with a purplish hue rather than a true purple.

'I'm no prince.'

'Neither am I.' Dr Zuniga settled into a comfortable chair and crossed his legs. 'But the royal houses of the world are prolific. Aside from those who turn into kings and queens, there are countless princelings, royal dukes and more remote relatives. That's not including all the lines of now-deposed royal houses and a whole host of bastard children. I myself was the grandchild of a king's mistress. People think royal blood is a rarity, but the world is littered with people of royal descent.'

'Oh.'

Herculano paced the room. Arriscado looked astonished by the news, while the alchemist remained sphinx-like. Something more than the discovery that he had royal blood was going on here.

There was a tap at the door and, without waiting to be invited, a tall, thin, elegantly dressed man stepped into the room. Herculano gasped and staggered back against the alchemist's desk, staring. The elegant man stood stock still, his eyes wide, his face white with shock.

Herculano pushed himself upright and muttered, 'Who the devil are you?'

'I could ask you the same question,' the man said.

'Your voice... it's so familiar.'

Herculano closed the gap between the two of them, peering at the man's face. He had the disconcerting but impossible feeling that he was looking into a mirror.

They were almost the same height, but Herculano was marginally shorter and more powerfully built. The man's face was handsome and instantly likeable. It was exactly the kind of face Herculano approved of. He was less sure of the person behind it. He felt a rage build up towards the man but couldn't understand why.

'Your Highness,' Dr Zuniga said in a quiet voice. 'What are you doing here?'

'A slip of a girl told me I should speak to you, so I came.' Juliano looked puzzled as he spoke, but his gaze didn't move from Herculano's face.

The door swung open again and somebody said, 'I heard you are harbouring a spy, Dr Zuniga,' and the Duque de Louredo stepped into the room.

Herculano hissed in air as he took in the latest arrival. His anger turned to hatred, and he clenched his hands into fists. What was it about this place? Why were these people more familiar to him than the staff of his own house? Why did he dislike this man more than all the rest?

'It was nothing but a misunderstanding,' Dr Zuniga said. 'There is no spy here.'

'No?' The duque's gaze took in the room and the two young men standing so close to one another. Then it flicked on to Arriscado. 'Do I know you?'

'Your Grace.' Arriscado bowed over nearly double, his corset squeaking as he did so, and stayed down as he muttered, 'I have never had the honour of meeting you.'

'Odd,' the duque said, but shrugged and turned back to the alchemist. 'If you haven't taken in a spy, then who are these people?'

'This is His Excellency, Herculano Escovar,' Dr Zuniga said with a wave of his hand. 'An eminent merchant of the city.'

'An eminent merchant?' The duque's eyebrow went up a notch. 'I thought I knew all the most important men of Lisbon. Why don't I know him?'

'He is the son of an old friend, Isaltinho Escovar, sadly deceased. I'm sure you remember him.'

'Ah yes, Isaltinho. I didn't know he had died. My condolences,' the duque said and looked Herculano up and down in a way that gave no sense that he regretted the death of the merchant. 'I am surprised to find you talking to merchants, Dr Zuniga. It isn't exactly your field.'

The duque examined Herculano and the prince once more before he nodded and walked out.

'I don't think you convinced him,' Herculano said.

'Would you prefer to be hanged as a spy?' Dr Zuniga asked.

'Wait, you mean he really is a spy?' Juliano said.

'I am not,' Herculano snapped. 'But neither am I a merchant.'

'According to Arriscado, you have no memory of what you are,' Dr Zuniga said as he returned to his desk and took out his needle again.

'Oh no, one prick was more than enough,' Herculano said and backed away.

'This time, it isn't for you. Your Highness, if you wouldn't mind.'

'You want my blood?' Juliano said and held out his hand.

Herculano wondered why he was being so obliging. Then again, why did the alchemist need to test the blood of one everybody knew to be a prince? Still, he watched as the alchemist dripped blood onto the same saucer, an inch away from his blood, and then cast the spell. The blood turned exactly the same colour as his own.

'Holy Mary, Mother of God,' Arriscado muttered and crossed himself several times over.

'That isn't right,' Juliano said. 'My blood should have turned entirely blue. What is going on here? Is this why I've felt so strange today? And why do you already have another drop of this peculiar mixed blood on the saucer?'

'That is his blood,' Dr Zuniga said, pointing at Herculano. 'Which presents us with a rather interesting dilemma.'

'What is going on here?' Herculano said. 'Why do I know all you people?'

'You know us?'

'*Know* might be too strong a word. You just feel familiar. That woman earlier, I like her. I don't mean because I saw her for the first time today and she was pretty. I feel as though I have liked her for a long time. And you, I know to be wary of you. I hate the duque, and him... I don't know what to make of him.' Herculano pointed at the prince and shook his head, and his gaze flicked over the man. 'My ring!' he gasped.

He shot to his feet, grabbed hold of the prince's hand and twisted it to get a closer look at the gold ring set with a red ruby engraved with a crest.

'What are you doing? This is my ring,' Juliano said and pulled his hand away.

'You don't sound so sure of that.'

'How could it possibly be yours? I've had it all my life.'

Herculano shook his head. This ring was his. He could picture it on his hand. Only his hand looked like that of the prince's, not the coarser fingers of his own hand.

'This isn't right!'

'Mmm,' Dr Zuniga said, nodding thoughtfully as he looked from one young man to the other. 'It is what I feared.'

'What you feared? You're speaking in riddles again.'

'I will explain. At this point, I don't have a choice. Please be seated.'

Herculano wasn't inclined to do anything the alchemist suggested, but as the prince sat down, he supposed he didn't have a choice. He noticed that Arriscado remained standing and was wringing his hands nervously.

'Arriscado, make sure we aren't disturbed,' Dr Zuniga said.

Arriscado went to the door, locked it and then leaned his substantial bulk against it.

'So, what is going on?' Herculano said and selected a more comfortable chair.

Dr Zuniga made a temple with his fingers and gazed at the tips for a while.

'Things went wrong after the earthquake.'

'Which earthquake? There hasn't been an earthquake in – wait, do you mean, The Earthquake?'

'Which other one could it possibly be? The royal family was at the Mass of All Saints when it struck and the cathedral came crashing down about us. It was so sudden and so violent that there was nothing I could do to stop it, or even to save the king and queen and the little princesses. It is ironic that the thing I feared most for the king was the scheming of the duque. In the end, it was an act of God that changed everything. It gave the duque the opportunity he always wanted.'

Herculano was pulled back to the traumatic events of the earthquake again. Why was the alchemist bringing this up? It was upsetting and explained nothing.

'The only one I could reach in all that chaos was Prince Juliano. He was pinned under the fallen great crucifix of the cathedral. Arriscado, as the prince's valet, was there too and he helped me get the prince free. We had just pulled him out of the wreckage of the cathedral when the tidal wave came crashing through.'

Herculano glanced at Prince Juliano who looked grave but not as harrowed as Herculano felt. He wished the alchemist would get on with it. Reliving these memories just brought pain to everyone.

'My magic couldn't withstand the force of the wave. Arriscado vanished, but I held on to the prince as we were swept away. By some miracle we washed up in a square all together: me, Prince Juliano, Arriscado and you,' Dr Zuniga said, turning to Herculano.

'Me?'

'We were half drowned and badly injured. I broke my arm and most of my ribs. The prince was unconscious and Arriscado was half buried under a pile of detritus. That was where he found you, moaning under the same remains. He pulled you out and dragged himself and you over to me with the intention of saving you.'

'That wasn't your intention?'

'My sole loyalty lay with the prince.'

'What does that mean?' Juliano asked.

'I could see that only the most powerful magic would keep you alive, Your Highness. It looked like he…' Dr Zuniga pointed at Herculano. 'It looked like he would die, so I decided to take any healthy tissue I could find in him and put it into you and take what was damaged, bones and organs, in you and put it in him.'

'You were willing to kill me to save him?' Herculano said.

'If I hadn't believed you were dying anyway, I wouldn't have done it. As it was, I decided it was better to save at least one rather than lose both.'

'And you chose to save the prince,' Herculano said, as bile rose in his throat.

'The kingdom needed him and you looked like a pauper. Your clothes were rags. I could see that even underneath the mud and the blood. Your life would have been miserable even if you had survived. So I cast my spell.'

'Why am I here, then? Why didn't I die?'

'I don't know. I could never work that out. I can only put what happened on that day down to my injuries and consequent lack of focus.'

'So, I'm a pauper. That doesn't explain the blood and my feelings about all of you.'

'And my confusion,' Juliano said.

'What happened next took a while to be uncovered,' Dr Zuniga said. 'Arriscado took you, Herculano, to one of the remaining intact churches. He told me he'd wait with you till you died, then return to me. I, in the meantime, did what I could to heal my broken bones and get the prince back to the palace.

'Miraculously, that had survived the earthquake and the tsunami. I slipped in amidst the chaos, carrying the prince and cleaned him and put him into my bed. The situation was too dangerous at that point to let anyone know he'd survived.'

Dr Zuniga looked to be far away and Herculano decided it was best to just let the story unfold the way the man wanted to tell it. Even though he wanted to grab the alchemist by the shoulders, shake him and roar at him over the dreadful thing he'd done.

'It took a few days for the prince to wake. When he did, he was detached and appeared not to care that his mother and father had died. He also seemed different, but I put it down to his injuries. That was until Arriscado reappeared and told me that the pauper we'd expected to die was still alive, awake and crying for his parents, the king and queen.'

'What!?' Herculano and the prince shouted.

'Somehow, I had not just switched blood and bone, but also your minds.'

'Good God!' Herculano said. 'But... why didn't you switch us back?'

'Do you think I didn't try? Magic isn't a simple thing. Using it to heal bodies takes a great deal of subtlety and skill. I had never even heard of magic that could switch two people's minds before. I did not understand how it had happened nor what to do about it. Arriscado and I brought the two of you back together and I tried to swap you back. But all I did was erase a bit of each of your memories.'

'Is this true?' Herculano said, turning to Arriscado.

'I'm afraid so,' the man said as he did an apologetic bow while remaining propped against the door.

'I feared what might happen if I persisted when I knew so little about what I was doing,' Dr Zuniga said. 'Which was when we came up with our plan. I would stay at the palace and look after the boy who looked like the prince and Arriscado went in search of a wealthy merchant. He agreed to take in the prince who now occupied the body of the pauper and bring him up in wealth and comfort. Arriscado remained to watch over the prince and train him.

'The plan was that I would find the spell to switch your minds back. Once I did, I would correct the mistake I had made. Little did I realise it would take me fifteen years to work the spell out.'

'What?' Herculano shot to his feet; his confusion was turning to rage. 'Are you telling me... Did you just cast that spell? Have I been living as Prince Juliano for the last fifteen years?'

'I'm afraid so. I also regret that while Prince Juliano has gained your memories and knowledge of life at court, it appears that his memories of growing up as a merchant that should have been transferred to you, have been lost.'

'So, you're saying that I'm a pauper who lived for the last fifteen years as a prince,' Herculano said. 'But now I am... what am I?'

Dr Zuniga shrugged and said, 'I don't know. The prince is back in his proper body. I can tell because your personalities have changed. You, Herculano, always throw yourself into things without thinking about it first. Like you did today. Coming into the palace was foolish but oh so typical.'

'While Prince Juliano has the personality of the boy I raised,' Arriscado said. 'He's cautious. He waits and he watches as he is doing now.'

'I don't remember you,' Juliano said, looking at Arriscado.

'There was no need for you to remember him,' Dr Zuniga said. 'We returned you to your rightful place with the skills you needed to be a prince. We gave Herculano the life of a merchant. It is more than he could have expected from his humble roots.'

'Don't make it sound like you were doing me a favour,' Herculano snapped. 'You only did that to ensure the prince grew up in comfort.'

'However, we now have a problem. The spell I used on your blood shows that you both have a mixture of each other's blood: some royal and some common.'

'That has nothing to do with me.' Herculano was so angry he could barely keep his tone even and short of a shout. 'You have already made it clear my role in this farce is over. I can walk out of here right now and into that life of a merchant.'

'Do you think you can do that without help, now that you have no memory of what it means to be a merchant?'

'I'm sure I'll work it out.' Herculano glared down at Arriscado and said, 'Are you coming home with me?'

'I can't,' Arriscado said, but looked like a man stuck in a dilemma. 'My first duty is to the prince.'

'Whom you brought up?'

'I was his loyal servant from the day he was born.'

'Fine, then stay here. I'm going.'

Arriscado looked imploringly at Dr Zuniga, but it was the prince who said, 'Let him go. We don't need him, and he is right about one thing. You treated him badly.'

Herculano wanted to snap at him to shut up and that he didn't need his permission to do anything.

'I've done all I'm going to do for you people,' Herculano muttered and pushed Arriscado aside.

'You're not going anywhere,' Dr Zuniga said.

An iron fist felt like it wrapped itself around Herculano, lifted him off the floor and dumped him back in front of the alchemist.

'Don't you push me around.'

With an effort that left Herculano's head throbbing and his teeth rattling, he shattered the force holding him in place and made another dash for the door.

'We can take your land and property away from you as easily as we gave them to you,' Dr Zuniga shouted. 'Aside from that, you are a subject of this kingdom. You owe fealty to your prince. You may not turn him down if he requires your service.'

'Yes, I bloody well can.'

'So you would like the duque to win, would you?' the prince said.

That pulled Herculano up short.

'What?'

'Don't you think that is the most likely outcome if you won't help me?'

Herculano turned slowly to stare at the prince.

'You and I... we've lived each other's lives. Don't you think it's low to use your knowledge against me?'

Juliano smiled and said, 'I've just realised that the intense hatred I feel for the duque is because of your memories. You might not remember the knowledge I now hold, but it is clear your feelings remain with you.'

'You made a right mess of this, didn't you, Dr Zuniga?' Herculano said, and glared at the alchemist. 'Tell me, did you at least warn us you would attempt the body swap?'

'I thought it best not to. If the spell had worked properly, neither of you would have been any the wiser when you woke up. I thought that would cause both of you the least pain.'

'So, how did you do it?'

'We waited till we had a thunderstorm, as I required the energy from the lightning for the spell. Then we drugged you both, brought you together and cast the spell.'

'Idiots,' Herculano muttered.

'I agree,' Juliano said. 'But what's done is done and now I need your help. This battle against the duque is a battle for my life and control over the kingdom. I fear it is coming to a head. At this moment, with my conflicting emotions and confusion about my role, I am more vulnerable than I have ever been.'

'What do you mean?' Dr Zuniga said.

'I may have all the memories a prince needs, but I feel like a man looking through a mirror and nothing feels real. I woke this morning to discover that my best friend has vanished. I fear the worst, but I don't know why, and the emotion feels false.'

'Lord Tiago Andrade has vanished?' Dr Zuniga said, and exchanged a worried glance with Arriscado.

'It appears so.'

'The two of you have been very secretive lately. What were you planning?'

'Something against the duque,' the prince said with a shrug. 'But try as I might, I can't remember what.'

'Do you remember?' Dr Zuniga said, turning to Herculano.

For reasons Herculano couldn't understand, he felt sick to his heart hearing that this Tiago had vanished, but he shook his head.

'That name isn't familiar to me anymore. I have no idea who he is, let alone what he was doing.'

4

Viriato Berenguer, the Duque de Louredo, closed the grand alchemist's door with a click. Then he stood and stared at it for a while. He would have given a small fortune to know what was being said in that room, but he knew from experience that it was impossible. Dr Zuniga used magic to block all attempts at eavesdropping.

The duque gave an accepting shrug, shook some imaginary dust from one silvery satin sleeve and proceeded on his leisurely way to the council chamber. As he made his way to the ground floor and past the throne room, he pondered what the grand alchemist might be up to.

Although Dr Zuniga and the prince were allies, they were careful not to spend too much time in each other's presence. Viriato couldn't understand why, when everyone knew they were close.

On a day like today, it had more significance still. Today, the prince had been distinctly different. It was such a profound change that even Lord Antelmo Carvalho, a singularly stupid man, had noticed the difference.

Then there was the other man. He felt familiar when he shouldn't have. He was clearly the merchant Zuniga said he was, and yet... and yet. What was his name again? Ah yes, Herculano Escovar. The duque would have to have his secretary, Diogo Martinez, look into him.

The two black servants who flanked the council chamber doors clipped their heels together in salute. Then they swung the double doors open with a crash. It was impossible to do it silently, which annoyed the duque. However, he was inured to that particular inconvenience of the ancient palace and strolled into the council chamber. He was not an anxious man by nature, but he'd cultivated an even more relaxed air to show enemies and friends alike that he was unshakable.

Now he slowed as he approached the large black table that occupied the centre of the room and whose legs were carved to resemble thick twisted rope. The table was battered with age. Viriato liked that. It spoke to the hundreds of years it had stood in this room, absorbing the conversation of the great and the powerful.

The windows in this room were large, but set so high that one couldn't look through them. The walls were covered in tapestries, the biggest of which adorned the wall at the foot of the table. It was an impressive image of Brazil, depicting vast, parrot-filled forests. So much of the dye from the Brazil wood imported from that far-off land had been used that it glowed a fiery red.

Viriato's pious and foolish brother-in-law, the king, had commissioned the tapestry. He'd died shortly after they had hung it in the council chamber, putting an end to the king's intention of moving the court to Brazil, much to Viriato's relief.

'Your Grace, it's good to see you again,' Lord Antelmo Carvalho said.

It brought Viriato back to his inner council. He'd selected some of these men for their intellect, others for their influence or wealth, one because he had to placate the church.

His Eminence Cardinal Caio da Gama, Patriarch of Lisbon, was his sole concession to the religious hierarchy that had held the city in its grip for so many years. The duque was determined to break their hold, weakened since the earthquake, but still omnipresent and influential.

The cardinal himself had, much to everyone's surprise, emerged unscathed from the wreckage of his ruined cathedral after the quake. Such a miraculous survival gave him more influence than the duque felt he deserved. The cardinal swept back his thick iron-grey hair with one spade-like hand and examined the duque as closely as he was being watched himself.

Viriato gave him a nod of acknowledgement before turning to Lord Carvalho standing to the cardinal's right. He was an ally of the old king and sided with Juliano more than the duque liked. He was also fat, always sweating, and stupid, but fabulously wealthy, so Viriato put up with his slovenly ways. Lord Carvalho removed his wig and hung it on the back post of his chair. His sparse grey stubble, beaded with sweat, distracted Viriato's gaze.

'Lord Carvalho,' he murmured, 'please, do sit down.'

The man beamed at him, oblivious to how repulsive Viriato found him, and eased himself onto his seat. His paunch strained against his buttons and it wasn't uncommon for one to go shooting off in the middle of a meeting.

The rest of the men around the table bowed and settled too, and Viriato examined each in turn. The most important to him was Lord Onofre Paiva, the Chancellor of the Exchequer. He was a thin, effeminate man who wore his long wavy white hair about his shoulders like a woman.

Viriato despised him, but his family had held the treasury for generations, and he was necessary. To ensure his compliance, Viriato had winkled out his disgraceful little secret and held it over the man. It made Lord Paiva jumpy and quick to obey, which made him tolerable.

Next was Lord Nicanor Ledo, a marquis who was fully behind Viriato's plans for the rebuilding of the city. He was efficient, ruthless and, next to Viriato himself, one of the most powerful men in the kingdom. Some teased him about his diminished stature, but he seldom cared what people said about him.

Finally, there was Lord Xavier Alardo, a young, fair man with useful military connections and, it was rumoured, Viking ancestry. It was odd that he'd allied himself with the duque when he was closer in age to the prince. Presumably he thought he could gain more power by supporting the duque. Viriato was willing to go along with him for as long as it was mutually beneficial.

'Good afternoon, gentlemen,' Viriato said. 'Before we begin, I wanted to ask whether any of you have seen young Lord Tiago Andrade today, or know of his whereabouts.'

'Has he gone missing?' Carvalho asked.

'So it would seem. It is the reason the prince isn't with us today.'

It was awkward that the young man had vanished. Viriato hoped it wasn't because of something linked to him. He'd have to look into it. In the meantime, he could ask his council.

'If he's only been missing since yesterday, I wouldn't worry about it,' Lord Ledo said. 'He's probably asleep in the arms of some young woman. Who amongst us hasn't vanished for a few days for that, or a spot of hunting?'

'I would say that's very likely,' Carvalho said.

'Perhaps,' Viriato said, 'but the prince was worried about his disappearance. Since the two of them are bosom companions, I also have my concerns.'

'Sometimes the prince is overly anxious,' Alardo said.

'No doubt you are right. So we will wait and see if he turns up. In the meantime, we have more important matters to attend to.'

'Your Grace, if you are after more funds, I can't give it to you,' Lord Paiva said in his reedy, high-pitched voice. 'I keep telling you, we no longer have the gold to support your rebuilding project.'

'The city was flattened, Onofre.' Viriato used the man's first name because he knew it would irritate him. 'It must be rebuilt and that will cost money.'

'Maybe so. But why must you sweep away the old city? Why must you put down ruler-straight roads radiating to the sea and line those roads with monumental buildings? What's wrong with replacing like with like?'

The duke sighed and tapped his index finger impatiently on the table. 'Onofre, we've had this conversation before. The old Lisbon was a decrepit medieval city. It looked backwards and was oppressed by the church.

'The new Lisbon needs to reflect a modern, enlightened era informed by science. Before the earthquake we had wealth, but the world looked down upon us because to come to Lisbon was to travel hundreds of years into the past. Our dark, superstitious little city was an embarrassment.

'Well, no more. Our capital city will reflect our glory. When strangers come to our shores, they will be in awe of this advanced country and its wealth.'

'Our wealth no longer exists. We suck our colonies dry and still you outspend what we bring in.'

'So you have said for the last decade. Yet we continue to find the money. I expect you to keep doing so without this never-ending nagging.'

'Lord Paiva has my sympathy.'

Cardinal da Gama spoke in the deep voice he'd perfected to awe the Sunday churchgoers.

It irritated the duque but he took the bait.

'Why does he have your sympathy?'

'Because the church continues to suffer under your management too, Viriato Berenguer. You are stealing from God to rebuild your city.'

The duque decided to ignore his offensive tone and casual use of his name for now.

'Would God prefer I leave his people homeless while I rebuild your fallen cathedrals? Would the church rather hold on to its treasure and allow the people to starve?'

'I am not saying that. But your regency, so far, has seen the church stripped of its influence and its money. For what? To emulate the godforsaken northern countries? What the people need is a place to pray and even deeper repentance.'

'I hardly think another auto-da-fé, where you burn more of our citizens, will be any help at all.'

'It may prevent another earthquake. It has so far.'

'But you were burning far more people before the quake and it didn't keep that earthquake at bay.'

'We should have been more diligent, not less,' Cardinal da Gama roared as he surged to his feet and slammed the table with his hands.

'How could we have been more diligent?' Viriato said, forcing himself to stay seated and his voice calm. 'I well remember returning from London as a student to discover so many heretics on pyres that Lisbon's sky was black with smoke and the city reeked of burning flesh. It is hardly the hallmark of a modern city. None of the great powers of the world would want to trade with a backward, superstitious country like that.'

He meant his words to enrage and they had the required effect.

Cardinal da Gama turned as red as a beet, leaned forward till he was face to face with Viriato and ground out, 'You will pay for your lack of faith, Viriato Berenguer, mark my words.'

'But not today, and while I am regent I will manage the kingdom as I see fit.'

'But for how long will this state of affairs remain?' Lord Carvalho asked as he mopped the sweat from his head with a large handkerchief. 'The prince is well past his majority and the people grow restless. They want him to take the throne. Even you can't put his accession off forever, Berenguer.'

Viriato was not in the mood for an argument, especially not on this subject, and from the only ally the prince had on the council. Fortunately, he was an inept one.

'How many times must I remind you, Carvalho, the king's will was clear: his son can take the throne once he is married. We have discussed all the potential options and even given Juliano the choice of two eligible young women.'

'One of which is your daughter.'

'Nothing wrong with that. It is now entirely in the prince's hands. As soon as he is married I will step down,' Viriato said, his gaze running over the councillors.

Some took him at his word, and others didn't. Either way, he was determined that the prince would marry Mafalda and he would keep control of the kingdom and ensure the rebuilding of Lisbon exactly as he had planned it.

Odete sucked on the end of her pencil, thankful that the shade had moved in her direction. The glare from the river was making her drowsy, but she resisted falling asleep. It wasn't often that she got time to indulge her passion and now she set to sketching a view of the river.

'Odete,' Mafalda whispered right by her ear.

Odete jerked back and looked at the young woman in astonishment. This was not how she usually behaved.

'Lady Mafalda?'

'Shhh, quiet, I don't want to wake the others,' Mafalda said, looking back at Pia and Maria da Luz, still fast asleep.

Maria da Luz was even snoring gently.

'I don't think there's much chance of waking them.'

'All the same.' Mafalda took Odete's hands and pulled her down so they were facing each other on the little stone benches. She leaned forward and said in an undertone, 'I need your help.'

'You do?'

The request, and Mafalda's furtive behaviour, surprised Odete. She'd never singled her out like this before.

'I need somebody I can trust.'

'And you think that's me?'

'Pia is Lord Paiva's daughter and Maria da Luz is Lord Carvalho's daughter.'

'Ah, I see. They are both in your father's council,' Odete said, and glanced back at the sleeping women. 'If it's any consolation, I don't think they speak to their fathers very often.'

'No, but you don't have a father, do you?'

Odete wondered why that statement of fact pained her so much.

'He died before I was born.'

'And you rarely see your mother.'

'She is ashamed of her impoverished state and has retired to the only property we have left, a palacete in Sintra. She stays away from the royal palace and her former friends.'

'My mother died in the earthquake,' Mafalda said. 'I sometimes wish it wasn't so. It would have helped if I'd had some brothers and sisters.'

'Believe me, they are rarely as useful as you might hope.'

'So you have brothers and sisters?'

'I do, but I hardly ever hear from them. They are all busy keeping body and soul together.'

'What about your mother?'

'I write to her once a week. She rarely writes back.'

Mafalda nodded and twirled her hair about her finger. Odete had seldom seen her in such a state of indecision. She'd never shown any interest in her ladies-in-waiting before either. To her, they were there to see to her comfort.

'I need you to undertake a dangerous mission for me,' Mafalda said.

'That sounds a little melodramatic,' Odete said and smiled to put the girl at ease.

'Can I trust you, Lady Odete?'

'Of course you can.'

'I need to know for certain that you won't betray me.'

Odete wondered what Mafalda could possibly have been up to that had got her so worked up.

'You can trust me. After all, who would I tell if I was going to betray you?'

'My father, maybe.'

'I would never betray you to your father,' Odete said, and took the young woman's hands in hers. 'What is troubling you?'

Mafalda eyed her dubiously for a moment. Whatever was worrying her was greater than her fear of discovery.

She took a deep breath and said, 'I was supposed to meet Tiago last night.'

'Tiago Andrade?' It was an unnecessary question, but Odete needed the time to assimilate the information. 'I knew you had a tenderness for him. But to have gone so far, Mafalda?'

'I know it was foolish and dangerous. But I love him and he loves me.'

'You really kept that a secret, didn't you?'

'You know my father is determined I will marry the prince. But I don't want to. I don't love him and he doesn't love me.'

'Your father will never permit you to marry anyone else.'

'That is why I'm so afraid. What if my father discovered what was going on? What if he did away with Tiago?' Mafalda said, her voice just a whisper.

'Lord Andrade is a powerful man. Your father wouldn't move against his son in such a blatant manner.'

'You may not think I notice things, but I know how ruthless my father can be. If he found out about me and Tiago...'

'So what would you like me to do?'

At the very least, the question gave Mafalda something else to focus on.

'Find him for me.'

'Tiago? How am I supposed to do that?'

'I don't know, but you have to find him. Please, Odete. I can't bear not knowing what has happened to Tiago. I fear this is all my fault for going against my father's wishes. I was so upset last night when Tiago didn't appear. I thought he'd decided against coming. I was going to scold him when next I saw him and instead... instead I hear he has vanished. That can't be a coincidence. Something is very, very wrong.'

Odete was starting to fear the same. It wasn't just that Tiago had failed to visit Mafalda; it was the strain on the prince's face too.

'Alright, I will see what I can do. But for that, I will have to go out on my own, and spend less time with you, Pia and Maria da Luz.'

'I know.'

'What should we tell them is going on? They will wonder if I am off on my own.'

'I shall tell them you are having an affaire.'

Odete blinked at Mafalda and said faintly, 'An affaire?'

'One I approve of, because I am a great romantic, you know. I will tell them I am allowing you time to see your lover.'

'Mafalda, I'm not sure I want my reputation sullied in that way. It is highly improper. If such a rumour were to get out, I would be ruined.'

'It's not as though you will ever get married though, is it? I mean, no man of consequence would want a penniless bride.'

Odete gasped at Mafalda's cavalier attitude. But she was young and worried about her own love, so Odete decided not to let it upset her too much.

'Let's just say I am running errands for you. Whenever I step out, I will make sure I come back with something useful.'

'But I have servants for that.'

'Then I will come up with something else.'

Odete indicated with her head to Mafalda that her sleeping ladies-in-waiting had started to wake. They were currently looking about themselves in bleary-eyed confusion.

Fortunately, a bevy of servants arrived at the same time, laden with trays of biscuits, dried figs, candied almonds and wine. They would provide sufficient distraction.

Odete tucked her sketchbook under her arm, gave her skirts a shake to straighten them out and made her unhurried way to the table to examine the treats laid out for them. Mafalda trailed along behind her, looking put out. Odete hoped she wouldn't say anything about the non-existent lover.

To distract everybody, she gave them all a bright smile and said, 'Shall I pour the wine?'

Herculano stood in the middle of the grand alchemist's room, three men watching him. He was a pauper. A disposable item whose blood, bones and guts were used as spare parts for a prince. He had no ties and no family, no value beyond what they had bestowed upon him.

Even now, he wasn't free. For now they expected him to leave the life of a merchant and move into the palace to support the prince. Damn, how was he supposed to reconcile these feelings?

Worse, what was he supposed to do with them? What was he supposed to do with the people he'd keep running into in the palace whom he wouldn't know, but he'd have an emotional reaction to?

There was that woman from outside the alchemist's rooms. He'd felt such joy to see her. He wanted to hold her. He wanted to love her. She didn't recognise him, though.

What could he do about her? Was it even possible to do anything? Did he have to suppress his feelings for her and walk away? Was that even possible if he kept running into her?

The bottom hadn't just fallen out of his world, they had grabbed it in one clawed hand and ripped it apart. Even the fiction he'd started to accept, that he was a merchant, was gone.

Everything was a lie, but if he were to survive, he would have to continue the lie.

'What do you want me to do?'

Dr Zuniga looked relieved even though Herculano felt that it was capitulation.

'It would be best if you remained close to the prince. I will continue to search for some way to further disentangle the two of you. The mixed blood you share is a symptom of the problem and a dangerous one for the prince. As a royal, his blood should be a pure blue.'

'Fine,' Herculano said, and ran his hands over his head. It felt like he was living through the longest day of his life. 'Does that mean I have to move into the palace?'

'It looks that way,' Juliano said. 'Come with me for now. We can sort the rest out later.'

It looked like Dr Zuniga wanted to object, then he apparently thought better of it.

'I'll let you know if I find a solution.'

'Follow me,' Juliano said.

Herculano caught a flicker of amusement from the prince and realised that he was laughing at the alchemist. The prince had intended to do exactly as he pleased, whatever the good doctor said. Herculano liked the prince better because of it.

He stepped out into the corridor and said, 'Where are we going?'

'My room,' Juliano said, picking up his pace. 'You may as well see it.'

'What of my fat valet?' Herculano asked, aware that Arriscado had remained with the alchemist.

'He can stay with you for now. Although it appears he is a servant to the royal family and I may well reclaim him.'

'You'd be welcome to him. He is more loyal to you than he is to me.'

'And that is how it should be.'

'I suppose so.'

The prince said nothing till they got to his quarters. He waved all the hovering servants away, closed the door on all of them and turned to examine Herculano.

'Are you aware of how casually you are addressing your lord and master?'

'You?' Herculano asked.

'Who else?'

'I can't say I've considered it.'

'Well, you'd better start. I can't have anyone being as familiar with me as you are. Not even my best friend and bosom companion, Tiago—' The prince cut himself off and said, 'I wonder if I actually ever met him. I am worried about him. I have so many memories of the things we did together and yet...'

'You were not the one doing those things,' Herculano finished.

'This is such a strange situation.'

'That it is,' Herculano said with a sigh and threw himself onto a wide, comfortable chair with silk-covered striped cushions and arms carved like the wings of a swan.

He liked this room. It didn't feel cramped like his own and he realised it was because this was the place he'd grown up.

'You're sitting in my chair,' Juliano said.

'Damn.'

Herculano leaped to his feet while he fought not to tell the prince to bugger off. The man was right, and he would have to learn his place in this new world.

'Why did you want to come here?' Herculano decided that he was being too abrupt and added a hasty, 'Your Highness.'

Juliano gave him a cynical smile and said, 'Actually, I want to go to your house, and to achieve that I need to change.'

'To achieve that?'

'How easy do you think it is for a prince to go out of the palace incognito?'

'I can't say that, in the short life of my current memory, I have considered it.'

'Well, once upon a time you knew it well,' the prince said as he threw open the door to a wardrobe that reached nearly to the ceiling.

It was painted white and had ornate scrollwork carved into it. Inside was row upon row of sombre suits.

'That's more like it,' Herculano murmured as his gaze travelled appreciatively over the clothes.

'It isn't really my taste. Why on earth would you have so many black coats? Why not have one of each colour?'

Herculano smothered an abrupt laugh and said, 'The wardrobe in my house is stuffed with coats in a multitude of colours. I disliked it instantly.'

'Mmm, so it appears that our tastes were always our own. As were our personalities and our mannerisms,' Juliano said as he went to the end of the row of suits and pulled out a plain brown coat, tan waistcoat and brown breeches.

'Brown?'

'I, or should I say, you, were used to don this outfit to go outside incognito. It goes with this rather fetching wig,' Juliano added as he pulled out a hatbox from the base of the wardrobe and retrieved a grey wig with a single row of curls.

'I see,' Herculano said. Then a thought occurred to him. 'What do you mean about our mannerisms remaining our own?'

'The duque asked me whether I'd hurt my feet this morning,' Juliano said as he stripped out of his navy blue suit and put on the brown one. 'Apparently, I was not walking the way I used to. I've watched you and you have a very purposeful stride that, frankly, I find exhausting. I stroll. I think I always have.'

'I see.'

Herculano turned to examine the room again to give the prince some privacy. It heartened Herculano to hear that his personality and mannerisms hadn't changed. It felt, in some small way, like he had retained his essence when the rest was stripped away.

'Ready?' Juliano said.

'As you see,' Herculano said, examining the disguise. 'I'm not sure that would fool many people.'

'People see what they expect to see,' Juliano said as he placed a plain brown tricorn hat over the wig. 'They don't expect to see the prince alone in the city, so they don't.'

'Maybe, but how will you get back into the palace looking like that?'

'How?' Juliano looked confused for a second. He scratched his forehead then snapped his fingers, crossed over to his desk, reached for the quill and the neat stack of papers and said, 'I will write us a letter each, granting permission to enter the palace.'

He wrote quickly, scattered sand over the ink to ensure it dried, and fixed his seal to the bottom of the letter. Then he slipped his signet ring into his waistcoat pocket.

'Here, you may as well keep this. It will enable you to come and go as you please,' Juliano said as he handed Herculano a letter.

'The many advantages of being a prince,' Herculano murmured as he folded his letter, pocketed it and followed the prince out of the room and through the palace.

Herculano was relieved to have the document. The prince might not have considered it, but Herculano had been feeling trapped. This letter, with its royal seal, gave him a way out if he needed it.

As they made their way through the palace, Herculano dropped back a bit to examine the prince. He was right about the way he walked. It looked like a leisurely stroll, although, with his long legs, he still moved swiftly. It just wasn't the way Herculano walked.

Maybe it would be good for the prince to learn how to stride and hide some changes that had come about with the swap of their minds. If that was even possible. On a whim, Herculano tried to copy the way the prince was walking and found it wasn't as easy to mimic someone as he'd imagined.

He was so intent on his effort that it took a moment to realise that they were now in the nether regions of the palace. It was the far less sumptuous part given over to the servants and the work they did. The corridor here was narrower and simple. Plain white tiles with a blue star and blue edge lined the walls, and the floor was a simple terracotta worn into dimples by the tread of many feet.

They passed the laundry, filled with women pounding the sheets in a vast sud-filled communal pool. It surprised Herculano to see Lady Odete near the door, deep in conversation with a washerwoman. He slowed down to watch her, filled with the same pleasure he'd felt when he'd first laid eyes upon her. She looked serious as a fragment of her conversation caught his attention.

'Tiago Andrade,' she whispered in the second he was close enough to overhear.

Then he'd walked on, the laundry and Lady Odete lost to sight and hearing. But what the devil was she doing there? Why was she asking after a man the prince was also worried about?

A desire to protect Lady Odete filled his heart. He was tempted to turn back and pull her away from whatever dangerous endeavour she was engaged in. Only he couldn't.

The prince was threading his way past the servants and nearly at the kitchen door. Discovering what Lady Odete was up to would have to wait. Herculano hurried to catch up with the prince and stepped out into the palace courtyard.

'Come on,' Juliano said. 'Getting out is easy. Nobody questions why you are leaving.'

That was true. The soldiers on guard at the end of the yard barely glanced at them as they headed out into the busy street that led to the Commercial Square. Herculano was about to tell the prince which way he needed to go, when he realised the prince had pulled ahead again and was walking as if he knew exactly where the Escovar house was.

That was interesting, so Herculano maintained his distance and followed, ignoring all the sedan chair carriers who offered him a ride. The prince picked up his pace and appeared unfazed by the steep climb as he wended his way ever upwards through the partially rebuilt streets of Lisbon.

Finally, the prince stopped at Herculano's front door, reached for the knocker, then stopped, turned and arched an eyebrow.

'Are you going to let me in?'

'How did you know this is the correct house, and how to get here?' Herculano said as he grabbed the heavy knocker shaped like the head of a lion biting on an iron ring and hammered it hard against the door.

Juliano paused, a thoughtful expression etched on his face.

'I just knew.'

'Well, you knew better than me. I'm not sure I could have got us back here on my own.'

'That is unfortunate,' Juliano said, as a servant opened the door.

Upon spotting Herculano, the footman stiffened to attention and bowed to let the two of them in.

'Welcome home, master.'

'It won't be for long,' Herculano muttered as he walked into what felt nothing like home.

Because he was irritated, he took the lead to his bedroom, playing host to the man who'd grown up in the house.

'It's odd,' Juliano said, once they were safely in Herculano's room. 'None of this is familiar to me, and yet it's all far more comfortable than the palace.'

'I felt the same in the palace,' Herculano said as he opened the door to his wardrobe.

The prince's eyebrows rose as he took in the rows of colourful suits.

'I see what you mean.'

'I presume I should pack some and take them to the palace, if I am to remain by your side.'

'That would be the sensible thing to do,' Juliano said as he strolled round the rest of the room, taking everything in.

He gasped as he came to the dressing table and snatched up the small portrait of the man propped against the wall.

'Do you know him?' Herculano said as he joined the prince, who was clutching the portrait so tightly his knuckles had turned white.

'My father,' the prince muttered.

'No.'

'I know,' Juliano snapped. 'But this man took me in and raised me. He showed me such great kindness. I now realise how great it was, for I was not his son and he knew it, but he never told me. He only spoke of my mother and brothers who were lost in the earthquake. And of how much of a consolation it was to him that I survived.'

'I see.' Herculano wished he could feel even a tenth of what the prince felt for the man in the portrait. 'Well, at least one of us remembers him.'

'Damn Dr Zuniga. He should have left well enough alone. From what I can tell, you were doing perfectly well as the prince.'

'I'm not so sure of that. The duque apparently stymied me at every turn and I somehow managed to lose my best friend. Maybe what the kingdom needs is to have you in charge. You are right, we are different. Maybe you can break the impasse I was stuck in.'

'I barely know what I am doing.' Juliano paced about the room, the portrait still clutched in his hands. 'How can I take on the duque?'

'Well, you can't let him win,' Herculano said and started taking out the suits he found least offensive in his wardrobe and flinging them onto the bed.

'What does that even mean?'

'Every ruler, no, every man, must make his own decisions. You might turn out to be a terrible king, but the faults should be your own. They shouldn't be as the result of a puppet master pulling the strings behind the throne. If people blame you for anything, it should at least be for decisions you made yourself.'

Juliano laughed and said, 'Spoken like a true ruler. You may have forgotten everything, but I think you still understand statecraft. Maybe it will be good to work together.'

'Do you think so?'

'We are stuck together, anyway. No two men in history have shared more than we have. We have lived each other's lives. We couldn't get any closer. So let's use that to our advantage and break the duque's hold over us and over our kingdom.'

'How do you propose we do that?' Herculano said, and found himself actually liking the prince.

'The first thing we need to do is find out what Tiago and I were up to. If the duque had anything to do with his disappearance, then it is a sign that we were on to something. It must be something so important that the duque had to act against us. It is imperative, therefore, that we work out what that is.'

5

Odete had been so distracted by her mission that she lost track of time. As a result, she had to scramble into her clothes for dinner and run to rejoin Mafalda, Pia and Maria da Luz.

'Where have you been? We will be late!' Mafalda hissed.

She slipped her arm through Odete's, pulled her close and set off for the dining room at a brisk walk. Odete glanced first at the footmen leading the way, then back at Pia and Maria da Luz who looked flustered, hurrying after Mafalda.

'I have been doing as you asked,' Odete said in an undertone. Heaven help them if she was overheard.

'So what have you discovered?'

'Just that Tiago went out early last night and hasn't been seen since. None of the servants in the palace have come across him. The maid who cleans his room told me his bed hadn't been slept in.'

'What if he was set upon by ruffians? Has a search been made beyond the palace?'

'Nobody is taking his disappearance seriously yet. I have it on good authority that his father thinks he's just off entertaining himself and he'll reappear in a couple of days.'

'But the prince is worried.'

'Aside from asking for Tiago this morning, it doesn't look like he has done anything else. Maybe he also thinks he will reappear in a couple of days.'

'But if he's in trouble, they might all be too late to save him. They can't afford to wait a few days,' Mafalda hissed.

'I know, but I am not done looking.'

Odete patted her arm. In part, it was to reassure her and in part to urge her to be quiet as they stepped into the dining room.

It was a large room, designed to seat a couple of hundred guests. The tables were laid with the finest silverware and practically translucent porcelain plates edged in gold. Massive silver centrepieces were placed at regular intervals along the long tables, and chandeliers with hundreds of candles blazed above, adding to the heat of an already stifling day.

They were so late that the room was full of courtiers. They were the richest of the country's nobility, attested by the glittering jewels and the fine silk dresses of the women, and the heavily embroidered, wide-skirted coats of the men. Worse still, the prince had already arrived. It was breaking etiquette to arrive after him.

Odete feared they were in for a reprimand as everyone watched Mafalda walk to her seat. The men bowed as she passed and the ladies curtsied. Odete let go of Mafalda's arm and dropped back a half pace as they reached the high table.

It surprised Odete to see that the man she'd confronted that morning by Dr Zuniga's room was now sitting beside the prince. In fact, he was occupying the place usually taken by Tiago Andrade. What was the meaning of that?

'So good of you to join us,' the duque said in a tone that relayed his displeasure.

'I apologise, we got a little held up,' Mafalda said and dropped her head, unable to hold her father's gaze.

'It is no matter,' Prince Juliano said.

This got a gasp from Mafalda and made Odete wonder again what was going on. He never stood up for Mafalda or involved himself in any conversation between the duque and his daughter.

His intervention annoyed the duque, who said, 'You, of all people, should know the importance of etiquette.'

'I'm sure Lady Mafalda won't do it again.'

Then, to everyone's astonishment, Prince Juliano turned away from the duque and indicated for the servants to serve the food. Never before had the prince dismissed the duque so casually, nor taken charge of dinner.

Odete wondered what was going on but was distracted when she realised the man sitting beside the prince was staring at her. As he was noticed, he smiled and looked away. What was the meaning of that? Odete was astonished by his brazen behaviour. And then to smile! How dare he?

But who was he? And how did he rise to his sudden position of prominence when just this morning she'd caught him with his ear pressed to the alchemist's door?

She wasn't the only person wondering. The courtiers were whispering amongst themselves and pointing at the man beside the prince.

The man himself appeared not to care and focused on his food. Every now and then, he glanced in her direction. Was he plotting his revenge because she'd called him a spy?

'Your Highness has brought a new guest to the table,' the duque said.

Odete held her breath and leaned forward so she could hear. It was tricky over the hubbub in the dining room, and because she had Mafalda and Lord Nicanor Ledo between her and the duque, while the prince was to the other side of the duque.

'I have,' the prince said. 'You met him this morning with Dr Zuniga. But if you wish for a second introduction, this is His Excellency, Herculano Escovar.'

'And what elevates a mere merchant to the position he has occupied at this table?'

Herculano Escovar stopped eating as the introduction was made and gave the duque a slight, cynical smile as he tilted his head in greeting. It was so calculated to offend that Odete gasped at his courage. Or perhaps he was a fool and didn't realise how dangerous it was to get on the wrong side of the duque. At this moment he was holding the duque's gaze and didn't look at all intimidated.

'I have a feeling I can learn from him,' the prince said.

'And this warrants him being at your right hand?'

'Until Tiago returns, he will remain here.'

To Odete, the prince's words sounded like a challenge or a threat. What was more surprising was that the duque was apparently lost for something to say on the matter.

The noise in the palace dwindled away as everyone headed for bed. It was well past midnight and the candles on the single candelabra he had lit were burning low, but Herculano couldn't sleep. He paced restlessly around Tiago Andrade's room, his temporary home until that noble lord reappeared. *If* he reappeared. Herculano worried that Tiago had met an even more drastic fate than he himself had.

From what he could see in the flickering light, it was a large room, larger than the room he'd occupied, albeit briefly, in the Escovar household. All the furniture was made from the dark, nearly black, wood that was the current vogue. There was a four-poster bed, a desk and accompanying chair, a wardrobe and a silk-upholstered sofa that was a match in colour, if not design, to the sofa in the prince's room.

As it was a room assigned and furnished by the royal court, it held no stamp of the occupant's personality. It also gave no clue as to his current whereabouts.

For the hundredth time, Herculano wondered what he'd stumbled into. It had all happened so quickly that it threw him. The more he thought about it though, the angrier he grew.

He had already realised that if he'd been taken in by Escovar senior, it meant that even Herculano Escovar was not the name he was born with or baptised in. If he'd been baptised at all. He had no idea whether his pauper parents had done that. It scarcely mattered, but his identity, the core of what he was, had vanished and he felt adrift.

People were anchored to their lives by their history. They were the sum of their name and the names and faces of their parents and siblings. The location of their birth, where they had been schooled, their local parish, the community that surrounded them, and the innumerable stories and incidents that peppered their lives. It gave them a connection.

Herculano had none of that. He didn't even have anyone who could tell him any of it. The life he was supposed to remember wasn't even the life he had lived. The life they had given him had gone back to its rightful inheritor.

Well, he had one thing: the memory of the earthquake. Maybe in time he could retrieve more. His deepest yearning was to go further back and know who he really was. He had no interest in either of the personas they had given him.

A crash beyond his door jerked him out of his introspection. More for something to do than any actual interest, he strolled out to see what had happened.

A small dark figure was dusting herself off beside an overturned side table. She reached for the copper vase lying on its side, the source of the almighty crash, righted the table and put the vase back on it. She was wrapped in a voluminous black cape with a hood pulled far forward so it was impossible to see her face.

Herculano was sure of who it was, though. There weren't many women on this floor and fewer of those had such a neat figure.

Herculano closed the gap between them and murmured, 'What are you doing here at this late hour, Lady Odete?'

Odete gave a shriek that she hastily smothered by clapping both gloved hands over her mouth as she swung round to examine Herculano. He gave her a smile and a bow and then waited. It was unkind of him to do so. He should have helped her, but he felt he owed her some repayment. She had accused him of being a spy, after all.

'Nothing, I'm doing nothing,' Odete said breathlessly.

'Indeed, and this nothing involves sneaking about the palace after midnight, wrapped in a black cloak?'

Odete pulled herself up to her not very impressive full height and said, 'What I choose to do, sir, is none of your business.'

'So you have been visiting a paramour,' Herculano said, and overwhelming jealousy washed over him.

'What? How dare you! I have done nothing of the sort.'

'Why else would a young woman be about, unaccompanied, at this hour?'

'I'm looking for someone.'

'A likely story.'

'About as likely as your own. I don't know how you inveigled your way into the prince's affections, but you, sir, are an imposter.'

'You have no idea,' Herculano murmured. 'But, while your diversionary tactic was a worthy attempt, you will not evade my questions. What are you doing away from your quarters?'

'I will never tell you.'

A thought struck Herculano and he said, 'You were on your way out, weren't you?'

'At this hour?' Odete hissed. 'That is most unlikely.'

'Is it? Where exactly were you headed then? For you have your back to your rooms.'

'I was merely going out for some air. It is very stuffy in the palace.'

'You were going out for some air?' Herculano said, as he crossed his arms and leaned his back against the wall. 'That is the most absurd reason yet. Perhaps, my lady, you are a spy, and you have been listening at my door.'

'Why would I listen at your door?'

'Because you have already accused me of being a spy and inveigling my way into the prince's affections. You are clearly of a suspicious inclination.'

'Well, I am,' Odete said with disarming honesty. 'And you are worthy of my suspicion, but I have no interest in you this evening.'

'Perhaps another evening then,' Herculano said, more in hope than belief.

Odete gasped, pulled her cloak more tightly about herself and said, 'I won't stay here to be insulted by you,' and she hurried away.

Herculano was astonished to see that she was still heading for the stairs, so he ran after her. A few strides got him in front of Odete and he barred her path by spreading his arms wide.

She stepped back, ensuring an arm's length between them and said, 'Now what are you doing?'

'I can't let you go. It is far too dangerous for a woman to be out on her own at night. Especially if you really do plan on leaving the palace.'

'I don't see why it would be.'

'Then you are more naïve than I thought you. Good God, woman, no lady would go out on her own even in full daylight. How much more foolish to do it at night?'

'Nobody will see me.'

'I saw you.'

'Well... well, then I shall adopt a disguise. I shall change and go out dressed as a man.'

Herculano laughed and said, 'You are far too short for that.'

'I will go out as a boy then.'

'You are too buxom to pass for a boy. Unless you wish to be mistaken for those man creatures that dress up as women.'

'Who do what?' Odete said, blinking at him in surprise.

'What?' Herculano said, and realised he was talking about something no well-bred woman would know about. 'Never mind.'

'I really don't think I'd be mistaken for a man dressed as a woman,' Odete said, giving him a hurt look.

'No, I don't suppose you would. But, as I've already said, it is inappropriate for any woman to be out on the street at night.'

'I have to go out.'

Herculano sighed. It seemed like nothing he said could sway Lady Odete. He hoped it didn't mean she was touched by madness. Herculano felt not. He didn't think his old self would fall for a deranged woman.

'Look, if you are determined to go out, at least let me accompany you.'

'You? But I don't trust you at all.'

'What is it exactly that you wanted to do outside? You must have some reason, and if it isn't a secret assignation, then there is surely no harm in telling me about it.'

Lady Odete at least looked swayed by his entreaty and nibbled on the edge of one black-gloved finger as she examined Herculano.

'If you must know, I am looking for someone. I intend to visit all the hospitals to see if they have brought in anyone matching his description.'

'Lord Tiago Andrade?' Herculano said, as pieces fell into place.

'How did you guess that?' Lady Odete said, taking a startled step back.

'Do you like him?' Herculano asked, puzzled by whether that was the case.

'I am worried about him.'

'So you like him.'

'That is none of your business.'

Herculano reflected that, since the prince had given him a similar assignment, it wouldn't be a bad idea to work with Lady Odete. At least that way he could keep an eye on her and try to keep her safe. For her to accept his protection would require some candour on his part too though, and that was a risk. Ah well, life was full of risks. At least this way he had a reason to be near Lady Odete.

'As it happens, my lady, the prince has tasked me with finding Lord Tiago as well.'

'He has? I thought he wasn't overly worried by his friend's disappearance.'

'Quite the contrary. But he is trying to be discreet.'

'Are you implying that I was not being discreet?'

'Perhaps you are not that experienced in spying.'

'And you are?'

'Well, no. Despite what you might think. I am no spy. But the prince has given me a mission that matches your own. Wouldn't it be best if we work together?'

6

For the second morning in a row, Herculano woke to find Arriscado's unlovely face gazing down at him.

'Oh, so you're here, are you?' Herculano muttered.

'I thought it best to remain here and support you.'

Herculano flicked his light coverlet off, sat up and rubbed his face to wake himself properly. It had been a restless night.

'You or Dr Zuniga?'

'It was my decision, although Dr Zuniga was in agreement.'

'So you can spy on me and make sure I do as I am told?' Herculano stood and stretched as he spoke and blinked in the bright summer sunshine. 'Who the devil thought it was a good idea to open the shutters? It looks like it will be a scorching day.'

'I opened them for some fresh air. Now that the room has cooled, I'll close them again.' Arriscado rose from his chair and, with great decorum, went to close the shutters. 'In answer to your suspicions, I asked to stay because I want to look after you. I wish the spell had worked properly so you could at least have the memories we owe you. The prince had a comfortable and happy upbringing as a merchant's son, while yours was harsher. You deserve at least the memory of happiness.'

'I'm glad I didn't get those memories,' Herculano said, as he stepped up to a blue and white porcelain washbasin and splashed water over his face. 'It wasn't the life I actually lived. Nor am I really Herculano Escovar. I am happier with no memories at all than false ones. Besides, the prince doesn't seem to be coping with the memories he has either.'

'It is perhaps because of your different characters. I wouldn't be surprised if the prince is struggling to square what he was likely to do in any given situation, with what he remembers actually doing.'

'You mean what I did,' Herculano said and started to get dressed into a plain pair of brown breeches and a white shirt. 'This is all damnably confusing.'

'Which is why I am here to support you. I can help fill in the gaps.'

'Maybe.'

'And you can help the prince by explaining why you did certain things the way you did. It might even enable you to work out what has happened to Tiago Andrade.'

Herculano felt like more of an interloper in this room than he did in the body he'd so recently reacquired. He picked up Tiago's shaving blade and gazed at the worn ivory handle. This was an implement its owner wouldn't have left at home if he'd planned a trip of more than a day.

'I can do that for you,' Arriscado said, taking the blade out of his hand. 'I always used to shave you in the morning.'

'Very well,' Herculano said and sat down before a mirror where he could watch the valet at work. He was reluctant to call him his valet just yet, but the thought of valets made him ask, 'Where is Tiago's valet? Has he been questioned about his master's whereabouts?'

'He was the first to raise the alarm about Tiago Andrade's disappearance. He went straight to the prince yesterday morning to inform him that his master hadn't come home.'

'So he was already worried?'

'It is unusual for a man of Lord Tiago's status to go away for any length of time without his valet. Especially as he said nothing to him of where he was going.'

'That doesn't sound good,' Herculano said with a sigh.

Arriscado nodded and said, as he applied a lather of soap to Herculano's face, 'Dr Zuniga suggested you go and see him once you're dressed.'

'Later,' Herculano said, glad that he could reject the suggestion. 'This morning I am going out with Lady Odete to visit all the hospitals in search of Tiago.'

Arriscado paused in his shaving and looked at Herculano via the mirror. 'Lady Odete?'

Herculano grinned at him, taking delight in sowing confusion.

'For some reason, she is also looking for the gentleman. I can only assume because she is in love with him.'

'You are going out into the city accompanied by an unmarried young woman? How do you even know her? Who is this Lady Odete?'

'She is a very suspicious woman who is one of Lady Mafalda's ladies-in-waiting.'

'Suspicious? You distrust her?'

'On the contrary, she distrusts me. In fact, she denounced me as a spy.'

'Oh, that woman. Well then, all the more reason not to go anywhere with her.'

'But if I don't, then I fear she will go out on her own with no protection. I can't allow her to do that.'

One of Arriscado's bushy eyebrows rose at that comment.

'Do you like the young lady?'

'I think I was in love with her.'

'Ah, I see. That is complicated.'

Much to Herculano's surprise, Arriscado reached under his collar and pulled a chain into view. Dangling at the end was a simple gold band. Judging by the small size, Herculano guessed it had belonged to a woman.

'Were you married?'

'A very long time ago.' Arriscado removed the wedding ring from the chain and held it out. 'If I might suggest – the young lady should wear this if she is going out only accompanied by you.'

'I can't take something that's so precious to you.'

'I know you will bring it back safe and sound.'

Herculano nodded and accepted the ring.

'Now, I will wait.'

'You aren't going to fetch her?'

'She gave me strict instructions not to go anywhere near her quarters for fear of what the gossips might say.'

'But what will they say to her knocking at your door?' Arriscado said. 'Whatever you do, you can't allow her to come inside. That would ruin her in an instant.'

Herculano was about to reassure Arriscado that he had no intention of allowing Lady Odete into his room when a timid scratching at the door stopped him.

He pulled it open to find Lady Odete, swathed in the same cloak she'd been wearing the night before, a wide bag slung over her shoulder, peering out at him from under her hood.

'You surely don't mean to go out like that.'

'Why not? Are you ready?'

'Nearly, just give me a moment to get my jacket.'

Herculano turned to find Arriscado standing directly behind him. He was holding out the jacket, but watching Lady Odete in undisguised curiosity. Herculano snatched the jacket away and hurried after Lady Odete, who'd not bothered to wait for him.

He caught up with her at the top of the stairs and said, 'Wait. I have something for you,' as he held out the ring.

Lady Odete looked astonished and said, 'What is the meaning of that?'

'My manservant thought it might occasion less comment if we went about as man and wife.'

'I see.' Odete snatched the ring out of his hand and slipped it onto her finger. 'It would be best if we don't walk together in the palace, though.'

'What should I do then?'

'Follow behind, but don't make it obvious,' Odete said in an undertone as she hurried down the stairs.

Herculano followed at a more leisurely pace and allowed the gap between them to widen. The palace was already filled with servants going briskly about their business. The occasional courtier also wandered the corridors although it was early enough to expect most of them to still be in bed or at the very most at their breakfast.

Herculano watched as Lady Odete showed a letter to the guards at the gate and judged it time to get closer to her again, so he picked up his pace. Moments later he'd shown the letter given to him by the prince and stepped out into the hot, bright, Lisbon streets.

It took a moment for Herculano's eyes to adjust to the glare and find Lady Odete. She was watching him from the shaded wall of the building opposite the palace. Herculano dodged a slow-moving carriage, side stepped a sedan chair being carried by two sun-browned men and crossed the road to join her ladyship.

Herculano slipped his arm through hers and tightened his grip as she jumped and tried to pull away from him.

'Relax, I mean you no harm. But if we stick together like this, we will look like a couple and that is for the best.'

'I feel like you have an ulterior motive,' Lady Odete hissed.

'Not at all,' Herculano said, trying to make his voice sound light and disinterested. 'Now, where would you like to begin?'

'The All Saints Hospital. It's the closest and the biggest.'

'Very well, lead on.'

'You don't know the way?'

Herculano toyed with confessing that he'd lost his memory, then decided against it.

'I never really paid attention to the locations of the hospitals. It would be best if you lead the way for now.'

'Very well,' Odete said and pulled him along in a determined manner as she started down the cobbled street.

She had her eyes fixed on the route and wasted no time looking up at Herculano. That suited him for the moment. He'd felt a surge of pleasure to be so close to this woman. His heart beat faster to hold her near, but he didn't actually know her.

As he looked down at her face, so focused on her task, he wondered what it was about Lady Odete that he'd liked so much when he was the prince. She was very pretty. But the palace was full of beautiful women, so why Lady Odete? Why had he fallen in love with her in the first place?

He also wondered whether things might change now. Would his love remain or fade in this new body? Would he fall more deeply in love or lose interest? Would it matter either way?

If she didn't love him, what could he do? Was he even a worthy suitor? Lady Odete could never have married the prince, their stations were too far apart. But would she be willing to consider a merchant for a husband? Or even a pauper? He doubted it.

Odete had never been as close to a man as she was to this Herculano Escovar and it was uncomfortable. He had a firm grip on her arm and she could feel the heat and bulk of his body.

Much as she'd wished it, she'd never been this close to the prince. The closest they'd ever been was when he'd kissed the tips of her fingers in greeting. Despite his royal status, though, Odete suspected that the prince's presence wouldn't be as overwhelming. This Herculano might be shorter than the prince, but his shoulders were wider and overall he carried more muscle.

To get away, she walked as briskly as she could. Thank goodness she was wearing her sensible shoes. She practically dragged the man along in her eagerness to get away, although he seemed oblivious to her discomfort.

Odete glanced up at his face and was shocked that he was examining her and he looked puzzled.

'What are you doing?' Odete said, breathless from her breakneck speed.

'I beg your pardon. I was just wondering about you.'

'About me?' Odete said, and squirmed under his gaze. 'What could you possibly wonder about me?'

'How long have you been a lady-in-waiting?'

'Why do you want to know that?' Odete asked as they reached a long set of broad stairs that would take them up to Figueira Square and the All Saints Hospital.

'I thought perhaps I should know, if I am to play your husband.'

'I doubt anyone at the hospital would want to know that much about either of us.'

Odete started up the stairs, dragging Herculano with her. It was infuriating that he was not in a hurry.

'But what if they ask? I feel we should have some kind of story for them. If not about ourselves, then about Tiago Andrade.'

'What?'

The question made Odete stop halfway up the stairs. She was a couple of steps higher than Herculano so that the two of them were now the same height and he was staring at her, an unreadable smile crinkling the corners of his eyes. The smile was pleasant, she realised with a shock. It improved an otherwise plain face.

'What should we tell them about Tiago?' Herculano said. 'What is our reason for searching for him?'

'We are family, just concerned family,' Odete said and went back to dragging this intractable man up the stairs.

'You or me?'

'What does that matter?' Odete said, exasperated.

'Well, we're married. So he's either related to you or to me. I think it would be best to say he's your brother. Then you can act like a concerned sister. I'll be the long-suffering husband, dragged along for support.'

'Dragged along!' Odete snapped and jerked her arm free from Herculano. 'Dragged along? I didn't ask you to come with, sir. You invited yourself. Then you came up with this ridiculous ruse of marriage and have been clinging to me ever since. Today, when it's so hot and I don't even know you, I have your sweaty body pressed against mine!'

'Peace,' Herculano said, holding his hands up in supplication and apology. 'I did not mean to make you uncomfortable. I'm sorry. But you know, I really did come out to keep you safe. As we are working on the same mystery, it also seemed sensible.'

'Maybe.'

Odete was uncomfortably aware they were creating a scene. The people passing them on the steps were watching and listening. One old woman, swathed in black skirts and a black shawl, was grinning at the pair of them. Odete decided it was best to get away and hurried on up the stairs.

'Alright, we can tell the hospital that Tiago is my brother,' she said, refusing to look at Herculano lest he give her a triumphant smirk.

The top of the stairs opened up onto a pleasant square, the centre of which was dominated by a large, shady fig tree. On three sides of the square were sparkling new buildings three stories high. They were tiled in blue and green with elegant wrought-iron balconies.

On the fourth side was the half-built hospital. The north wing was complete, as was an imposing central entranceway. The south side was still being constructed.

Judging by the small number of men at work and the limited supplies of bricks stacked out front, it looked like another project that had stalled due to lack of funds. The city was littered with so many such projects that Odete barely noticed and made straight for the hospital entrance. Over the door was a massive stone cross. On either side were carved saints depicted healing the sick.

A sizeable crowd of the needy were gathered at the entrance. These were the people who were too poor to buy their way in. They had to wait till someone inside took pity on them. Their clothes were ragged and their faces thin.

Odete avoided looking them in the eye. She already knew they would be filled with desperation. Two nuns walked purposefully amongst these people, examining each in turn and deciding whether to grant them entry.

For the first time, Odete looked back in search of Herculano. He was standing directly behind her, his expression far graver than she'd seen up till now as he examined the unfortunates.

'Can I help you, Your Excellencies?' a hospital porter said as he spotted Odete and Herculano. He was a thin, sinewy man with a blood-smeared white apron protecting his clothes.

It was typical that the porter asked the man Odete was with, rather than speaking to her. It was yet another reason Odete would have preferred to visit all the hospitals on her own. That way, they would have been forced to speak to her.

'Yes, you can help,' Herculano said with a nod at the orderly and a gleam in his eye that implied he'd noticed Odete's irritation. 'My wife is looking for her brother. He has failed to come home for two nights in a row, which is most unlike him. Tell the porter what he looks like, my beloved.'

He said the last words with unholy glee and Odete decided he'd need to be punished for it. She'd just have to work out the best revenge. In the meantime, the orderly was looking at her expectantly.

'I can do better than just tell you,' Odete said, giving Herculano as severe a glare as she could. She took her sketchbook out of her bag and flicked it open to the drawing she'd made of Tiago and held it up for the porter.

'I think my brother came out in plain clothes. But they will have been of good quality. He is of average height, with curly dark brown hair that he ties back with a black ribbon. He has a dark complexion and... as you can see here, a small mole to the side of his left eye.'

'Mmm,' the orderly said and stared at the sketch as he considered all the patients. 'I can't recall such a man.'

'Would it be possible to see for ourselves?' Herculano asked.

'If you wish, Your Excellency. I doubt he'll be here, though. We've not had any member of the quality brought in over the last couple of days. I always remember quality,' the porter said and held out his hand expectantly.

'Money!' Odete hissed at Herculano's blank look and rammed her elbow into his side.

'I am embarrassed to admit, I don't have any,' Herculano whispered into her ear.

'You came out with no money?' Odete said, staring at Herculano in astonishment.

Then she tutted with impatience, reached back into her bag, pulled out a reticule, loosened the strings to get at her money and pressed a couple of reais into the orderly's hand.

'This way please, Your Excellencies,' the man said, rolling his eyes at Herculano as he slipped the money into the deep pocket of his apron.

He led them into a large hall-like room filled with four rows of beds from one end to the other.

'You just take a look around. There's two more rooms like this one on the floors above. We usually put the quality on the middle floor. We reserve the top floor for female patients,' the orderly said, and, with a bob of his head, he walked off.

Odete wondered whether now was a suitable moment to chastise Herculano for being so astonishingly unprepared. But no, there would be plenty of time for that later. For now, she would focus on the job at hand. Herculano was already doing that as he'd made his way to the first person in the first bed.

It turned out to be an old man drooling onto a grubby pillow. Odete shuddered and pulled the side of her hood across her face to cover her nose and mouth. The smell in the hospital was a mixture of vomit, human waste, sweat and blood that made her feel queasy. She dreaded to think whether it carried a contagion. Much as she wished to help Lady Mafalda and the prince, she didn't want to fall ill.

Herculano seemed less worried by the sights of all the sick men in their rows of beds and went methodically from one to the next, checking each face. Odete was grateful that she wasn't the one pulling back sheets and getting up close. Just the coughs, groans and occasional screams were enough to make her want to flee.

❧

'We should head back,' Herculano said as they emerged back into the bright sunshine from the fifth hospital. They were all filled with the same misery of sick people. He wasn't sure he could take much more of it.

'There are still two hospitals to visit,' Odete said, but she looked tired and didn't sound that eager to go on.

'I'm beginning to feel like this is a waste of time. I don't think Tiago has wound up at a hospital.'

The one advantage of going through all the sick was that it had been so stomach-churning that Herculano had not wanted lunch when it reached noon. That was probably just as well, since he'd forgotten to come out with money.

He realised that he'd not considered money since he'd woken in his new body. He had no idea whether he even had any. He'd have to ask Arriscado. Maybe the old man would be useful after all.

Herculano was so absorbed in his own thoughts he hadn't noticed that he'd lost Lady Odete till he looked down to speak to her. He turned around and found her standing stock still, her arms folded and a stubborn set to her mouth.

'Are you going to force me to go to the last two hospitals?' Herculano said with a sigh.

'What if he is at one of them? What if we gave up and he died because we were tired and hungry and not bothered to go on?'

'Aren't you tired?'

'Of course I'm tired. And I'm hot. I never want to see another sick person again. But how can I go back and tell Lady Mafalda that I haven't found Tiago?'

'Lady Mafalda? What the devil has she got to do with this?'

Odete slapped her hands over her mouth. 'Nothing, no, nothing,' came her muffled reply.

'So... it's Lady Mafalda who likes Tiago, is it?' Herculano said, considerably cheered to discover that fact.

'I never said that,' Odete said guiltily.

'Mmm,' Herculano said.

They'd just come up some stairs and arrived at another of the hundreds of little squares that made up the city. It had a road that passed east to west along its nearest edge. Herculano would have liked to take the road as it followed the contour of the hill. He had the resigned feeling that they'd be crossing the square and continuing their upward path as the stairs continued beyond the square. His suspicion was confirmed when Odete crossed the road in a beeline for the next set of stairs.

They had planted a row of lemon trees to either side of them. Their dark green leathery leaves looked almost black in the bright sun. Herculano assumed someone had planted them after the earthquake, as the trees were only slightly taller than he was.

'Let's at least pause for a drink.' Herculano said as he made his way to the fountain. He was parched, but he also worried about Lady Odete who was flushed from the heat and looking tired.

The fountain was little more than a permanently running tap set into a tiled wall, with a trough below. The stairs went up the outside of the fountain, taking pedestrians to the next level of Lisbon. A handful of peasant women stood around the fountain, each holding a large, narrow-necked water jug.

They waited as a girl of around eleven filled her jug. She was skinny and had her skirts hitched up so that her bare feet, ankles and calves showed. The soles of her feet were thick and cracked and stained with dust. All the women were dressed similarly in faded and threadbare clothes that had evidently been thumped and scrubbed to this state in the local washing pools, as they were all clean.

They stepped back from the fountain so that Herculano and Odete could drink. Herculano wondered what he'd have thought of that when he was the prince. Then he laughed inwardly. When he was the prince, he'd never have been alone in a Lisbon square drinking from a fountain.

He scooped the water that dribbled out of the fountain into a cupped hand and drank. It was lukewarm, but thirst-quenching. He wiped away the water that spilled down the side of his mouth. Then he filled his hand again and held it out to Odete. So far she had rejected any help he offered, and she did the same now.

She crouched down to hold her hands under the fountain. Odete brought her cupped hands to her lips and drank so carefully that she didn't spill a drop. She wiped her hands down her skirt, straightened up and looked expectantly at Herculano.

'We have to go to the next two hospitals.'

'I will, if you tell me the truth. Are you doing this for Lady Mafalda?'

'I don't need you to come with me,' Odete said as she headed for the steps, although she sounded less confident.

A day spent with him had apparently changed her mind. Most of the hospitals' staff were more willing to speak to Herculano than to her and he'd noticed how afraid she was to approach the people in their sickbeds.

'I won't allow you to wander these streets alone, especially not so late in the day. If we go to the next two hospitals, it will be dark before we get back to the palace.'

'Then we'd better get moving. I can't afford to be late for dinner again.'

'So, are you going to tell me what's going on?' Herculano asked as he fell into step behind Odete.

She picked up her pace, to get away from him, he'd realised, which hurt.

'I swore I wouldn't tell a soul.'

'From that, I will assume it's Lady Mafalda who has tender feelings for Tiago. That way, you can't be accused of telling me.'

Odete looked dubious but issued no denial.

'I thought Lady Mafalda meant to marry the prince.'

'That is what her father wants. You know how difficult he is to deny.'

'Even for his daughter?'

It astonished Herculano to discover that Lady Mafalda wasn't interested in the prince. The loathing he felt when he heard Lady Mafalda's name made him wonder whether he'd known it when he was the prince.

'You don't know the duque very well, do you?' Odete said.

'How would I? Until yesterday, I'd never met him.'

'That means nothing,' Odete said as she sidestepped a one-armed tramp who sat slumped against a house wall, his remaining hand held out in supplication. 'How can you not know what the duque is like? All of Portugal knows you must not cross him, for his vengeance is excruciating and final.'

'Is it?'

Odete swung round to stare at Herculano, her eyes wide in surprise.

'Are you even from our kingdom? How can you have lived in Lisbon and be so ignorant?'

Herculano shifted uncomfortably under her gaze. He got the impression he was coming over as a nincompoop.

'What is it about him you are referring to, exactly?'

'Everything,' Odete said, flinging out her arms in emphasis to encompass all of Lisbon. 'He does exactly as he wants.'

'Do you have an example?'

Herculano lengthened his stride to keep up with Odete. Her inner agitation was being expressed by an increase in walking pace.

'An example? You really don't know?'

'Would I be asking if I did?'

'It isn't safe to talk about him. Especially about sensitive matters.'

'Don't mention his name, then.'

Odete let out a deep sigh and she examined the street she'd stopped in. It was narrow; the houses rose to three stories about them and the lines of washing overhead cast them in a deep and pleasantly cool shadow. A pair of women were holding a loud conversation across the road to each other from their respective windows. Below, a group of children were playing with a dog. The dog had a rag in its jaws and the children were trying to pull it away and dragging the dog back and forth in their attempts, accompanied by howls of laughter.

Much to Herculano's surprise, Odete slipped her arm into his and pulled him closer. She spoke in such a low voice that Herculano had to lean his head down to hear her. To any passer-by, they must have looked like a couple engaged in an intimate conversation.

'You must surely know about the Marquis of Portima?'

'What about him?'

'Really? You don't know?'

'I'm afraid I don't.'

'When he was younger, the duque asked the marquis for his daughter's hand in marriage. Owing to a feud between the two families, the marquis turned him down. After the earthquake, the marquis also objected to the duque's reconstruction plans for the city. It angered him that the duque wanted to take some of his land. He said the money being offered as compensation was paltry. He said it was an insult to his dignity. Two months later, the marquis and his eldest sons were arrested and accused of treason. They were taken away and tortured until they confessed...'

Odete stopped as they crossed the open doorway of a workshop. It was filled with men hammering away at making barrels. There was no way they could hear her, but she maintained her silence until they were clear of the men.

'The marquis confessed to all that the duque had accused them of. But the duque wasn't done. He ordered a public execution in the Chiado. He arrested the marquis's wife, too. She was strangled before the baying crowd. Then the marquis and his sons were tortured and finally killed. The whole spectacle took all day.

'Some people believed the story of treason. But many whispered that it was the duque taking his revenge for being turned down as a suitor. I don't know if that is true. All I do know is it is dangerous to snub the duque.

'He never forgets an insult. He takes his time getting his revenge, but he always gets it. He used similar ruthless measures to break the power of the church. He hasn't stopped, either. Anyone he sees as an enemy is doomed. The numbers of executions and burnings in the Chiado are hardly fewer than when the Inquisition was purging heretics. Only now it is the duque who is in charge of the slaughter.'

7

It was dark by the time Herculano and Odete got back to the palace. Herculano just had enough time to dress for dinner, but the prince still arched his eyebrow at him for being out all day. The meal, or rather the packed banquet hall, saved him from further interrogation, though, as he couldn't reveal what he'd been up to with so many potential eavesdroppers around them.

It was a battle for Herculano not to nod off, despite the raucous laughter at the antics of a group of performing dwarfs. Try as he might, he couldn't find them funny.

'Follow me to my room,' Juliano murmured when they finally processed out of the dining room at the end of an interminably long evening.

'Now?'

'It isn't a request,' Juliano said with his slight smile.

'As you wish, sire,' Herculano said with a resigned bow.

'How goes the search?' Juliano asked as soon as Herculano closed the door on the two of them.

Herculano made his way to what he hoped was an acceptable chair. It was less ostentatious, but also less comfortable than the swan sofa, and he dropped into it with a sigh.

'I'm afraid I have nothing to tell you. We visited all–'

'Wait,' Juliano said, holding up a finger. 'We?'

'Ah, yes, I should have mentioned, Lady Odete accompanied me.'

'Why?' Juliano said as he poured himself a glass of wine from a gold and cut crystal decanter.

Juliano held the wine up in query and Herculano shook his head. He couldn't face more drink. He'd supped far too much while trying to kill time in the banquet hall.

'Lady Odete was worried about Tiago's disappearance, too. I thought it best to go out together.'

'Odd,' Juliano said. 'I thought she liked me.'

'Did you?'

'You don't remember?'

'I'm afraid not,' Herculano said, and kept to himself how he felt about Odete.

A day spent in her company had proven interesting but not definitive. It didn't adequately explain why his heart beat faster when he saw her, nor the wish to hold her close at every opportunity.

'Well, I got that impression when I met her yesterday. That was further reinforced by reading my diaries.'

'Diaries?'

Herculano lifted his head from where it had been lolling against the back of the chair and looked around. Juliano waved in the general direction of a pile of about a dozen books neatly stacked on his desk.

'I... you... we have been keeping a diary since the day we recovered sufficiently to do so. I suspect Dr Zuniga insisted upon it as a backup, should his reversal spell fail.'

'You have been keeping a diary,' Herculano said. 'Let's not complicate matters. My head hurts enough simply wondering about what happened. I can do without trying to allocate actions to our alternate selves.'

'Fair enough.' Juliano took a sip of his wine and washed it about his mouth before he swallowed. 'My diaries are quite interesting. I remembered everything as I read, although sometimes my actions as described were inexplicable to me.'

'Our different natures,' Herculano murmured.

'What is more interesting still, is that I wrote certain sections in code.'

'No doubt to prevent prying eyes from reading your most private thoughts.'

Herculano smothered a yawn. The low light of the flickering candles placed around the room were a powerful soporific.

'It took me a while to work out the code,' Juliano said. 'You'd think I would remember, but it wasn't that easy. You can imagine how much I was cursing you today.'

'But you managed in the end?'

'I did. I'm curious to know whether you could read the code, though.'

'Mmm,' Herculano murmured, and silence reigned. The prince cleared his throat and Herculano's head jerked up again. 'Now?'

'Of course.'

'Really, Your Highness, could we not do this tomorrow?'

'Tomorrow I must spend the whole day with my uncle at a very tedious council meeting. That, in part, was why I was reading my diaries. The least you can do is obey your prince and see whether you can decipher the code.'

Herculano got up with a groan, made a big show of staggering over to the desk and opened the book at the top of the pile. He flicked through a couple of pages.

'It all looks perfectly simple to me,' Herculano started, then spotted a page that looked like it was filled with gibberish. He squinted at the words, mouthing them to try to make sense of them, turned the book upside down and finally held a page up to the candlelight. 'Nope, I don't know what to make of that.'

'So you can't decipher it?'

'It is beyond me,' Herculano said as he replaced the book. 'Maybe, given time, I might work it out, but not today.'

'You might have more of a chance to figure it out than most, but it relieves me that you can't read it,' Juliano said, and finally sat down on his swan sofa, one long leg crossed over the other.

'Does the diary say anything about Tiago Andrade?'

'Not enough to prove useful, I'm afraid. In it I say that Tiago is investigating Onofre Paiva,' the prince said, and waited, watching Herculano closely.

'If you're hoping the name rings a bell, I'm afraid it doesn't. No, wait, Lady Odete mentioned he's Lady Pia's father.'

'Did her ladyship also tell you that Paiva is the kingdom's treasurer?'

'I don't think she mentioned that.'

'He's one of the duque's council so I'm guessing he was being investigated to discover the duque's hold on him,' Juliano said, gazing at his wine as he swirled it round his glass.

'I'll look into him in the morning.'

Herculano hoped this would signal the end of the conversation. Unfortunately, the prince seemed in no hurry to dismiss him.

'What do you make of Lady Mafalda?' Juliano asked.

'I can't remember her. What should I make of her?'

'She's quite pretty, really.'

'No!' Herculano snapped, surprised at how angry he grew just considering the prince marrying the duque's daughter. 'She will be used against you for your whole life.'

'Somehow I knew you'd say that,' Juliano said with a slight, cynical smile. 'In fact, you did in the diaries, all too often. But you have forgotten the alternative.'

'You know I have.'

'You mention her too. A Habsburg princess.'

'Why would that be a problem? Aren't the Habsburgs the most powerful royal family in Europe?'

'Ah, so you haven't forgotten everything. You are correct. They are immensely powerful and fabulously rich. They are also legendary for their hideousness. I have a miniature of the proposed princess in my desk drawer. Go take a look.'

Herculano wanted to snap that he'd been on his feet all day examining sick people, but he knew better than to whine about it. So he heaved himself up, dug around the drawer and pulled out a small portrait of a woman in a gilt frame. She had a tiny mouth with a grotesquely protuberant lower lip, an immense jutting out chin, a long nose and weak, pale blue eyes.

'You see?' Juliano murmured. 'And please consider that the portraitist will have done his best to make her look good. If that is what she looks like in a miniature, I shudder to think how she will look in the flesh. I couldn't marry her, really, Herculano, no.'

'All the same,' Herculano muttered, unwilling to concede, even if the alternative was hideous. 'It's just more of the duque's manipulation, isn't it? He's given you the choice between a nice-looking girl and a monster.'

'Sadly, he didn't even have to work hard to do it. Your diaries make it clear that you searched for alternatives. None could make a more compelling case than the Habsburg monstrosity.'

Viriato Berenguer ambled through the palace listening to the click of his heels. As he approached, people stopped talking, turned and bowed to him. They held their tongues as he walked past and until they were certain he could no longer hear them. Most would then hurry away, continuing their conversations in an undertone.

It was unnecessary to be so careful. He already knew all their secrets. Still, it was a reflection of his power and he appreciated it.

Now, as he'd nearly arrived at the council chamber, he paused for a moment to examine his mauve floral coat with the row of brass buttons. It contrasted nicely with his frothy white cuffs. Then he withdrew his pocket watch and checked the time. He was fifteen minutes late. Perfect.

He gave a nod to the waiting footmen who opened the door with the usual crash, drawing the attention of the men inside.

'Good morning, gentlemen.'

'Your Grace,' came the collective reply.

Lords Paiva and Ledo had been holding a low-voiced conversation on one side of the room. The fat Lord Carvalho had already divested himself of his wig and was sweating away in his usual seat halfway down the enormous council table. Young Lord Alardo was also seated at the table but pointedly ignoring the fat man by polishing his dagger. Cardinal da Gama was apparently lost in rapturous inspection of the tapestry of the forests of Brazil. So deep was his attention that he was slower than the rest to turn and acknowledge the duque.

It was a deliberate snub and the duque would make the cardinal pay for his insolence, even if he had to wait twenty years to do it. In the meantime, he had something more surprising to consider.

'The prince isn't here yet?'

'As you see,' the cardinal said, waving both hands to encompass the room.

'Mmm,' the duque murmured.

On the days when the prince was summoned to the council he always arrived early. Viriato amused himself by keeping him waiting. In fact, once, he'd deliberately arrived an hour late just to show the young man who was in charge. The prince was fully aware that his uncle did this and yet, without fail, he'd get to the council chamber first.

With a bang that would make a lesser man jump, the double doors swung open again and the prince strolled in.

'Your Grace,' he said, giving his uncle a slight nod.

'Your Highness,' Viriato said, astonished at the hint of amusement in the prince's voice.

He was even more surprised by his appearance. The prince was wearing a white silk suit embroidered with green vines. On any other man, especially a prince, this cutting edge of sartorial fashion would have drawn no comment, but on the prince, it was entirely out of character.

'I hope I didn't keep you waiting,' the prince murmured as he strolled down to the foot of the table. 'Allow me to introduce His Excellency, Herculano Escovar. Herculano is a merchant, and I have asked him to teach me about business.'

'Business?' Viriato said, examining the Escovar fellow again.

Since he'd seen him in the alchemist's rooms, he'd accompanied the prince nearly everywhere. This, too, was out of character. The prince had few friends and even fewer hangers on. He had never taken an unknown nobody into his inner circle. This man was dressed entirely in black, just as the prince used to do. He was also glowering at Viriato as if he had a personal dislike of him, much as he'd done at dinner the night before.

'The kingdom needs money, doesn't it?' the prince said as he gave the rest of the men in the room a nod of acknowledgement then sat down.

Viriato almost lost his temper at that. Although Juliano was the prince, he'd always deferred to his uncle and waited for him to sit down first. Now he'd dispensed with that and he'd made a dig about money.

'Are you implying that I am mismanaging the kingdom and the empire?'

'How would I know, Uncle? You have kept me away from the treasury and all their records.'

Juliano leaned back in his chair as he spoke and a slight, wry smile played on his lips. This was so wrong that Viriato just stared at him, at a loss to understand. This wasn't how his nephew behaved.

He was blunt and abrupt. He'd slam his hands on the table for emphasis. He'd smoulder with rage and be argumentative. He'd jump up and stomp about the room. What he would never do was be relaxed in his uncle's presence.

His new companion was sitting forward in his seat, his arms crossed on the table, glaring at the duque. That should have been his nephew. It was disconcerting that it wasn't.

'What do you think a merchant can teach you that your tutors and Lord Paiva, the head of your treasury, can't?'

'I will tell you as soon as I discover that,' the prince said, his smile broadening as he gave Paiva a penetrating examination.

Viriato had no idea what had got into his nephew, but it was a mystery best considered at his leisure and away from the watchful eyes of the council.

'Shall we get down to business?'

'Certainly,' Juliano said with a gracious wave of the hand.

Again, this was out of character. Viriato had the odd sensation of watching himself. That was the way he behaved.

'We have to discuss which property to prioritise for reconstruction. Since Lord Paiva has failed to source the revenue we need for a complete rebuilding of the city, and Lord Carvalho is incapable of finding sufficient skilled craftsmen, we are left with the unenviable task of deciding what gets built and what is left to crumble to dust.'

'The Church of St Joseph urgently needs restoration. We have had scaffolding holding up the walls for the last fifteen years,' Cardinal da Gama said. 'Not a single stone has been replaced as yet.'

'The Church of St Joseph?' Viriato felt an immense weariness come over him. 'While the church you mention may not have been repaired, countless others already have been. In fact, correct me if I'm wrong, my Lord Ledo, but didn't we calculate that we already have a sufficient number of rebuilt churches to house the entire population of Lisbon?'

'You are entirely correct, as always,' Lord Ledo murmured.

Viriato gave him a thin smile of thanks. He was a reliable ally.

'I propose we build an additional wing at the University, dedicated to the study of Natural Philosophy.'

'Another godless object,' the cardinal said, flinging up his hands. 'Not only do you ignore the spiritual needs of your subjects, you–'

'*My* subjects,' Juliano said quietly.

There was a collective intake of breath, and everybody turned to Viriato. He only just maintained his neutral expression as he said, 'Not quite yet, Your Highness.'

To add insult to injury, the prince smiled at him. It looked like a challenge.

'His Excellency, Herculano Escovar, informs me that the All Saints Hospital is only half built and in desperate need of more supplies and builders to allow for completion. Isn't that right?' Juliano said as he turned to Herculano.

That man was staring at the prince with his mouth agape. So, Viriato thought, Juliano and he hadn't planned this challenge to his authority together.

'The hospital is operating adequately. There is no hurry to build the second wing.'

'You could say the same thing about the university,' Juliano said. 'No lives will be lost for the lack of a building for your natural philosophers. While countless lives could be saved with a larger hospital.'

'While the health of the kingdom's subjects concerns me as much as it does you, Your Highness, I believe we can no longer flounder around in ignorant darkness. We need educated young men to rebuild the nation and make us a leader in the world.'

'You would be better teaching theology in that godless university of yours,' Cardinal da Gama said. 'What use will natural philosophy be to any man if he lands up in hell?'

'Let's put it to a vote, shall we?' Viriato said, tired of this pretence that anyone actually had a choice in the matter. 'Raise your hands if you believe we should spend our precious funds on the Church of St Joseph.'

The cardinal's hand shot up and no other.

Viriato gave an accepting nod.

'Who wants the money to go to the hospital?'

The prince raised his hand and gave his uncle a wry smile. He knew full well that he and his father's old ally, Lord Carvalho, would be the only ones to vote for the hospital.

'Finally, a show of hands for the university,' Viriato said, raising his hand.

The rest of the men at the table followed suit, as he knew they would.

'Fine, that's agreed then. Now on to the next item of–'

The doors crashed open and Mafalda stormed into the room, her trio of ladies-in-waiting trailing behind her and apparently failing in their endeavour to prevent this intrusion.

'Lady Mafalda?'

Viriato noted his daughter's flushed face and heaving bosom with surprise. He loved Mafalda with a fierce passion. He'd lost his wife and son in the earthquake and now took every precaution to ensure his daughter's safety and prosperity. Viriato would destroy any man who ever did her harm. However, he would never show his feelings to anyone, not even Mafalda.

'What brings you to the council chamber?' he drawled, and gave the ladies-in-waiting a menacing stare.

'I demand to know what you are doing to find Tiago Andrade.'

'My lady, this is neither the time nor place to raise such a question.'

Viriato was angry that his daughter had appeared at all, let alone with this foolish question. He had no idea what Tiago Andrade meant to his daughter and even less interest in finding out.

'He's gone missing and none of you seem to care,' Mafalda said, and her voice faltered and grew softer as fear started to creep in.

And well it might. Viriato gave the ladies-in-waiting another meaningful glare which, this time, they seemed to understand, at least the clever one, Odete Salema, did.

She took Mafalda by the arm and whispered, 'Speak to him later,' as she pulled Mafalda backwards.

The other two ladies joined in, but it was unnecessary. Mafalda's momentary burst of passion had evaporated.

'Nobody has seen him in two days,' she said, on what came perilously close to a sob, then she turned and hurried away, thankfully at a walk, not a run.

Viriato realised she would require a stern talking-to and an even sterner one for the women who were supposed to keep her in check. For now, he would behave as if nothing extraordinary had happened.

'As I was saying, our next order of business is continuing the clearance of the land for the grand avenue.'

'Your Grace,' Lord Paiva said, apparently seized by fear, if the sudden pallor of his face was anything to go by. 'I must apologise for my daughter's lack of discipline. As Lady Mafalda's lady-in-waiting, it was her duty to ensure such an outburst never occurs.'

'I am aware,' Viriato said, and gave the man an icy stare that he hoped would stop him from enlarging upon the issue. The less that was said about it, the better.

Unfortunately, the stupid Lord Carvalho blundered in with a muttered, 'My daughter should also have done her duty.'

'I don't care about them,' Viriato snapped. 'I want to know what you will do to rid me of that damned merchant. What was his name? Orlando Jusarte, who is refusing to give up his property that sits right in the middle of my new road!'

8

L ady Mafalda, what do you think you were doing?' Maria da Luz cried, the moment they'd dragged the young woman out of the council chamber.

It was exactly the wrong thing to say, although Odete was wondering the same. Up till now Mafalda had kept her passion for Tiago a secret. Apparently, the fear of what had happened to her lover had now overruled her concerns about what her father might do about the relationship.

'What was I thinking?' Mafalda shouted as she backed away. 'Nobody cares about how I feel. My heart is broken and all you think about is my father!'

With that, she took off with a swish of her blue taffeta skirt down the long corridor, as servants and courtiers threw themselves frantically out of her way. Maria da Luz and Pia ran after her, both hitching up their skirts to an undignified height, revealing their shoes and stockings.

Odete followed along behind, adding no more than the odd hurried skip to her brisk walk to catch up. She was trailing far enough behind that nobody would think her part of the group who were currently screeching at each other. The ladies-in-waiting begging for some decorum and Mafalda in a full-blown despairing rage, tears streaming down her face as she wailed that nobody understood her.

Odete did feel sorry for her. But what motivated her, and the other ladies-in-waiting, was fear. If not for their lives, although the duque was dangerous enough for that to be a possibility, at least for their livelihood.

Odete hated the fact that the duque had been right about her: she was of no interest to any young man and their ambitious parents. She had learned that from numerous amorous men who were perfectly happy, no, eager, to enjoy a momentary dalliance, but who left her in no doubt that marriage was out of the question.

If she lost her position at court, she'd be forced to return to her mother. Then she would no doubt die a spinster, making a living by seeing to the needs of her aged relatives. The very idea made her shudder as she swept up the stairs, determined that they get Mafalda back to her room and provide as little spectacle as possible. She was being overly optimistic to hope they had prevented a major source of gossip. The palace would be alive with eagerly whispering courtiers trying to find out exactly why Lady Mafalda had been in such disarray.

Finally, they reached the top floor and Odete watched as Mafalda and Pia battled to get through the door of their quarters simultaneously but hampered by their wide skirts. Maria da Luz pushed them from behind in her determination to get everyone out of the public gaze. Like a cork erupting from a champagne bottle, the three women broke free and tumbled into the room. Odete brought up the rear and shut the door behind them with a snap.

'Lady Mafalda!' Maria da Luz said as she folded her arms.

Odete guessed there was a tapping foot below her floral skirt and Mafalda's expression darkened in anticipation of being scolded.

'Lady Mafalda, let's get you to bed,' Odete said as she took her firmly by the elbow and hurried her past Maria da Luz.

'I don't want to go to bed. Don't tell me what to do!'

'Do you want a telling off from Maria da Luz?' Odete whispered in her ear.

'Oh, Lady Mafalda, what have you done?' Pia wailed.

'Or the waterworks from Pia?'

Mafalda looked back, her rage subsiding as she considered the alternatives.

'I'm going to my room. Don't you dare bother me,' Mafalda said, and ran for the bedroom, dragging Odete with her.

She pulled Odete inside, slammed the door shut on the other two women who had started after them and twisted the key so that it locked with a loud click. Then she threw herself face down on her bed.

'He's dead, I just know it!'

'You don't know that,' Odete said in a calm voice, although she feared Mafalda might be right.

'So why haven't you found him yet? And why are you intending to look amongst the dead?'

'As I explained last night, those are the first and easiest places to search. It is merely a formality,' Odete said to Mafalda's back.

She'd pulled her pillows to herself and was hugging them tightly.

'If it's merely a formality, why do it? You're wasting time when Tiago may be languishing, injured somewhere.'

'I can't honestly think what else to do.' Odete prayed that wouldn't set Mafalda off again. To stave off accusations of incompetence, she said, 'Where would you look?'

Mafalda rolled over and sat up, but kept her arms wrapped around a pillow.

'The prince must know.'

'Why has he got that man Herculano Escovar searching for Tiago if he knows?'

Odete had informed Mafalda about Herculano's help the day before, as the girl had demanded a detailed report back on everything she, or as it had turned out, they, had done.

'Don't you think it's suspicious that they have given him Tiago's room?'

'It is odd. In fact, that Escovar fellow is very strange. I felt like he was staring at me every time I looked away. It was unnerving. But it's best we keep him where we can see him. At least till we know what he and the prince are up to. Otherwise, we will have no way of finding anything out.'

'So you will get information out of him that benefits us.'

The idea seemed to please Mafalda, if the cunning smile that spread across her face was anything to go by.

'At the very least, he will prove useful to us because he can get into places that we can't.'

'That's true. But we can also get into places men can't.'

'Can we?' Odete said, and wondered what crazy endeavour Mafalda was dreaming up now.

'I can seek out Tiago's mother. She must surely know where her son has got to.'

Odete had her doubts about disturbing a lady who could well be frantic with worry about the disappearance of her son. But she decided, as long as she wouldn't be required to go along, not to say anything against the idea. It was up to Mafalda, after all. She had very little chance of changing her mind when she was set upon accomplishing something.

'What else do you think we could do?' Odete asked, to keep Mafalda from worrying too much.

Mafalda put the corner of one striped pillowcase in her mouth and nibbled thoughtfully on it as she considered.

'We could put up missing posters.'

'Ah... I don't think Tiago's parents would like that,' Odete said, kicking herself now for asking for more suggestions. 'That is one you'll have to ask Lady Andrade about before we take it forward.'

Mafalda scowled, then her mood flipped completely and a tear slipped down her face.

'Oh dear,' she sobbed. 'I'm so worried about him.'

Herculano gazed out of his window at the vendors in the square below. They were all happily going about their business, oblivious to the dramas in the palace.

'You look very serious, sir,' Arriscado said.

Herculano wondered how long he'd been standing behind him. He'd been nowhere in sight when he'd got back from his meeting with the prince which had followed the council meeting.

'Did you get my message to Lady Odete?'

Arriscado bowed, which resulted in a squeak from his whalebone corset. The man was so fat, no amount of physical bondage could disguise it, and yet his vanity still drove him to this discomfort.

'The young lady thanked you for your message and said she'll be at the entrance to the palace at two o'clock precisely. She entreats you not to be late.'

'She does, does she?'

'Her maid relayed the information. I believe the woman is under the erroneous impression that she is assisting a clandestine romance.'

'Ha!' Herculano wondered whether that was true. He was still confused about his feelings for Lady Odete.

'Well, I suppose I'd better go if I am not to keep the young lady waiting.'

'You might find this useful as well, sir,' Arriscado said, holding out a simple pocket watch on a gold chain.

'Another heirloom of yours?'

'One of yours, sir, from your father. It was his father's before him.'

Being reminded of the merchant who'd brought him up added a spark of anger to Herculano's already sombre mood.

The man wasn't his father. They weren't related by blood and, although he'd looked after the body he now had, it wasn't his mind that the merchant had nurtured. He wasn't going to have an argument with Arriscado about that though, so he just slipped the watch into his coat pocket.

'Thank you. What about the other matter?' Herculano asked, aware that now he was being hypocritical.

'Your money, sir,' Arriscado said, and held out a bulging purse.

Herculano would have felt less guilty about taking money from someone who had no relation to him if it had been a smaller amount.

'Really? Isn't that excessive?'

'His Excellency, Dr Escovar, was an extremely wealthy man. He was known as the King of Merchants by the local businessmen.'

Herculano hefted the purse and felt the considerable weight of gold coins. He should have realised that the prince wouldn't have been placed with any old merchant. They would have wanted to ensure he had all the luxuries his rank demanded.

'His house didn't give an impression of extreme wealth.'

'He was a modest man. But he believed in quality. You will find no better decoration, furniture or food in any house in Lisbon, and that includes the palace.'

'I see.' Herculano had to rearrange his mind to take full account of this new information. Somehow, he'd just accepted that he was a penniless pauper. 'Ah well, I'd better get going if I'm not to keep Lady Odete waiting.'

The church bells across the city were chiming precisely two o'clock when Herculano stepped out of the palace into the baking heat. The bell nearest him was so loud it was impossible to hear the merchants shouting their wares to the passers-by.

Herculano crossed the street to take shelter in a narrow strip of shade that barely made it all the way down the wall of the building. He leaned his back against the warm tiles and watched the door, expecting Lady Odete to emerge every time it opened.

While he waited, he considered the morning's council meeting. He must have sat through hundreds of such affairs and yet none of it felt familiar. It had been infuriating, though. Each time the prince proposed something, the council ranged themselves behind the duque. The duque had such an iron control over the council the prince had no hope of achieving anything.

For the first time in his new life, Herculano felt tremendous relief that he wasn't the prince. He stopped to examine that feeling. Everything had happened so suddenly that he'd not really considered this. He'd lived as a prince. That had been snatched away from him and yet, he felt no envy towards Prince Juliano.

The palace door swung open and Lady Odete stepped out into the sun. She opened a fetching pale blue frilled parasol and looked about herself.

'What time do you call this?' Herculano said, without bothering to move from his place against the wall.

'Two o'clock,' Odete said, giving him a surprised look.

'It's half past two.' Herculano held out his pocket watch so that she could see the face, just as the church bells chimed their confirmation. 'You said not to be late.'

'I'm sorry. I've been trying to distract Lady Mafalda.'

What could he say to that after the scene in the council meeting? Herculano grunted a grudging acceptance and took a firm hold of Odete's hand.

'Come on, you and I need to talk.'

Herculano tightened his grip on Odete's hand as she tried to pull it away, and drew her closer to him.

'Remember, we're supposed to be married.'

'I remember,' Odete said, holding up her left hand with the plain gold band on her ring finger. 'But you seem to have forgotten that we are supposed to be looking for you-know-who's body and you're heading away from the cathedral where we said we'd start.'

'Talk first,' Herculano said as he led Odete into a side street.

The buildings all around were so tall and so close together that they provided welcome relief from the sun. A couple of bridges crossed the road above, making it shadier still.

'Where are we going?'

'Here.'

Herculano stopped at a glass-fronted shop where gold lettering painted on the door proclaimed it was a coffee house.

'I don't think that's a good idea.'

Odete looked like she might dig her heels in, so Herculano said, 'I have some news that needs to be imparted away from prying ears, and I've been reliably informed that we will be safe in here.'

With that he pushed open the door and a wave of tobacco smoke and coffee-scented steam assailed their nostrils as a bell tinkled to announce their arrival.

A waiter with a long white apron stepped up to them and said, 'Can I help you, Your Excellencies?'

'We want a quiet corner,' Herculano said.

The waiter looked from him to Lady Odete and gave a smirk, as if he knew precisely what they were up to. Thankfully, Odete was too busy shutting her parasol to notice. It suited Herculano to be misunderstood, but he doubted Lady Odete would like it.

'This way, Your Excellencies,' the waiter said, as he led them between rows of tables at which men sat with the wide skirts of their coats spilling out into the walkway as they puffed on long white clay pipes and sipped from elegant little coffee cups.

The waiter stopped at a cool blue and white tiled and vaulted alcove and said, 'What would you like to order?'

'Coffee,' Herculano snapped.

What else did one get at a coffee shop?

'Hot chocolate,' Lady Odete said, giving him an icy stare. 'I hope today you have brought the funds for this extravagance, because I refuse to pay.'

'I don't make the same mistake twice,' Herculano said, waving the waiter away.

He'd paused at the possibility that his customers might not have any money.

'So what do you have to say to me, sir?'

Lady Odete was at her frostiest and Herculano wondered whether that was all his doing.

'Have you had a difficult morning?'

She looked surprised by the question, then gave a deep sigh and some of her tension eased.

'What do you think?'

'We were astonished to see Lady Mafalda's performance, and I suspect it continued even after she had been removed.'

'I suppose you could call it a full-blown tantrum,' Odete said, and she looked about the coffee shop to make sure they weren't overheard. 'But I can hardly blame her. It seems she was sincerely attached to Tiago.'

'Still, it was a foolish thing to do.'

'We are all aware of that, especially Lady Mafalda. The duque is punishing her for it too.'

'He's already seen her?'

'Not yet. Which is a greater punishment. If he just got the meeting over and done with, it would be easier. As it is, he's leaving us all to stew.'

'Is he likely to do something to you too?'

It was a question that caused Herculano far more concern than what might happen to Lady Mafalda.

'I honestly don't know,' Odete said, and rubbed her eyes in a gesture of tiredness. 'Lady Mafalda has never stood up to her father before. On occasion I've overheard her shouting at him, but that has always been behind closed doors and between the two of them.'

'The duque didn't shout?' Herculano said, but felt he had a sufficient measure of the duque to know how he would behave.

'I don't think I've ever heard him raise his voice,' Odete said with a shudder.

It was an appropriate reaction, Herculano thought.

'So,' Odete said, fixing Herculano with her I-will-not-be-distracted-from-my-mission stare, 'what do you have to say to me?'

'Ah, that.'

Herculano paused as the waiter arrived. With a flourish he scooped Herculano's coffee off a silver tray and laid it with loving attention before him, then he did the same for the taller cup of hot chocolate he placed before Lady Odete. He gave a brief bow, clicked his heels together, and spun off.

Herculano waited till the man was sufficiently far enough away before he said, 'It turns out the pri—' He stopped, he had to be careful what he said even if there was a comfortable hubbub of conversation to mask their own, and sufficient smoke to make them difficult to spot in their alcove. 'Juliano has been making enquiries of his own.'

'Has he? I suppose that isn't surprising. He was never one to sit around waiting for others to do his work for him.'

'Wasn't he?'

Herculano realised with a pang that Odete was speaking about him, and her voice held a strong note of approval.

'He is a man of action,' Odete said.

'I suppose so.'

Herculano wished she didn't look quite so pleased. How was he supposed to compete with the prince?

'What has Juliano done?' Odete asked, snapping Herculano out of his musings.

'Ah yes, he went to see Tiago's father. It turns out Lord Andrade was worried about his son's disappearance. He has had his people scouring the city. They have already visited all the hospitals and churches as well as the prisons.'

'The prisons?'

'Just in case. I must admit, I hadn't considered searching the prisons.'

'And he has found nothing?'

'I'm afraid not,' Herculano said, and took a sip of his coffee. It was still hot and tremendously bitter, which caused him to curse.

Odete gave him a meaningful look as she dropped four cubes of sugar into her chocolate, using the dainty silver tongs that hooked onto the side of the sugar bowl, and then gave it a vigorous stir.

'This begins to sound very serious. What can have happened to Tiago? Do you think he left the city?'

'If he did, it wasn't voluntarily,' Herculano said, and added a couple of cubes of sugar to what remained of his coffee. 'He took no toiletries.'

'None at all?'

'Nothing. Arriscado checked with his valet and the man says none of his clothes are missing either. At least, only the suit he had on the last day anybody saw him.'

'The fact that he didn't take his valet with him is also alarming,' Odete murmured. 'This information is serious, and honestly, leaves us with nothing to do.'

'On the contrary, we now have to work out why he went out rather than where he went.'

'Surely the prince knows the answer to that.'

'I wish he did.'

Herculano also wished he could tell Lady Odete about the body swap and loss of memory, which would explain this lapse. But he didn't know her well enough for that.

'I am astonished that the prince doesn't know. He and Tiago were the closest of friends.'

'The salient fact is that he doesn't. No amount of surprise is going to change that.'

Odete stiffened to be told off and said, 'Then what do you propose we do next?' in a frosty tone of voice.

Herculano liked that. He wanted a strong woman, not one who simply gave in and accepted whatever a man told her to do. He also realised an apologetic tone was now required to get back into Odete's good graces.

'I would be grateful if you could sound out the ladies Pia and Maria da Luz about their fathers.'

'Their fathers? Have you gone completely mad? What relevance do their fathers have?'

'Must you know?'

'Of course I must. You are becoming more nonsensical by the moment.'

'The thing is…' Herculano said, and looked about himself once again, checking on the other patrons of the coffee house. Fortunately, a group of five men were having a robust political discussion that was sure to drown out everything else. 'What we are about is extremely dangerous. The less you know, the safer you will be.'

Odete leaned across the table and said, 'By which I infer you suspect the duque is involved.'

Herculano gave a noncommittal sideways nod.

'In which case,' Odete said, 'the mere fact that I am looking for Tiago would be enough to send me to the pyres if the duque so wished. So there's no point in trying to hide anything from me.'

Although she spoke in an offhand manner, Herculano could see her fear.

'I shouldn't have dragged you into this.'

'You didn't, Lady Mafalda did, and she won't rest till she knows what has happened to Tiago. I fear, however, that it looks like he is dead. So now, will you tell me everything you know?'

There didn't seem to be any point in holding back, so Herculano said, 'Juliano suspects that Tiago's disappearance has something to do with the power struggle in the palace. After this morning's council meeting, it is clear that the duque has a firm hold on all the men except, possibly, Cardinal da Gama and Lord Carvalho. Tiago was tasked with finding out what that hold might be. We think, if we can discover that too, it might give us some idea of what Tiago might have found out and, therefore, what danger he was in.'

'And maybe who is behind his disappearance?'

'Precisely.' Herculano was impressed with how Odete kept her calm. 'If I were you, I'd start with Lord Onofre Paiva. He seemed unusually jittery in the meeting and quicker than anyone else to accept whatever the duque proposed.'

Herculano kept to himself that the prince and Tiago had specifically targeted Lord Paiva, possibly for the same reason. It was probably safer if Lady Odete conducted her inquiries without making it obvious who their target was.

The duque was angrier than he'd ever been with his daughter and it took considerable discipline not to send for her immediately after the meeting. He needed time to calm down so that he didn't do something he would later regret.

In the meantime, he retired to his private study. It was a small circular room that jutted out of the palace on one corner. In an era that was long past, it had served as part of a defensive tower.

That was why he liked it. The walls were thicker than a man lying down and therefore impossible to listen through. The windows were slits, useful for an archer or a rifle shooting from within, but difficult to attack from outside. Even the door was thick, iron-plated wood. It provided absolute silence when required, although he usually left it open so that he could communicate with his secretary in the adjoining room.

The furnishings were comfortably modern. The rows of books that lined the walls were from the pre-eminent thinkers of the day and covered natural philosophy, politics, statecraft and commerce. He was proud of the fact that there was not a single theological book in his study.

But even his books couldn't soothe his temper today. It wasn't only Mafalda's astonishing intervention that was troubling him. The prince had changed out of all recognition.

Worse than that was the disappearance of Tiago Andrade. He had hoped the young man had merely gone off on a spree. But his spies, of which he had many, had already informed him that the prince and Lord Andrade himself were making discreet but strenuous enquiries after the man.

He suspected, therefore, that this had to do with the prince's ongoing efforts to unseat him. The only puzzling thing was that the prince was equally in the dark about his friend. Surely, if they'd been plotting together, Juliano would know where Tiago was.

Much as he was loath to do it, it was time to call in his most trusted agent. A man only he knew about and whom he used to do his darkest deeds, which included assassination. He scribbled a note, rang the silver bell he had on his desk, and waited for his secretary to appear.

He'd chosen Diogo Martinez for his impeccable and secular education, as well as his discretion, and he had worked for the duque for well over thirty years. This grey little man was as familiar to the duque as the palm of his right hand and as reliable.

'Your Grace?' Martinez said on a deep bow.

'I have two jobs for you. The first is to get me all the information you have on one Herculano Escovar. He's a local merchant and, for some unfathomable reason, the prince is keeping him close.'

'Yes, Your Grace.'

'The second is to deliver this note to the Church of Baby Jesus.'

Martinez knew exactly what that meant. He took the note and bowed deeply as he backed out of the study.

The duque turned to the massive book that had a permanent place at his left elbow. When it was open it was exactly the same width as his desk. Within its pages were the maps of Lisbon as it currently was, as well as the plans for what it would become.

It was infuriating that his grand vision was taking so long to come to fruition but he was determined that nothing, especially not the prince, would prevent him from reaching his goal. At least leafing through the pages of his dreams always had a soothing effect.

It was a good three hours later when there was a discreet tap at his half-open door and Baltasar Lopez stepped inside.

The duque indicated with one long index finger that he was to close the door, which Lopez did. Then he turned to watch the duque. He made no attempt to sit and the duque didn't invite him to do so either.

'You wished to see me, Your Grace?'

'I did,' the duque said, and examined his man.

He was a priest, and, until he'd started working for the duque, one of the Inquisition's most zealous investigators, which amused the duque deeply. He was wearing a black cassock and had a black felt, four-peaked biretta on his head.

Even though the duque had known him for years, he was always surprised by how nondescript Lopez was. He was of average height and average build, with brown hair that he tied back with a black ribbon. Aside from his clothes, if anyone was asked to describe him later, it would be impossible to get a useful description. Even the fact that he was dressed as a clergyman wasn't that helpful in a city that had hundreds of priests.

The only thing that might make him stick in a person's mind were his eyes. They were brown too, but had a flat, lifeless quality that was unnerving. Fortunately, a man would have to get very close to see that. If they did, it would most likely be the last thing they ever saw.

'I am troubled by something, Baltasar,' the duque murmured. 'A young noble has gone missing.'

'Do you want me to find him?'

'Not necessarily.' The duque picked up a letter opener in the shape of a slim dagger and examined its highly polished surface. 'This young man may have been interfering with my work. However, his father is influential and it will be inconvenient if anything untoward has happened to him.'

Balthasar's right eyebrow flickered briefly upwards. It was the only sign he ever gave of being disconcerted.

'When did he go missing?'

'It would appear it was four nights ago.'

It disturbed the duque to see that flickering eyebrow for a second time.

'Four nights ago I was about your other business at the docks,' Baltasar said, being vague despite the fact that it would be impossible for anyone to eavesdrop on them.

'Quite successfully too. I was pleased.'

'Not so successfully,' Baltasar said, and his face hardened.

The duque wondered whether he was seeing fear from this most implacable of his henchmen. 'What went wrong?'

'A young man saw me at a critical moment in my mission. He looked like he'd been hiding, maybe even following me.'

'You were followed?' the duque said, and even he couldn't keep the surprise from his voice.

'There was a violent storm raging at the time, otherwise I would have noticed him sooner.'

'I see. What then?'

'When he realised he'd been spotted, he ran. So I ran after him.'

'That isn't good news. What happened next?' the duque asked as he pushed the point of his letter opener into the soft pages of his map book.

'We fought. He was a skilled swordsman but, in the end, not skilled enough.'

The duque let out a long, thoughtful sigh.

'Did he have any distinguishing features? I'd rather not jump to any conclusions as to who he might have been.'

'He had a mole below his left eye.'

'Ah! Then there can be no doubt that was Tiago Andrade. How unfortunate. But if he had taken what he saw to the prince, that would have caused even more difficulties. What did you do with his body?'

'I sealed it into a barrel of wine beside a nearby warehouse. I expect it is on its way to foreign lands as we speak.'

The duque considered the information. It wasn't the best news, but the situation had been dealt with and he couldn't see how any of it could be traced back to him.

'Very well, what's done is done.'

'Is there anything else you need me for?' Baltasar said.

'Not as yet. Just keep an eye on our, ah, package for the moment.'

Baltasar gave another nod and then bowed himself out.

The duque gazed at the space he'd occupied while he weighed up the situation. His silent battle of wills against the prince was bound to lead to one or more deaths at some point, he supposed. He regretted it as an inconvenience, but maybe it was for the best.

The loss of his friend had diverted the prince from his other investigations. These appeared to have been more thorough than the duque had given him credit for. No doubt his reasoning was laid out in his diaries. The duque was annoyed that, as yet, he'd been unable to decipher the code the prince used.

Another advantage was that Tiago Andrade was removed from his daughter's orbit. He'd had no idea that Mafalda had developed a passion for the young man, but that could be the only conclusion to be drawn from her hysterical performance. It was very tiresome when he was trying to achieve a marriage for her with the prince. That would be to all their benefits, even if neither young person was ready to see it his way yet.

9

Odete left the coffee house feeling warmer towards Herculano Escovar than she had thus far. At first, she'd been suspicious of him. To make matters worse, his unexplained appearance at court coincided with Tiago's disappearance and the remarkable change in the prince.

Then there was his behaviour towards her, which was inappropriately familiar. He spoke to her and gazed upon her as if they were old friends. No, that wasn't quite right. It was more like they'd been friends a long time ago and were getting reacquainted. Only she'd never seen him before the day she spotted him eavesdropping on Dr Zuniga.

'Shall we return to the palace?' Herculano said, and waited as Odete opened her parasol before he offered her his arm.

She took it with less reluctance than she had until now. Today he had pleased her by both having money and a plan.

'I will own,' Odete said, looking up at Herculano as they strolled downhill towards the palace, 'I am relieved that I won't be required to examine any dead bodies today.'

'You and me both. Nor did I fancy being dragged to every single church in Lisbon, for it would have been a fruitless search.'

'And exhausting. My legs still ache from all the walking we did yesterday,' Odete said, watching the man's swarthy face.

It was so different to the prince's aristocratic fine, pale features. But Herculano also had the directness that she'd always liked in the prince. On top of that, he seemed perfectly happy to go along with her investigation. No, more, most men would have taken over and told her to return to Lady Mafalda and the safety of the palace. None of them would have taken her to a coffee shop, a scandalous place for any woman, nor spoken to her as an equal in their endeavour.

'Your Excellency,' a voice called out. 'Your Excellency, Mr Escovar.'

An old man with flyaway white hair was hurrying up the road towards them. His frame was square and hinted at power, but old age had withered the muscle so that the skeleton looked bigger than what was currently needed. His clothes, a smart, plain, dark green suit, also looked too big for him and hung in loose folds. He was flanked by two tough-looking men who had the appearance and the sweat-mingled-with-fish smell of dockworkers.

'Your Excellency, thank goodness,' the man said as he spotted Herculano and paused, leaning one hand against the wall as he mopped his face with a giant white handkerchief.

'Yes?'

The way Herculano spoke was guarded and in sharp contrast to the old man who'd addressed him like an aged and faithful retainer.

'It is I, Pero de Mello, your man of business,' the old man said in an undertone clearly only meant to be heard by Herculano.

'Why have you come in search of me?'

Odete was struck by his continuing wariness, as if he were on unfamiliar ground, which shouldn't have been the case.

The old man straightened up and folded his handkerchief away.

'I'm afraid we have an emergency, Your Excellency. The moment Paolo and Joachim told me about it, I headed straight for the palace.'

The two dockworkers nodded corroboration. Despite their size and their muscular arms tattooed with icons to ward off evil, they looked uncomfortable.

'Arriscado told me I might find you at the coffee shop.'

'And you did. What's the problem?'

'We've found a body, sir,' de Mello said in dramatic tones. 'Stuffed into a barrel in one of your warehouses.'

Odete stifled a gasp by slapping her hand over her mouth and stared at Herculano in wide-eyed surprise. He'd also turned to her and looked equally astonished.

'A body?' Herculano said, and shifted his gaze back to his man of business with apparent difficulty. 'A person?'

'If it had been a rat or a dog, I wouldn't have bothered you with the news, Your Excellency,' de Mello said, conveying just the right amount of dignified hurt to be so misjudged.

Herculano let out a sigh and apparently considered the situation. Then he nodded.

'I'd best take a look.' With that, he tightened his grip on Odete and set off again.

'Do you think..?' Odete whispered, hoping nobody would hear her but Herculano.

'I don't know,' Herculano said, but he looked grim. 'The odds must surely be against it.'

'All the same.'

Herculano shook his head, unwilling to delve further into the mystery.

As they had neared the palace, he said, 'You should go inside. I'll report back, I promise.'

'No!' Odete said and tightened her grip on Herculano's arm, determined that he wouldn't get rid of her so easily. 'I must see this with my own eyes. It's the only way I'll be able to convince Lady Mafalda.'

'But we're going to the docks. It's not an appropriate place for a lady.'

'Neither is a coffee shop,' Odete snapped, glaring up at Herculano.

He looked for a moment like he might turn his suggestion into an order, then he shrugged.

'Alright, but I thought you didn't want to look at dead bodies.'

The idea unsettled Odete, but she was determined to see this mission through. Besides, it was only one body and she'd been screwing up her courage to examine hundreds today.

Displaying more of that straightforward and swift decision-making Odete admired, Herculano kept his hold on Odete's hand as they turned right at the palace and walked down a lane that ran parallel to the river and, Odete knew, would eventually lead to the docks. A multitude of companies ran the docks and owned the vast wood and brick warehouses that thronged the riverside.

As a well-brought-up lady, Odete had never gone near the docks, although sailors were notorious for drunken debauchery. It sounded like a wild and dangerous place. But as they turned left and the road widened out into a sunny space filled with rippling sunshine that bounced off each wavelet on the water, the docks looked like a busy and industrious place.

Vast wooden ships loomed over them and vied for space along the quayside, creaking and groaning under the weight of their loads. Sailors and porters, most stripped to their waists, their skin burned to a dark leathery brown, hairy and dripping with sweat, heaved at ropes and worked a perpetual line of goods being walked onto one vessel. Another line unloaded its neighbour. The backs of the men were scarred by their work, worn red by the rough sacks and wooden boxes, and some were dripping blood.

Nobody seemed to notice her. The sailors on the wooden behemoths shouted orders to each other. The porters did the same, swearing in a manner that made Odete blush all the way to her ear tips.

'Watch out!' a man shouted as a rope slid at speed along the ground.

Odete looked down as a loop that had been lying still, tightened and pulled around her ankle. Odete shrieked as it whipped her foot out from under her. Herculano's grip tightened as he swung around, wrapped his right arm around her waist and swept her into the air. The rope ripped away from her foot, taking her shoe with it, splashing into the water where it was pulled into the deep by a departing ship.

Herculano put her back on her feet but for a dizzying and intense moment he kept his arms about her while her blood drummed in her ears and it felt as if the world shifted about her.

'Whoa, you were lucky,' the big, tattooed Paolo said. 'I once saw a man dragged right off the quay and drowned when his foot got caught in a rope.'

Odete felt sick and her grip tightened on Herculano as he gently pushed her back to examine her face.

'Are you alright?'

'Yes, I'm fine.'

Odete was damned if she was going to show how shaken she was by this near escape from what could have been a grizzly end.

'Your ankle?' Herculano asked as he retrieved her shoe lying some distance away on the quayside and helped ease it onto her foot.

'It's fine.'

It was aching and Odete was certain the hairy twine had burned her skin, although her stocking currently hid that. She wanted everyone to forget what had just happened and spare her further embarrassment. She needn't have worried. Their concern about the body meant they had already turned away and were headed to what looked like the largest warehouse on the quayside.

The walls were built from a red brick with an exposed wooden framework and a red-tiled roof. Three massive double wooden doors stood open and as many porters were streaming through these as there were from any other warehouse. Evidently, finding a body didn't bring business to a halt.

'This is your warehouse?'

The size of it surprised Odete.

'So it would seem,' Herculano murmured, his gazed fixed on the back of his man of business as they stepped inside.

Odete wondered whether Herculano was being sarcastic. It didn't feel like he was, but he'd given her a strange answer. Odete had also assumed, because of his lack of funds on the first day, that Herculano Escovar wasn't wealthy. She was having to readjust her first impression.

It was cooler inside the warehouse, but not by much. Wooden barrels, massive bales and sacks, as well as boxes, were stacked all around her and towered overhead. The smell of spices, leather, fish and wine filled the air and was overwhelming in its intensity.

At the end of one row of goods stood a group of men who looked out of place because they were so still. They were all holding handkerchiefs up to their faces. A balding man with a fuzzy rim of black hair tied into a skinny ponytail stood with his back to them.

'Pedro Alvaro, the manager of the warehouse,' de Mello murmured to Herculano.

Odete wondered why the explanation was necessary and then dismissed it as the stomach-churning smell of decay washed over her. It was coming from the man-shaped mass on the floor that somebody had thankfully covered with a tarpaulin. An open barrel stood beside the body, the lid propped up against its side. Somebody had drawn a cross on the tarpaulin and a couple of the men were clutching charms to ward off evil.

'The boss is here,' one man in the silent circle said, with a tilt of his chin.

'Your Excellency,' Alvaro said, and swung about.

He looked green to the gills, Odete thought, and like he was on the verge of throwing up. A deep red liquid, mingled with a thicker brownish sludge, had seeped out from under the tarpaulin and, up close, the stench of a rotting body was intense.

'It's a man, is it?'

Odete admired the fact that Herculano showed neither fear nor distaste.

'I'm afraid so,' Alvaro said.

'How did you find the body?'

'We were about to send these barrels out on the carts. One of the men noticed the smell, and, when he got closer, saw it was oozing. They're sealed well. They don't leak unless there's a problem.'

'So you opened it?'

'Someone had clearly tampered with it because the lid came off too easily. This didn't happen at the vineyard.'

'When do you think it happened?' Herculano said as his gaze swept over the covered body.

Alvaro scratched his bald patch and considered.

'I've checked the records and these barrels arrived on Tuesday. They landed up sitting outside overnight as we had to clear a space for them, and that night there was a thunderstorm. I'm willing to bet that's when it happened. Our bloody night watchman must have taken shelter from the rain and that moment, when the barrels weren't guarded, must have been when the body was put inside.'

'I see,' Herculano said, still looking cool and composed.

Odete doubted she was managing to do the same. Tuesday night was when Tiago had vanished. She was feeling increasingly sick about the mysterious body.

'Alright, let's take a look at him,' Herculano said.

The smell of decay intensified as the men pulled back the tarpaulin and Odete shut her eyes, dreading what she might see.

'I think it's him,' Herculano murmured in her ear.

'Oh no!'

Now Odete forced herself to look. Only the head and shoulders were visible. They were stained a dark purple that added to the horror of the bloated face and the grimace that exposed stained teeth. Thankfully, all she had to look for was the mole by his left eye. It was as well he had such a distinguishing feature, because it was impossible to discern much from the mashed and stained face.

'It's him,' Odete said, and hastily turned away as she groped for her handkerchief and pressed it against her mouth.

'Do you know this man?' de Mello asked, and, even in her distressed state, Odete heard the surprise in his voice.

'I believe he is Lord Tiago Andrade,' Herculano said. 'Do what you can to clean the body, then have him wrapped up and... Where is the nearest church?'

'That would be Our Lady of the Sea.'

'Fine, take him there. I will inform the gentleman's father, so tell the priest to wait and not bury him.'

'You were looking for him?'

'It's a long story. I'll give you more information as soon as I am able. But for now, please, just do as I tell you.'

'Yes, Your Excellency.'

Odete was grateful Herculano had taken over again, but the thought of telling Mafalda about the body sent a tremor of fear through her.

'This is going to cause an uproar,' she said softly, so that only Herculano would hear her.

He nodded, then something else apparently occurred to him because he turned back to his people.

'Do we know how he died?'

'It's hard to say,' Andrade said, 'but it looks like he may have been stabbed in the belly.'

'So no accident.'

'It isn't usual to stuff the bodies of accident victims into barrels.'

'Mmm. Get a priest to bless the area. And a witch. No harm in using both,' Herculano said, and his words seemed to reassure the men. Nobody wanted the restless spirit of a murdered man wandering the warehouse. 'I have to return to the palace now. I'll leave the rest to you.'

Herculano nodded a farewell to his people, took Odete more gently by the arm than usual and led her back outside.

De Mello hurried along after him and said, 'Your Excellency, this stay at the palace... is it going to last long?'

'I honestly don't know,' Herculano said, as he stopped on the quayside and took a deep breath.

Odete understood why. Even the fishy air out here was a vast improvement on the smell in the warehouse. Not that it could shift the scent of decay entirely. It lingered in her nostrils.

'In the meantime,' Herculano continued, 'please carry on looking after business. I will come and visit you as soon as I am able.'

De Mello nodded acceptance, but to Odete, he looked troubled as he headed back to the warehouse.

Herculano examined Odete thoughtfully and said, 'How much of an uproar do you think finding Tiago Andrade's body will cause?'

'I'm not entirely sure. His father will be devastated, as will Lady Mafalda. That's not even to mention the prince. He and Tiago were best friends.'

'Yes.'

Odete was struck by the fact that Herculano looked bereft. It was odd because he'd claimed not to know Tiago and he'd needed her to identify the body. So why was he hurt?

'I suppose you'll have to tell Lady Mafalda,' Herculano said.

'I'm afraid so. I'll be in serious trouble if she hears of it from anybody else. If you think her tantrum from this morning was bad, you can't imagine how much worse it will be when she hears the man she loved is dead.'

'I'm sorry, you are going to have a hard time. At least I know the prince won't fall apart at this news.'

⁊

Herculano had no memory of Tiago, but he felt a great pain in his heart as he walked silently back to the palace with Lady Odete. Perhaps it was a blessing that he didn't have all his memories, for the pain would be even worse.

For now, he had to look to the future and what it meant to have found Tiago. Even worse, for the body to have been on his property. Was it mere coincidence that it must have gone into the barrel on Tuesday night, of all nights?

'Damnation!' Herculano muttered, then hastily looked down, an apology ready for any offence he might have caused.

But Odete wasn't paying him any attention. She was pale and limping and looked worried.

'I'll get you a sedan.'

Herculano waved over a pair of men who'd been loitering on the corner, their chair sitting on the ground beside them.

'It's not necessary, really, not when the palace is so close,' Odete said, but she looked wan and not in the mood to put up a fight.

'Get in.' Herculano pushed aside the curtain that closed off the chair. Inside was a threadbare red velvet chair that let off a musty smell. It wasn't appealing, but Herculano was determined. 'No more walking,' he said, and led Odete to the seat.

'Don't leave me with these men,' Odete hissed as the men took up their position between their poles and hoisted her off the ground.

'I will walk beside you,' Herculano said, and realised that Odete's anxiety reflected how shaken she was feeling.

Was it worse than his own despair? It wasn't just about finding the body. Until he'd arrived at the warehouse, the full weight of his own responsibilities had not been clear to him. He'd been annoyed at the prince for insisting he had to remain at the palace. But, in a way, that had been a reprieve, a holiday from his actual duties.

At some point, he was going to have to learn about the mercantile empire he'd inherited. He wondered whether the prince had been a good student and competent manager. He suspected he was, which would only make his life more difficult as he bungled his way through. Herculano gave an inward shrug at that. There were more immediate concerns for now.

He looked up from his introspection and realised that Odete was peeping at him through a crack in the sedan curtain. Her expression was one of concern and suspicion. He could hardly blame her, but, since they'd arrived at the palace, Herculano paid the chair-men and helped Odete out.

As he led her to the palace door, he leaned up close and said, 'Don't tell Lady Mafalda anything.'

'What?'

Odete swung round to stare at him in uncertain surprise.

'Not before dinner.'

'She'll be furious if I delay.'

'After the display she put on this morning, do you really think it's wise to have her all in pieces before her father at dinner?'

'You have a point.'

Odete suddenly looked so young and vulnerable and scared that Herculano desperately wanted to wrap her in his arms and reassure her.

Instead, all he could say was, 'He has been missing for three days. Another couple of hours won't make any difference. Bring her to the prince's room this evening after dinner and we can tell the two of them at the same time.'

When Prince Juliano and Herculano were strolling back to their rooms through the candlelit halls after dinner, he said, 'There's something I need to tell you.'

'It's nothing good, I'll warrant,' Juliano said.

'No.'

'I feared as much. You scowled all the way through the meal. Then again, it wasn't a particularly cheerful affair. The duque said next to nothing, and it looks like Lady Mafalda was still distressed about this morning.'

'I suppose so.'

Herculano had been more worried about Lady Odete and hadn't given Lady Mafalda much thought.

'Speaking of which,' the prince said, and tilted his head to indicate someone ahead.

Herculano looked up to see the ladies Odete and Mafalda heading their way.

'Ah yes, I suggested they come too.'

'For the love of God, why?'

'You'll see.'

Juliano gave him a sceptical arched eyebrow and Herculano wondered whether this was indeed the best strategy. He'd only been thinking of shielding Odete when he'd suggested she bring Lady Mafalda. Now he realised how awkward that might be.

Fortunately, the prince didn't deny the ladies entry to his room. He merely waved them in as the footman stood to attention at the door.

'What is this about?' Lady Mafalda said, the moment the door closed on the little gathering.

'Presumably not about your extraordinary display this morning,' Juliano said, looking Mafalda up and down. 'What did your father have to say about the matter?'

'Nothing yet,' Mafalda said, and examined the prince warily. 'Not that I thought you'd care either way.'

'No, I don't suppose I do.' Juliano settled in his swan-shaped chair and crossed one elegant leg over the other. 'Now, my dear

Herculano, are you going to tell us why you've gathered us all together?'

'It's about Tiago Andrade.'

Herculano shared a look with Odete who looked pale and like she was bracing herself.

'I was afraid it might be,' the prince murmured. 'Don't tell me you managed to do what Lord Andrade failed to do.'

'We found his body.'

'No!' Lady Mafalda gasped. 'No, no, no, no, no, you can't have.'

'I'm afraid there can be no doubt. The mole below his left eye is quite a–'

'No! How is this possible? He can't be dead, he can't.'

Odete wrapped her arms around the young woman and said, 'I'm sorry.'

'No!' Mafalda said, as she sagged into Odete's arms and burst into tears.

Odete took her weight and led her to a nearby sofa, where she helped her to sit and kept an arm wrapped about her shoulders, patting her gently as she sobbed.

'You'd better tell us everything,' Juliano said, and his usually neutral expression now looked grave.

So Herculano did, glancing towards Odete for corroboration now and then.

'You found his body in a warehouse?' Lady Mafalda said, looking up at him with a tear-stained face when Herculano finished explaining.

'I'm afraid so.'

'Whose warehouse? Surely that person must have killed him. Why else would the body be on his property?'

'Ah, well, the barrel was in my warehouse.' Herculano wished he didn't have to admit that. 'But the barrels were standing outside on the night that Tiago was probably killed.'

'When was that?' Juliano said.

'Tuesday.'

Herculano gave the prince a rueful grimace. He'd know that neither of them would have been around on that night and certainly in no position to murder anyone. Lady Mafalda was having none of it, though.

'His body was in your warehouse and you appeared the day after Tiago was killed and suddenly you're living in his rooms. This all sounds suspicious to me.'

'I assure you, my lady, I had nothing to do with Tiago Andrade's death.'

'His murder!' Lady Mafalda jumped up and advanced on Herculano. 'And you're bound to say that, aren't you? But I still think this whole business is fishy.'

Odete jumped up and followed her, trying to get her to sit back down.

'It is suspicious,' Juliano said, as he gazed up at the rest of the company gathered about him.

Herculano blinked at him. What the devil was he up to?

'It's an enormous warehouse with hundreds of people working in it. Anyone could have stashed a body there. Besides, it is far more likely to be an outsider than me or one of my men. The last place we'd hide a body is on my property.'

'Quite,' Juliano said, before Mafalda could object. She had already opened her mouth, clearly intent on giving everyone her opinion. 'We shall have to consult Dr Zuniga.'

'I don't understand,' Mafalda said. 'What has he got to do with anything?'

'Far more than you know,' Juliano said.

10

Just as he managed to drop off, Herculano was shaken awake again. He pushed away the hand that had taken a painfully firm grip on his shoulder and opened his eyes. His words of complaint died on his lips as he found himself staring up at the prince.

'For the love of God, what are you doing?' Herculano asked, as he realised it was so early that the sun was only just coming up.

'Don't tell me you could actually sleep,' Juliano said, watching to make sure he didn't close his eyes again.

'Not really.' Herculano sat up and rubbed his head vigorously. 'What do you want?'

'I have been worrying about where Tiago's body was found. It's suspicious that it was at your warehouse.'

'So you implied last night, but I don't see why. I, or rather, the old Herculano Escovar,' Herculano said, pointing at the prince, 'had nothing to do with the duque or the succession. If Tiago did indeed die on the Tuesday night, that was the time of the body swap. Neither of us could have been involved and there would have been no reason to frame me.'

'That's what I kept telling myself,' Juliano said, as he took a turn about the room. 'Still, it bothers me. Not only for what it could mean, but for how the duque might use it.'

That possibility hadn't occurred to Herculano and it felt like a stone fell into his stomach to be suddenly in so much more danger.

'And what if, in the process of trying to link me to one crime, he stumbles upon our secret?'

'You mean the body swap? It's such an outrageous circumstance that I doubt anyone would even believe it. I don't believe it myself sometimes.'

'All the same, the court must be wondering about my sudden appearance, and the changes they see in you. Even I could tell that the duque was puzzled by your behaviour in the council meeting.'

'And he kept looking at you as well,' Juliano said with a sigh. 'But what can we do about that?'

'Keep apart from one another so that no comparisons can be made and I fade from their memories.'

Herculano surprised himself to realise that, although it was a sensible suggestion, he was hoping the prince wouldn't agree.

'You would abandon me to the sharks of the court, would you? Now, when I am at my most vulnerable.'

Juliano spoke far more calmly that Herculano could have managed.

'You see, that's precisely the problem. If I was in your situation I'd roar at you for being a traitor. People notice this kind of thing. Heaven only knows what the people of the Escovar business empire will think of their suddenly impetuous master. How can you not care whether those in the palace will notice? It's enough for us to be sentenced to death for impersonation or, at the very least, have you stripped of your crown.'

'It worries me too, Herculano, and you may think this weak of me, but right now, I need you. Trying to deal with my uncle

and Tiago's death on my own... It's not like I can tell any of my
other friends about it, is it?'

'You have a point, and I may not want to leave just yet either.
I take it as you've dressed simply I should do the same.'

'Good man,' Juliano said, as he gave Herculano's shoulder a
grateful squeeze. 'I sent a message to Tiago's father to meet us
at the church.'

'You've already told him about his son?'

'Not yet. I intend to tell him at the church. But before we do
that, we have to see Dr Zuniga.'

'I don't think I ever want to see Dr Zuniga again,' Herculano
said, as he hurried to his washstand and began his ablutions.

'We need to know when he performed his spell and how long
it took. I need to work out where the two of us were exactly on
Tuesday night.'

'And you need to do this at dawn?' Herculano asked,
watching the prince via his mirror as he rubbed his face with a
damp flannel.

'We're running out of time. Tiago's death will cause an
uproar. Tiago's father won't take it quietly, nor should he have
to. He'll blame the duque, for the two of them are bitter, if
silent, enemies. But he may well blame me too, and with good
reason. I have no doubt that whatever Tiago was up to, he was
doing it for me.'

Herculano gave a noncommittal grunt and towelled himself
down. He was guiltily aware that if anyone was responsible for
sending Tiago to his death, it was him. Whatever the prince and
Tiago had planned, it had to have been done before the body
swap.

He would probably have pointed that out if their positions
were reversed. He didn't know what to make of the fact that
the prince wasn't blaming him. They really were quite different
people.

'Do you still have no memory of what happened in the few
days leading up to Tuesday?'

'Nothing,' Juliano said, with a frustrated shake of his head. 'It seems the closer in time we come to Tuesday night, the worse my memory becomes. I can remember the week before that better, but with gaps. I can remember the month before perfectly. I don't suppose you have remembered anything?'

'I'm afraid not.'

Herculano looked around to find his clothes and Arriscado appeared with smalls and a freshly laundered white shirt, which he helped Herculano into.

'Will Dr Zuniga even be up at this hour?' Herculano asked, as he shrugged himself into the same black coat he'd worn the day before.

'I sent a man to tell him to be ready. He'll see us,' Juliano said, already heading for the door.

'He has no choice,' Herculano muttered, as he followed behind. Such was the power of royalty.

Prince Juliano and Herculano were shown into Dr Zuniga's laboratory by an anxious-looking young servant who bowed nearly double to the prince before rapidly effacing himself.

Dr Zuniga was up and swathed in a deep red velvet dressing gown tied at the waist with a twisted gold cord.

'Your Highness, Your Excellency Mr Escovar,' he said as he bowed, then lit the lamp beneath a wide-mouthed glass beaker filled with water. The flame fizzed and sputtered blue sparks before it lit.

The laboratory was what Herculano expected from an alchemist. The table upon which the beaker sat was long and wide and had multiple scorch marks partly obscured by a multitude of pestles and mortars, knives, cutting boards and a collection of glass beakers in a variety of shapes and sizes, many of which were connected by thin glass tubes.

Behind the alchemist was a bookshelf so crammed with books that some had been stuffed on top of the orderly rows. Charts filled with mysterious symbols hung from the shelves and walls. Another set of shelves held jars of coloured powders and liquids plus an array of animal parts. One jar was filled entirely with eyes. Above them, swimming through a flotsam of dried herbs, large black iron cauldrons and shiny copper pots, was a stuffed crocodile.

'Thank you for seeing us at this hour,' Juliano said, and sat down on one of the laboratory stools.

'Did I have a choice?'

Dr Zuniga spoke without heat as he reached for a plain white pottery jug. It had blue writing on it, but his hand hid too much for Herculano to read what it held.

'The matter is urgent,' Juliano said.

'I am sure it is, as I have been told you are not one to do anything impulsive.'

As he spoke, Dr Zuniga glanced across at Herculano who flushed. Herculano already knew he was the sort to rush in and think about consequences later. It was what made him worry that it was his fault Tiago was dead.

'Herculano found Tiago Andrade's body yesterday. It was stuffed into a wine barrel in one of his warehouses,' Juliano said.

Dr Zuniga paused. The spoon of black granules he'd just scooped out of his jug trembled ever so slightly before he overcame his surprise and emptied the contents into the water-filled beaker. Herculano watched as the granules drifted downwards, releasing inky brown trails.

'That complicates the matter somewhat.'

'So you also think the duque might use it to his advantage?' Herculano said.

'Your question presupposes that the duque had something to do with young Lord Andrade's death.'

'He is bound to be behind it,' Juliano said.

'I fear you are right. Either way, he'll be curious about Herculano and his sudden appearance at court. With this connection to the body, his interest will be piqued even more. Whether or not he was involved, I would not put it past him to benefit from this incident.'

'It looks like Tiago was killed on Tuesday night. With that in mind, could Herculano have done it?'

'Mother of God!' Herculano said.

The prince merely gazed calmly at him, then turned back to Dr Zuniga.

'Tuesday night?' the alchemist said, and stirred the concoction that had started to bubble and give off the pleasant aroma of coffee. 'No, that would have been quite impossible.'

'Why?'

'Because there was a storm on Tuesday night.'

'Are you always this obscure?'

Herculano was annoyed to be suspected even though, with his loss of memory, he was in no position to clear his name or even know whether he had been involved.

'In answer to your question,' Dr Zuniga said, with an amused smile, 'yes, I am always this obscure. An air of mystery is useful in my profession. But to answer the prince's question, I needed the energy from a storm to attempt my spell of getting you back to your rightful bodies.

'As soon as I saw that one brewing on Tuesday, I sent word to Arriscado. He had been in daily expectation of the event and immediately slipped a sleeping draught I had sent to him into a drink. I did the same here.

'Then Arriscado had your sleeping body transported to the palace. The moment the lightning started, I began the spell, and I kept going for the full duration of the storm. After that, it was a matter of getting you both back to your respective beds. Arriscado and I kept watch over you for the rest of the night. Which is why you both woke up with us by your sides.'

'That I do remember,' Herculano muttered, and the prince nodded his agreement.

'So you are our witnesses, should we need them,' Juliano said.

'I suppose we are.' Dr Zuniga placed three smaller glass beakers in a row before his boiling beaker and snuffed out the flame. 'The thing is, we would have to explain how it was that we were by your bedsides all night and that might lead to further questions.'

'I'll worry about that should it happen. In the meantime, we have to get ahead of the duque, and for that we have to figure out what Tiago was doing, and why that made him such a threat he had to be done away with.'

'Indeed,' Dr Zuniga said, and poured his concoction through a sieve into the three beakers. 'Before you go, though, have some coffee. I suspect you're going to have a long day.'

The bells had just finished chiming eight o'clock when Herculano and the prince arrived at the church where Tiago's body was being kept. Herculano paused at the bottom of the circle of steps that led up to the doors to the church of Our Lady of the Sea and looked up at the whitewashed facade. It was so bright that the walls shone in the early morning sunshine. The church had an elegant gable and twin bell towers, creating perfect proportions. The doors stood wide open, welcoming any who needed succour. Herculano had never felt less like going into a church in his life.

The prince showed no such hesitation and looked back at Herculano with one eyebrow arched impatiently. Herculano had to give him his due, he wasn't the type to procrastinate.

An acrid waft of incense curled up Herculano's nose as he stepped inside, followed by the less pleasant aroma of decay. This wasn't surprising. All the dead of Lisbon were buried inside their churches, so the stench of death was omnipresent. As the city continued to grow, the space for burials was becoming problematic, to say the least.

In this church, the walls were tiled in blue and white depictions of the fourteen stations of the cross, ornamented by fruits and the beasts of the earth. A plain, pale stone altar stood in a modest semicircular chancel. It seemed that any money given to the church had gone into a massive carved altarpiece entirely covered in gold leaf that glistened in the flickering light of a pair of sturdy candles.

'Your Highness,' a quiet voice said, and a man who'd been sitting so motionless he hadn't been noticed stood up and turned to face Herculano and the prince.

'Your Excellency, Lord Andrade,' Juliano said and bowed low to the older man.

A quiver of guilt-filled fear ran through Herculano as he bowed just as deeply then straightened up to examine a thin, average-looking man. He was dressed sombrely and wore a modest grey wig. His eyes were filled with pain, but it didn't show on his face.

'You got here before me, my lord,' the prince said as he straightened up.

'I feared the reason for your requested meeting.'

Lord Andrade spoke in tight, clipped words. He already knows, Herculano realised. This wasn't a man fearing the worst, this was a man who'd already confirmed it.

'I'm afraid I couldn't wait for your arrival, so I spoke to the priest and he...'

Lord Andrade stopped. A quiver of pain marred his face for an instant and then it was gone.

'I am very sorry, my lord,' Juliano said. 'There are no words to make this easier to bear.'

'No,' Lord Andrade said, and turned away. 'If you wish to see him, you need to go through the door on the right of the altar.'

Herculano had no wish to see the disfigured remains of what had once been his closest friend, but he realised the lord had suggested it to gain himself some time to collect his feelings.

The prince nodded and headed up the stairs into the chancel and through the open door into a small side room. It was simply furnished. A dark wooden cupboard occupied the entire length of the far wall. A large wooden table took up much of the rest of the space. There was no lid on the simple pine coffin that occupied the table, but it was painted with a mixture of crosses and sigils intended to ward off evil. Herculano gingerly stepped up to it and looked inside.

The church officials had done a good job of wrapping the body in a plain white shroud so that only the face was visible. It was blackened and, despite what must have been a considerable amount of scrubbing, still stained by the wine.

This time a tsunami of grief crashed into Herculano and he staggered backwards.

The prince caught him by his elbow and murmured, 'Easy now.'

Herculano grimaced at him, the best he could do for acknowledgement, and forced himself to look away from Tiago's hideously disfigured face.

'I thought the second time would be easier.'

Juliano nodded, then turned his attention to the ancient priest who'd started towards them when they'd stepped inside.

'Forgive me, I didn't realise he was nobility,' the old man said in a quivering voice. 'I would have found a nicer coffin had I known.'

'You did your best.'

Herculano admired Juliano's calm. He would have been roaring at the priest to do better. Not because he blamed the old man, just as an outlet for his pain.

'I assume his father has made arrangements for him to be removed?' Herculano managed to say, although it cost him a lot to do it.

'The family has a mausoleum on their grounds. His lordship will send his men to collect the body.'

'Good,' Herculano said, desperate to get away from this claustrophobic room.

The prince gazed calmly down at the body, made a sign of the cross, nodded a farewell to the priest and headed back into the church.

Lord Andrade had regained control over his emotions by the time they re-joined him and looked the prince and Herculano up and down more thoughtfully this time.

'Do you know how this happened?'

Lord Andrade was careful to show no anger. It wouldn't help his cause and, even if he blamed the prince, it would be dangerous to say so.

'I'm afraid I don't,' Juliano said, matching the lord's neutral tone.

'So it wasn't because of something the two of you cooked up?'

'It might be indirectly connected, but I am still trying to find out how.'

Lord Andrade nodded, looking Herculano up and down as he did so.

'Is this the man you installed in my son's rooms at the palace?'

'Forgive me, I should have introduced him earlier. This is Herculano Escovar. He has been investigating Tiago's disappearance. Needless to say, this was not the outcome I had hoped for.'

'But why is the richest merchant in Lisbon involved at all?' Lord Andrade snapped, his pain coming out in that brief flash of impatience. 'Especially when my son's body was ultimately found in one of his warehouses.'

'You've investigated me?'

Herculano was so surprised he couldn't keep it to himself.

'Of course I did. You are by far the strangest aspect to this case.'

'And one I can't explain just yet,' Juliano said.

Herculano was grateful for his intervention since he was so flabbergasted he had no words.

'I promise, however, that I will explain once this whole business is resolved.'

'When could that be?' Lord Andrade asked, flinging up his hands. 'You and the duque have been in silent battle since you reached your majority, Your Highness. Now my son has paid the ultimate price, as I always feared he would. When will you put an end to that tyrant's hold upon your kingdom?'

'I hope to do so soon. Like you, I suspect the duque is involved.'

'But you have no proof.'

'Not yet.'

Herculano watched Lord Andrade as he paced about the church. Since he'd been at court his whole life, he was impossible to read.

'I assume Tiago was trying to find out what sort of hold the duque has on the members of his council.'

'That much I do know.' Juliano motioned with his hand for Lord Andrade to join him on the pew. 'My uncle prevents me from taking control of the kingdom by the simple expedient of controlling the council. We both thought that if we could break that hold, or turn some of the council to my side, I could finally take over.'

'I would say that's a waste of time, Your Highness.' Lord Andrade flicked the tails of his coat outwards so that he didn't crumple them when he sat down. 'As you know, I have spent my life trying to undermine the duque, but he is far too well entrenched.'

'Are you telling me it's impossible?'

'Not impossible,' Andrade said, 'but extremely difficult. My friend, the Marquis of Portima, was found guilty of treason purely based on lies from the duque's men and a confession forced out of Portima through torture. Since his very public execution, nobody has been willing to stand openly against the duque.'

'Which was why I was trying to win round the council.'

'I fear you will need far more than that.'

Andrade sighed and his gaze drifted about the church's simple interior.

'What will I need?' Juliano said, and for once his voice did reflect his frustration.

'Something spectacular,' Herculano said, as realisation dawned and he leaped back to his feet. 'A crime, plain and simple, with all the evidence of the duque's involvement laid bare for all the world to see.'

'Precisely,' Lord Andrade said. 'And I'm sorry to say that my son's death may have provided you with exactly that.'

'So I must prove somehow that the duque ordered Tiago's death?' Juliano said.

'If he is guilty of that, then yes. It is what I will work tirelessly towards myself. Don't you owe it to Tiago to do the same?'

'Of course. Although it won't be easy.'

'My boy, you have been battling the duque for nearly a decade. Now may be your best chance to finally beat him.'

Herculano felt excitement building inside him even though his sensible side said he would be wisest to walk away from the prince and his plotting. He couldn't. His hatred for the duque was stronger than the prince's.

'In the meantime,' Lord Andrade continued, 'you need to build up your allies. It's sensible to start with the merchant class.' He waved in Herculano's direction. 'The duque thinks of the lower classes only as a source to be squeezed for money to rebuild the city. I feel sure they would flock to your side, especially as you have His Excellency Herculano Escovar on your side.'

'Do you think I'm that influential?' Herculano said with a laugh.

'If money is power, then you are four times more powerful than I am,' Lord Andrade said, looking Herculano over coolly. 'And I have been told that you are a canny businessman as well, and one not to be crossed.'

Herculano couldn't help looking at the prince in surprise. Juliano gave him a slight, wry smile.

The prince turned back to Lord Andrade and said, 'Your advice, as always, is worth more than gold. Rest assured that I will bring Tiago's murderer to justice.'

⁓

Odete woke with a heavy head. Her dreams were filled with wine-stained bodies, treacherous entangling ropes and sobbing ladies. She sat up and blinked at the bright slits of light that pierced her shutters. The sun was already bright and baking hot. Usually she wouldn't have been able to sleep in, but she supposed Mafalda was a huddled mass of misery in her own bed and likely to remain there for the day, if not longer.

The last thing Odete wanted to do was make another attempt to console the young woman, but that was her job. She stepped out of bed and winced. Her ankle was swollen and red with a stippling of scabs where the rope had ripped the skin away. She contemplated binding it with a bandage, then dismissed the idea. Her stocking would hide what was really a minor injury.

She shuddered to think what might have happened had Herculano not grabbed her in time. Then the memory of being held in his arms brought a blush to her face. She shook the thought away impatiently. She had work to do and it would be best to get it done before Mafalda emerged.

Just because Tiago's body had been found didn't mean an end to the investigation. Both the prince and Mafalda would be determined to find out what had happened to him.

A snort drew her eye to one of the other two beds in the room. Maria da Luz was apparently taking this opportunity to catch up on her other favourite activity: sleeping. Pia's bed wasn't only empty but already made. Now was, therefore, the best opportunity Odete was going to get to talk to Pia on her own.

All in all, Odete thought, as she hurried to bathe and dress herself before her maid realised she was awake and insisted on helping her, Pia and Maria da Luz weren't bad roommates. At home she'd shared the nursery with seven other sisters and a handful of brothers, until they grew too old to remain with the girls. They'd shared beds and clothes and bickered like only siblings could. Odete much preferred the quiet of the ladies-in-waiting's bedroom.

She smoothed down the simple dress she'd selected for the day. It was a pale yellow but, more importantly, the most lightweight fabric she owned. It was the best she could do to survive the humid heat of Lisbon. She fastened the deeper yellow belt into a fetching bow at her side and, hoping she'd have some time to herself, took her sketchbook and drawing implements with her into the sitting room the ladies shared.

As expected, Pia was the only one there. She was seated near a window whose shutter was half open, letting in light but not too much heat. Her head was bowed over a length of pink satin that she was embroidering.

Pia was by far the most accomplished needlewoman amongst the four of them. Odete knew she was embroidering a border that would soon adorn one of Mafalda's many dresses. In the light from the window, her fuzzy light brown hair glowed golden. She was a pretty girl, but a weak chin prevented her from being considered a true beauty.

Pia, sensing she was being watched, looked up and smiled as she saw Odete.

'You're awake.'

'Only just.'

'You should ring for some coffee and toast. It's late and you must be hungry.'

'Mmm.' Odete wasn't in the mood for food.

She'd only just woken up and it was too hot to have anything. She'd long since learned that Pia and Maria da Luz used food for comfort, but she didn't feel the need herself. Odete settled in the armchair opposite and drew her feet under her as she opened her sketchbook. People tended to let their guard down when they thought she wasn't giving them her full attention. At least Pia went back to concentrating on her embroidery.

'How is it progressing?' Odete asked.

'It should be finished in the next couple of days,' Pia said, holding up a length of fabric to display the intricate border of voluptuous pink and red roses.

'It's beautiful. I wish I could embroider that well.'

Odete lowered her head back to her drawing and searched for some way to broach the subject of Pia's father. The ladies seldom spoke of their fathers, so there didn't seem to be a natural way to go about her questioning.

'I had hoped to finish it by tomorrow,' Pia said, 'but what with everything lately, I haven't been able to concentrate.'

'Everything?'

Odete was surprised that Pia was the one to have started them down this useful line of conversation.

'Well, you know, you haven't been around much. Mafalda won't tell us why. And then that whole episode,' Pia faltered and looked towards Mafalda's closed door. 'The duque must be furious. He still hasn't summoned Mafalda, and who can blame him? I mean, I can't even imagine crashing into any meeting my father is holding, and he's far less intimidating than the duque. And then there was last night.'

Pia faltered and cast Odete an anxious look.

'She got some very bad news.'

Odete knew it would hardly explain why she'd had to carry a sobbing Mafalda back to her room.

'I've never seen her crying like that before and we have seen plenty of her rages,' Pia said, back to her fast, breathless, run-on sentences. 'But last night she seemed broken-hearted. I mean, usually she falls into a rage, and she screams and throws things at us. She doesn't collapse and need to be put to bed and sleep till past ten.'

'It's past ten?' Odete said in surprise. 'Have you been in to check on her?'

'I can't. She's locked the door. Heaven only knows what we'll do if the duque summons her and we can't get her up.'

'We'll worry about that later. Did your father say anything to you about Mafalda's appearance at the council meeting?'

'My father?' Pia said, giving Mafalda a surprised, blank stare. 'Why would he say anything?'

'Well... he was also at the meeting. I thought he might have said something to you about it.'

Pia looked like she didn't know what to make of such a strange question, then she bent back over her embroidery.

'I keep forgetting you don't have a father, otherwise you'd know they don't tend to speak much to their daughters. I doubt I've exchanged two words with my father in the last year.'

'Really?' Odete was surprised, despite the fact that she had spent the last two years with Mafalda, Pia and Maria da Luz. Thinking back, she realised that they rarely met with their families. When they did, it was usually with their mothers or other female relatives. 'So your father is a stranger to you?'

'I suppose so. He isn't a particularly paternal individual.'

'But he doesn't seem intimidating. That is, what I've seen of him.'

'Oh no, he's not intimidating, just uninterested, really,' Pia said with a sigh. 'My mother is always complaining about that. She said there's a good reason she's only given birth to three children, and the fault is not hers.'

'There's only three of you?'

Odete had thirteen living siblings and her family was by no means unique. In fact, if her father hadn't died, there would have been even more of them.

'I have two older brothers whom I rarely see. I am the only daughter in the family and with my father's rank and standing as head of the treasury, you'd think he'd find me a suitable husband, but no, he hasn't even tried.'

Odete wondered whether it was such a terrible thing to have an apathetic father and decided it was. They were all better than a father who was no longer around to disappoint her. She also thought Pia wouldn't have to worry much longer about finding a husband, as Lord Xavier Alardo always paid her particular attention when the duke appeared with his council. Now was not the time to discuss that. She had to keep her focus on her investigation.

'Has your father not made the slightest push to marry you?'

'He seems to think it's better for me to be a lady-in-waiting. My mother said it's just typical, when we could be improving the family lot with a wealthy and an influential man for me. Instead, he's content to see me wither into an old maid. Mother said he isn't interested enough in the family. She says he only cares for Mollies, whatever that means.'

'But he is very dedicated to his work, isn't he?' Odete said, trying to get Pia to think about other things.

Being an indifferent father would hardly be enough of a flaw for the duque to use it against Lord Onofre Paiva.

'Oh yes, he's very proud of the fact that he's the treasurer. He likes to brag that the duque couldn't have achieved half of what he has done for the city without his help.'

'So he is proud of helping?'

'It makes him feel important, but my mother says he's delusional. She says the duque only keeps him as the treasurer because he's easily swayed. When she's feeling most bitter, she calls my father the duque's lapdog, but–' Pia gasped and clapped her hand over her mouth. 'What am I saying?'

'Don't worry,' Odete said, trying hard to hide her disappointment. 'I doubt that anything you've just told me is a secret at court.'

If Maria da Luz had an equally unassuming father, Odete thought, then she would be no help at all with the prince and Lady Mafalda's investigations.

11

Herculano and the prince walked back to the palace in silence, which suited Herculano. The meeting with Lord Andrade had given him a lot to think about. So much that he barely noticed that they had arrived and presented the letter that gave them access.

It still surprised Herculano that the guards didn't instantly recognise the prince. But apparently they didn't. Either that or they were pretending not to. It probably would cause them less fuss.

'Come to my room,' Juliano said, as they wended their way down the wide corridor dotted about with servants, functionaries and a smattering of courtiers, and on up the stairs.

Herculano didn't bother to ask why the prince still wanted him. He would find out soon enough and in the privacy of his room.

So he waited till they were safely behind the closed door before he said, 'Is there something else you want to do today?'

'Of course.' Juliano headed for his dressing room and waved his valet away. The man retreated with a deep bow. 'As I said, we must act quickly if we are to get the upper hand over the duque.'

'I have been thinking about that.' Herculano settled on a straight-backed chair with blue striped silk padding, as the prince stripped out of his simple brown suit. 'Lord Andrade said you must work on your allies.'

'I've been running everyone I know through my memory and trying to work out how to approach them. It will be best to have a core network of people I can trust and get them to talk to their friends and allies for a larger, looser alliance.'

'That sounds reasonable. I should probably find out more about my merchant friends and allies. I must have some.'

'Merchants?' Juliano turned, halfway through doing up a dazzling white shirt with spectacular lace at the cuffs. 'What help would they be?'

Herculano couldn't suppress a cynical laugh as he said, 'I have no idea yet. I don't remember any names, let alone an opinion of those men. But Lord Andrade got me thinking: merchants have money and money equals power, yet they have no say on the council. Maybe that should change.'

'Do you want a seat at that august table?' Juliano said, as he went back to his dressing.

'Do you not think I deserve one?' Herculano said, swinging one crossed leg negligently, making sure he didn't look too invested in the suggestion.

'It's unheard of.'

'You're the prince. Make it happen. At the very least, the duque will be given a reason for my presence here.'

'You were at the council meeting yesterday,' Juliano said, and opened his cupboard to examine the array of sombre suits before him. 'You saw how every suggestion I made was stymied. The duque will block your appointment with a mere shake of his head.'

'The merchants may have something to say about that.'

'Oh they might, might they?' Juliano said, and stopped just short of laughing in Herculano's face.

'They might.' Herculano, after all, had no idea what they actually thought about the matter either. 'At the very least, it is an option you should consider, Your Highness.'

'Do you have any way of finding out?'

'As it happens, I too have kept a diary all my life. Arriscado told me about it last night. I suspect it was his and Dr Zuniga's back-up plan, should the body swap fail. I've asked Arriscado to bring me a selection so that I may get up to speed.'

'Fascinating.' Juliano inspected one black-embroidered-on-black coat, turning it back and forth, examining the silver embossed buttons. To Herculano it looked rather good. The prince's dismayed expression told him that he thought otherwise. 'I suppose Dr Zuniga did have to plan everything carefully.'

'Speaking of planning, there is perhaps another ally you should consider.'

'More palace outsiders?' Juliano said, as he replaced the coat and continued flicking through the wardrobe.

'Lady Mafalda, actually,' Herculano said, and waited to see the prince's reaction.

'Have you completely lost your mind?' the prince said as he spun round.

'Not at all. She was in love with Tiago, so I am certain she will want to uncover who was behind his death.'

'Not if it's her father, she won't.'

'Then don't tell her whom you suspect.'

'That would be a cruel thing to do.'

'Only if it turns out that her father is behind everything.'

'If he is, and I manage to get him arrested, it won't end there. To be truly safe, I would have to have him executed.'

'Or exiled.'

'I don't know, he is my uncle. Our connection makes this so much more difficult.'

'Do you think he would hesitate to have you killed if it suited his needs?'

Juliano shrugged and ran his hands through his hair.

'Maybe Lady Mafalda would be useful. If nothing else, it might look to my uncle like I'm reconsidering marriage to Mafalda.'

'I'm not sure he'd believe you. But it might buy you some time and at least you can reject the Habsburg princess. I have to admit her portrait has been haunting me.'

This time the prince did laugh.

'No more than she is haunting me, I assure you.'

'Would you marry Lady Mafalda if you actually liked her?'

Herculano was curious about how different he and Juliano were. Part of the impasse between the duque and the prince was due to his steadfast refusal to marry his cousin, after all.

'I might consider it.' Juliano pulled out yet another black coat, but this one trimmed in gold. It was apparently acceptable to him as he shrugged himself into it. 'Although the church generally frowns upon cousins marrying each other, they overlook it for royal families.'

'I wasn't thinking of that. More of the hold the duque would have over you.'

'It might work both ways. I would have more of a hold on him too. I have a feeling, and it's nothing more, mind you, that the duque is actually quite fond of his daughter.'

'He has a funny way of showing it.'

'Why? Because he wants her to marry a prince? On the contrary, that's exactly what makes me suspect he likes her. Otherwise, he might simply decide to take the kingdom for himself. He could easily do that.'

'Do you know, I might actually prefer being a merchant,' Herculano said. 'I can at least marry whomever I like.'

'Lady Odete?' the prince said, as he made for a locked cupboard and opened it with a key he retrieved from his dresser drawer.

'I doubt her noble family would be interested in her marrying down.'

'It all depends on what you call down.' Juliano opened his drawer and drew out a long, flattish, wooden box ornamented with a sturdy, twining, silver frame from his drawer. 'The salacious gossip is that her father, Lord Salema, died in flagrante delicto, in the process of conceiving Lady Odete. On top of that, his inheritance had not been large, and his inability to manage it properly brought them to the point of destitution. I understand it was the duque who provided work for the two eldest boys, as secretaries in the palace, and also took Lady Odete in as a lady-in-waiting.'

'Why did he do that?' Herculano asked, surprised by the news.

'Because my uncle is a snob. The Salema family are descendants of one of the old royal houses of Portugal. Also, he can keep any potential claimants to the throne under his watchful eye, lest they dream of taking over.'

'With such illustrious heritage, they are even less likely to consider a merchant,' Herculano said gloomily.

He couldn't bring himself to point out that he was born a pauper.

'But they would be very interested in your money,' the prince said, as he used a small silver key to unlock his wooden box.

Inside, nestled on a blue velvet cushion, was a matching pair of long-nosed flintlock pistols. The smell of gunpowder and oil drifted over to Herculano who stood up to take a closer look.

'Duelling pistols?'

'Apparently I am considered a deadly shot.' Juliano lifted one of the pistols and sighted along the barrel. 'And, according to Arriscado, you are too.'

'I don't recall that. Although it seems they took no chances with training you for the role. It appears they gave us an identical education containing much that would be of no use to a merchant.'

'One wonders what they would have done had the body swap failed,' Juliano said. 'All the same, I thought it would be interesting to see how good we actually are. Maybe we should invite the ladies out to adjudicate on our skill.'

'The prince wants what?' Lady Mafalda said.

Odete was equally surprised and the two young women stood, midway through dressing Mafalda, staring at the maid who had brought the message.

'His Highness requests you join him in the ballroom to help judge a contest of skill.'

'Now? Does he have no idea of how I feel? Or does he simply not care?'

Odete was aware that Pia and Maria da Luz, who'd both remained in the sitting room in a cowardly attempt to avoid Mafalda's grief, were listening intently.

'It's one way for us to meet without suspicion,' she murmured, and hoped nobody else heard.

'What?'

'It may be a way for the prince to be able to talk to you,' Odete said, trying to keep this louder pronouncement deliberately vague.

The last thing they needed was for gossip to get out about how Mafalda had really felt about Tiago Andrade. Mafalda looked confused for a moment, and then her eyes widened as she understood.

'Well then, we'd best not keep the prince waiting.'

More quickly than Odete had ever seen, Lady Mafalda was dressed, and the two young women were heading to the ballroom. Odete had mixed feelings about meeting there.

The ballroom was the biggest, grandest room in the palace and the space had the feeling of a cathedral, except that gilt mirrors hung where a cathedral would have religious icons. The crystal chandeliers were far more ornate and looked like gigantic, twinkling, glass-encrusted flowers. At least they did at night. During the day, they were a little dusty and stained black from the smoke of the hundreds of candles they held. The room itself was dim, as the windows were of secondary importance for a place used mainly at night.

The reason Odete wasn't fond of this hall was the misery of being ignored through all the balls she'd attended. First, she was penniless and with no one influential to back her. Second, she was a lady-in-waiting to a young woman everyone knew would marry the prince, so there was no point in cultivating Odete as a means of getting to Mafalda.

Because she was pretty, men would dance with her, and some made the outrageous suggestion that an affaire would be amusing. Odete would never countenance that. She later heard from her maid that the spurned gentlemen had labelled her a prude. That hurt, but she reminded herself that it was better than becoming mistress to any of those jaded gentlemen.

Today, the great echoing ballroom was occupied only by the prince and Herculano Escovar. Not for the first time, it filled Odete with envy that men could go about unchaperoned. Her second, more surprising thought, was that she was happy to see Herculano. Happier even than to see the prince.

The two men turned as they approached and the prince swept them an elegant bow. Herculano gave the ladies something closer to a nod than a bow. It pulled Odete up short because it was exactly the acknowledgement the prince used to give them. She couldn't recall ever seeing the prince give a deep bow. When he came up, the prince gave both women a vague smile, but his gaze lingered on Mafalda.

The warm glances he used to cast Odete were gone. She might have been a stranger to him the way he behaved now. Herculano, on the other hand, was smiling at her in a way that felt so familiar and comforting that it unsettled her.

'Thank you for joining us. Herculano and I thought it might be amusing to discover which of us is the better shot.'

Juliano waved his hand toward a table that had been pulled into the middle of the room, upon which lay an open pistol case.

'Shooting?' Mafalda said. 'You invited us to watch you shoot?'

'Among other things,' Juliano said, and waved the accompanying maids back to the door to wait there.

Mafalda watched their retreat and said, 'I really don't understand you.'

'Well, play along and we might come to an understanding,' Juliano said, as he picked up one of the pistols.

Mafalda scowled at him, and Odete prepared to step in. Mafalda wasn't used to anyone other than her father treating her in this offhand manner.

The prince picked up one of his pistols and approached the wall on the far side of the ballroom, where an array of playing cards had been pinned.

'I understand it's all the rage in Paris and London to attempt to shoot the little spades, diamonds, hearts and clubs out of the cards as a test of skill.'

Mafalda looked at him in amazement and said, 'You will shoot a hole in the wall as well.'

'That doesn't matter. It's my wall, and easily repaired.'

Herculano grinned at the prince's nonchalance and Odete felt this deserved a set down.

'It is highly irresponsible to shoot holes in any wall, even if it is yours,' she snapped.

The prince turned round with a surprised look and Odete realised what she'd done.

Before she could apologise, though, Herculano said, 'I believe ladies aren't as cavalier when it comes to matters of hearth and home. I, however, am willing to test myself against you, Your Highness.'

The prince gave his new henchman a knowing smile and, thankfully, dismissed Odete's criticism.

'I will aim at the black cards. You can take the red ones. We'll have ten shots each. That should demonstrate, without question, which of us is the better shot.'

'As you wish, Your Highness.'

Herculano lifted the second pistol out of the case and proceeded to load it, first measuring and pouring some gunpowder down the barrel.

'We'd best get further back,' Odete said to Mafalda, as she took her by the elbow and walked them towards the wall that was perpendicular to the one the cards were attached to. 'My brothers used to do this indoors on occasion as well. The bang is quite deafening. My mother landed up with severe palpitations whenever my brothers practised their shooting.'

From this safer distance, Odete watched as both men tamped down their shot and then filled the pan with the gunpowder which would ignite the rest.

'Cover your ears, my lady,' Odete said, as both men raised their pistols.

Herculano and the prince were standing on either side of the table, which they were using as a guide to ensure they were shooting the same distance. Herculano sighted down the long nose of the pistol, his arm held straight out and parallel to the ground, his body turned to the side as duellers did, to present a smaller target.

He squeezed the trigger. There was a flash of light as the pan exploded, followed by a roar as the powder in the barrel caught fire and shot the bullet outwards in a great puff of flame and smoke.

'Holy Mary, Mother of God!' Mafalda gasped and crossed herself a couple of times.

Odete sneezed as the strong smoky smell of gunpowder rolled out towards them.

'It is a bit frightening the first time you see a pistol fired at close range.'

Mafalda nodded, but her fascinated gaze remained on the men who were reloading. Odete realised that all of Mafalda's attention was on the prince. Was that because Herculano was a non-entity to her? Or was there a deeper reason? She had to ask herself the same question. Why was she more interested in watching Herculano?

As both men's arms rose to fire again, she decided to watch the prince. He truly was stirring in his handsomeness and the elegance with which he hefted the heavy pistol and pointed it, with no difficulty, at his target. So why wasn't she distraught that he'd lost interest in her?

Was she so fickle? Could she move so easily from being hopelessly in love with one man to being intrigued by another? To try and dredge up the excitement that seeing the prince used to bring, she watched him some more.

The prince didn't flinch as the pistol jerked and roared. In the past that would have been enough to excite her, now she felt like she was watching a stranger. It was so different to watching Herculano who, despite being less powerful and not as good-looking, absorbed her attention as he let off another deafening shot.

Odete sincerely hoped they had warned the guards about this exercise, or they'd soon be descending upon them to discover what the racket was all about.

By the time the tenth round had been fired, Odete's ears were ringing, even though she'd covered them.

'Well, ladies,' Juliano said from inside the haze of iron-grey smoke he and Herculano had generated, 'shall we inspect our handiwork?'

'Certainly.'

Lady Mafalda's voice was shaky, but she was the descendant of a powerful line and was determined to act as cool as everyone else.

For the first time in her life, Odete was glad that she'd had so many older brothers and was inured to the way men behaved.

She followed after Mafalda and so was the last to arrive at the wall. It had suffered spectacularly from the assault. Chips of plaster and even stone lay scattered on the now dusty floor. Odete raised her skirts so that they wouldn't collect any of the dust and peeked at the shredded cards. Some had fluttered to the ground, but the majority were still pinned in place, although now they had holes torn through them.

'Let's see now,' Juliano said, as he looked over the black cards. 'Seven pips are completely obliterated, two where I only nicked the pips and one with a clear miss.'

'Not bad,' Herculano said.

Odete had found herself looking at the red cards first, so she already knew that Herculano was the better shot.

She held her breath as he said, 'Eight perfect shots, two near misses.'

Both ladies turned back to the prince to see how he would react to being bested.

'Give me those cards.' Juliano held the red cards up so that the light shone through the holes. 'Not bad, Herculano. But I would say that we were very close to each other in skill and if we were to test ourselves again, I might well come out on top.'

'I'm sure you are right, Your Highness,' Herculano said, with his slight nod-cum-bow.

The prince laughed.

'It must be hard for you to simply concede.'

'Not at all,' Herculano said, with an answering smile.

Odete wondered what the meaning was below the words. For men who had just met, they had an astonishing understanding of one another. At times, they seemed like complete strangers, but at other times, like now, they clearly understood each other very well.

Now the prince gave an almost imperceptible nod to Herculano who approached Odete and said, 'Why don't we step away for a moment?'

Odete wanted to demand an immediate explanation as to why she needed to leave Mafalda with the prince, but she knew Herculano well enough already to just follow him as he strolled further down the ballroom, increasing the distance not only from the prince but also their chaperones.

He stopped below the magnificently carved, gilded and painted platform that the orchestra occupied during balls and gazed up at its colourful magnificence.

'How are you faring today? You look tired.'

'Mafalda is broken-hearted,' Odete said, and glanced back at the prince and Mafalda.

They had retired to the other end of the ballroom. To Odete's surprise, the prince appeared not only to be listening to Mafalda, but to be touched by the young woman's distress. In the past, his interest in another woman would have upset her. Now, she was unmoved, which, again, was odd.

'But I was grateful to be spared the role of telling her about Tiago. It meant all her rage was focused outwards.'

'To the prince?'

'Not as much as I expected. She is determined to find the assassin, though.'

'So are we.' Herculano turned from his examination of the room to give Odete's face an uncomfortably close inspection. 'Have you got anything from Ladies Pia and Maria da Luz?'

'Nothing of use, I'm afraid. Both fathers are close to being strangers to their daughters. From what I know of Maria da Luz and what I have seen of her father, they are neither of them very bright. Lord Antelmo Carvalho is wary of the duque, but not wary enough, and too busy basking in the glory of being on his council.'

'That is the prince's opinion too. What of Lord Paiva?'

'Also nothing. His only weaknesses are, apparently, vanity and a penchant for prostitutes, which hardly marks him as unusual.'

'Not unusual at all,' Herculano said, and his gaze also drifted across to the prince and Lady Mafalda.

The prince pulled a handkerchief out of his pocket and handed it to Mafalda, who dabbed at her eyes.

'She called the prostitutes Mollies,' Odete said. 'It isn't a phrase I've heard before. But then, I am not an expert when it comes to such matters.'

'Mollies?' The comment drew Herculano's gaze back to Odete. 'Really?'

'So you have heard of them?'

'I have.'

'Lady Paiva blames those creatures for the fact that she has only given birth to three children.'

'Yes,' Herculano said, and rubbed his chin thoughtfully. 'That would not be surprising.'

'Wouldn't it? Is that because of the diseases prostitutes carry? I have heard that if your husband brings such a thing home, it can put paid to any wife's ability to bear children.'

'I'm not sure this is an appropriate conversation to have with a lady.'

Odete thought Herculano had blushed, but in the dim light of the ballroom it was difficult to tell.

'I assure you, we women might not say much, but we are fully aware of what men get up to.'

'Not fully. For as it happens, Mollies are male prostitutes who disguise themselves as women.'

'For the love of God,' Odete gasped. 'Male prostitutes?'

'Which is a very useful piece of information indeed,' Herculano said with a wide grin. 'Might I also make a request?'

'You want something from me?'

'A sketch of Lord Paiva. I have a feeling I'm going to have to visit a few rather specialised brothels and having his image will help.'

'I will give it to you on one condition,' Odete said, rather pleased that she could help, and that she had something to bargain with.

'I absolutely refuse to take you anywhere near a brothel.'

Herculano spoke with such finality that Odete realised she wouldn't be able to shift him. She wondered for a moment whether she should threaten to withhold the sketch, but decided against it. Pettishness was neither endearing nor useful.

'Very well, I will make a sketch for you.'

'Thank you,' Herculano said with a nod and a slight smile that seemed to say he'd understood what she'd been thinking.

Not wholly, she thought, for she was determined to continue her own investigations.

12

Viriato looked his daughter up and down as she stared, half defiant, half frightened, back at him. He had not invited her to sit and she was swaying from side to side now, much as she'd done as a child. At least her gaze no longer wandered round his office as if she didn't care about what he thought. She was giving him back stare for stare.

'The older you get, the more you resemble your mother,' Viriato said.

Mafalda would know it wasn't meant as a compliment. Viriato had married for money and power but he'd disliked his wife, who was pious beyond reason and attributed everything that befell her, both good and evil, to the will of God.

Viriato wondered what she'd make of the fact that she and his brother, the two most pious people at court, had perished during the earthquake while he had survived. He'd never made a secret of his lack of faith and his wife lamented it and nagged him about it at every opportunity.

'I'm sorry,' Mafalda muttered.

If he was still angry with her, he might have forced her to explain her ambiguous apology. But the prince had informed

him of Tiago Andrade's death the evening before, and
Mafalda's puffy eyes told their own tale.

'I am also sorry about your friend. However, it won't do
to make a scene. As far as the court is concerned, you had no
connection to young Andrade.'

'Alright,' Mafalda whispered, and her gaze fell to
contemplating his beige and blue Arraiolos rug.

'I understand the prince informed you of Tiago's death
on Friday night.'

'Yes.'

'You'd better sit down,' Viriato said, irritated by Mafalda's
lack of spirit. 'I'm surprised he told you. In the past,
he'd have left that duty to me. Did he know about your
relationship with Andrade?'

'No,' Mafalda said, looking back up at her father. 'Tiago
said it was best the prince didn't know. Although, once,
Tiago said Juliano would probably give me to him with his
wholehearted blessing.'

'That sounds most probable,' Viriato said, and tapped his
finger on the desk.

The way the situation had panned out irritated him. If
only the body had never been found.

'Mmm,' Mafalda said, nodding in vague agreement.

Viriato realised his daughter had clearly been banking on
Tiago winning the prince round to his cause.

'Now we have nothing to do but find the killer. Juliano
said I can help him do that,' Mafalda said, and her defiant
spark flared to life again.

Normally Viriato would have been pleased to see it, but
he'd just been taken by surprise.

'Juliano said you and he would look for Andrade's killer?'

Mafalda gave a firm nod.

'We won't rest till the killer is brought to justice.'

Viriato realised he'd clenched both fists and forced himself to calm down. He stretched one hand out in front of him, examining his nails instead.

'Juliano said that, did he?'

'He said normally he wouldn't let a girl get involved in such a dangerous endeavour, but that I had as much right as him to find out the truth.'

That sort of manipulation was the kind of thing Viriato might do himself, but it enraged him to see the prince deploying a similar tactic with his daughter.

'He should have discussed the matter with me first. Juliano might not have a care for your safety, but I do.'

'What could anyone do to me?' Mafalda said, turning wide, surprised eyes on her father. 'They know you will destroy them if they try anything.'

For the first time in his life, Viriato was bereft of words. He hadn't realised how obvious he'd made his power. It was one thing to cow the nobility. It was another to see his daughter's absolute certainty.

It made his rage towards his nephew build once more. That bastard must surely believe he was behind Andrade's death. He must surely know he was using Mafalda as a weapon against her own father.

Would he also know that Mafalda would tell him? Again, using a loved one against his enemy was a tactic he would use. It was a blow to the heart. It was also entirely out of character with everything Viriato had come to know of his nephew.

'Did Juliano tell you all of this yesterday when he was blowing holes in the ballroom wall?'

'I knew you'd disapprove. But Juliano said it would be easy to fix.'

Viriato was thrown for a minute till he realised Mafalda was referring to the damage. It would be a lot harder to repair the trap Mafalda had been pulled into.

'Juliano has really changed,' Mafalda murmured as her gaze drifted over her father's shoulder.

'In what way?'

The change had to be great for Viriato's self-absorbed daughter to notice.

'Most of the time, he behaved like I wasn't even in the room. And when he did bother to say hello, he'd smile at Odete, but not at me. Now he's ignoring Odete and he's being really kind to me. He even wiped my tears dry when I started to cry.'

'Juliano dried your tears?'

'He was very gentle,' Mafalda said, with a reminiscing smile.

There was a time, only a few days earlier, when this change in his nephew would gratify Viriato. Now he was certain that nothing but malice towards him lay in his nephew's sudden change. It made no sense.

Juliano had always been a straightforward man. He spoke his mind and always did what he said he would. This underhanded behaviour was entirely out of character.

'What do you make of his new friend?'

'The merchant?' Mafalda said, and gave a disinterested shrug. 'He definitely likes Odete.'

It would be pointless to try and get more, Viriato realised. His daughter viewed the world through her own self-centred lens.

'You'd best get ready for church. I have ordered the priest to make it a memorial service in honour of Tiago Andrade, although I doubt his father will thank me for it.'

That last, Viriato said more to himself. The aspect that worried him most about the death was what Lord Andrade the elder would do.

Mafalda curtsied her farewell and hurried away, probably already forgetting his stricture to not make a scene in the chapel later on. There was something about fifteen-year-old girls, Viriato decided, that just couldn't be controlled.

The moment Mafalda had left not only his study, but his secretary's room beyond, Viriato rang his bell and Diogo Martinez arrived before the last tinkle had ended.

'What can I do for you, Your Grace?' Martinez said, with a deep bow.

'Tell me what you have discovered about Herculano Escovar.'

Martinez cleared his throat and began a singsong recitation.

'He is the sole surviving son of one Isaltinho Escovar–'

'Wait!' Viriato said, putting up his hand as he searched his memory. 'He was mentioned the first time I met him, but I was too distracted to realise. You don't mean, *the* Isaltinho Escovar? The Merchant King of Lisbon?'

'The very one, Your Grace. Herculano was his middle son. His wife and all the other children died in the earthquake.'

'I see. And when exactly did Isaltinho Escovar die?'

'Two years ago, Your Grace. Since that time, his son has run their business empire. By all accounts, he's been an effective heir and his fortune continues to grow.'

'Does he pay his taxes?'

'Without fail. In fact, I would say he and his father were unusual in how little they tried to evade tax.'

'Odd.' In Viriato's opinion, any man would be a fool not to attempt to hide his profits. If he was a merchant, he felt certain he'd make every effort to ensure no man laid a hand on his gold. 'What else?'

'Not much else, I'm afraid. Herculano had an excellent education that included three years in Paris and London. He has also travelled extensively on business and made many connections. The merchants all seem to like him and respect his work ethic.'

'So how did he come to know the prince?'

'That I have been unable to ascertain. As far as I can make out, the two of them never met before Wednesday.'

'And yet now they are bosom friends,' Viriato said, rubbing his chin thoughtfully. 'It is all very odd.'

What with the death of Tiago Andrade, the change in the prince and the appearance of a merchant at court, Viriato was feeling his control slipping. That wouldn't do.

'Martinez, prepare to move the court to Sintra. The weather is becoming insufferably stuffy in Lisbon.'

'Very good, Your Grace,' Martinez said, and bowed himself out.

His face gave away nothing of what he thought and Viriato wondered exactly what that was right now. Perhaps paranoia was creeping in, but Viriato felt like he needed to cut whatever Juliano was planning off at the roots before it could develop any further.

Herculano yawned over the diary he was trying to read. It was nearly twilight, which probably explained his increasing difficulty in making out the letters that blurred and slipped around his vision.

A knock at the door had him on his feet so quickly the diary fell in a flurry of pages onto the floor. He left it and raced to reach the door before Arriscado. He'd been brought up as a prince and presumably had servants seeing to his needs all day, every day, but for some reason he disliked being served and was determined to get to the door first.

Arriscado's hand slammed down on the handle and swung the door open just as Herculano reached for it.

'Bollocks,' Herculano muttered, as the opening door revealed a startled prince.

'Is that any way to greet me?' Juliano said with a smile that implied amusement, but also that an apology had better be offered.

'Forgive me, Your Highness,' Herculano said, and executed a bow. 'I wasn't swearing at you.'

'Why were you swearing, then?' Juliano said, as he strolled inside and Arriscado closed the door behind him.

Herculano glared at his valet's smug expression.

'It isn't important.'

The prince apparently considered the reply as he settled on Herculano's favourite chair. It was slightly shabby compared to the rest of the furniture in his allocated quarters, but by far the most comfortable in the room.

'If you say it wasn't important, I believe you. We have more pressing things to talk about anyway.'

'The court's move to Sintra?' Herculano settled in the armchair opposite the prince and, because he felt he needed to establish he was still the boss, muttered, 'Light,' to Arriscado.

The valet gave another stately nod and set about lighting the candelabras in the room, starting with the one on the table by the prince's elbow.

'Exactly, Sintra,' Juliano said. 'We made a move and my uncle made a countermove.'

'Maybe drawing Mafalda into the investigation wasn't the best idea after all.' Herculano stretched his legs out before him to get into a more comfortable position. 'It looks to me like the duque is removing her from Lisbon because of it.'

'I told you we wouldn't have much time after Tiago's body was found. Whether or not we involved Mafalda, the duque would probably do this. He needs time to clean everything up so that we can't find any evidence to incriminate him.'

'That's assuming he was behind Tiago's death. I mean, it happened at the docks. The only place in Lisbon that sees more death than the docks is the Inquisition's auto-da-fé in the Rossio.'

'If he had nothing to hide, he wouldn't have announced at Mass this morning that we are all leaving the city tomorrow,' Juliano said, leaning forward as he spoke. 'It's a logistical nightmare to move the entire court to Sintra. I'm willing to bet, despite what he said about the increasing heat, and Dr Zuniga's pronouncements on the auspicious astrological significance of the date, that is not the reason he's moving in such a hurry.'

Herculano agreed, but worried they were overly eager to blame the duque. It wasn't like him to be cautious, and he had good reason to dislike the duque, but he feared they could be making a mistake.

He was about to say so when there was a timid scratching at the door. More out of pique than anything else, Herculano didn't even bother looking around as Arriscado opened the door. The prince watched him though, and waited as a whispered conversation was held.

Arriscado approached the two men with a folded square of paper and bowed low.

'Please forgive me, Your Excellency, but the young woman at the door insisted I hand this over immediately.'

With that, he held a note out to Herculano. He took it with an accepting nod and placed it on the table at his right elbow.

Arriscado cleared his throat.

'The young lady is waiting for a reply, sir. She says she can't leave until she has one.'

Herculano swore under his breath, then, at a nod from the prince, he snatched the note up and read the brief contents.

'I gather it's a matter of urgency,' Juliano said.

Herculano could swear he was enjoying himself.

'Lady Odete wants to meet with me tonight. No doubt to discuss Lady Mafalda.' He turned back to Arriscado and said, 'Tell the maid that I will see her ladyship tomorrow morning.'

'Very good, sir.'

Arriscado made his stately way to the door and another whispered exchange followed. Then Arriscado closed the door on the maid, who was still whispering entreaties.

'I will now arrange some refreshments,' Arriscado said, then bowed to the prince and Herculano and removed himself.

'I don't mind if you see her now,' Juliano said.

'Not today. I'm going back to the docks tonight and that is no place for a lady.'

'No, I don't suppose it is.'

Herculano was struck by the distinct lack of interest in the prince's tone.

'Do you have no feelings for her now?'

'None. I've read my diaries and I am aware that I was rather infatuated with her, but now... there is nothing. It's probably just as well, as I would never be allowed to marry so far below my station. You should just offer for her and see what happens.'

'I want to be sure of what I think of her before I do anything like that.'

Juliano nodded acceptance.

'I'm afraid that all my plans were upended by the announced move and I've had to deal with a hundred irritating little irrelevant details.'

'So much for Sunday being the day of rest,' Herculano said.

'My uncle is notorious for not caring about the church and what it thinks. In fact, he probably enjoyed making us all work today. I hope you have been equally diligent.'

'I have been busy,' Herculano said, keeping his cool even though it irked him to be bossed around. 'Lady Odete gave me a decent sketch of Lord Paiva and one of Tiago. I spent some time at my warehouse talking to my people and trying to discover whether they had ever seen either of the two men around.'

'Had they?'

'They were unknown to any of the men. That's why I'll be returning to the docks to speak to its less salubrious denizens,' Herculano said and then waited as Arriscado reappeared with a bottle of wine and two goblets on a tray.

He watched as the valet poured out a glass of wine for the prince, which he placed with exaggerated care at his elbow. Then he poured Herculano a glass and put it down with decorum but less care. Clearly, his loyalty and admiration were more for the prince. Herculano supposed that was natural, as the man had helped bring the prince up.

'What else have you done today?' Juliano asked.

'Should there have been something else?' Herculano said, because he couldn't resist pushing back against the prince's bossiness.

'I would hope there was, although I'm aware that I am asking a great deal of you.'

The last concession drew an amused snort from Herculano, who waved at the three massive piles of books on his desk.

'I made a start on my diaries. As you can see, you were a meticulous notetaker. I suppose I should be thankful for the fact that you made such detailed observations of every one of your days, but it has left me with a mountain to go through.'

'My diaries? Why? They can have no relevance to this investigation.'

'As it happens, you are right. They have no relevance to the matter at hand itself. We were kept entirely separate and your days were filled with the business of trade. But my trip to the docks made me realise that I have a vast empire of my own with all the dependants that come with it. I've been wandering around, doing your bidding, and leaving my people to fend for themselves.'

'What is happening in the kingdom will affect everyone,' Juliano said, and sounded more defensive than Herculano had heard before.

'I am aware of the impact a power struggle will have on everyone. Even so, I have responsibilities of my own. Reading through the diaries made it clear you understood and cared about your people too.' To anyone else, Herculano might have snapped and spoken more brusquely, but he had to win the prince round. 'Besides, responsibilities aside, you also mention all the most influential men you dealt with, and they might prove useful. I will have to meet them myself and sound them out.'

'About what?'

'About whom they would prefer to have running the kingdom.'

The prince let out a hiss of annoyance and said, 'That's tantamount to sedition.'

'Your Highness, I need to know what they really think to find your true allies. If I go into each meeting making it clear I support you, they will only tell me what I want to hear, which will be no help at all.'

The prince frowned deeply as he lifted his goblet and took a sip of wine.

'You are speaking as if you intend to remain in Lisbon.'

'I can do nothing in Sintra. I know little about the court and have no allies within it. But I can continue to investigate in Lisbon. I might even be able to do more than I could when the duque is around.'

'Be careful, Herculano. The duque might be leaving town, but his agents will still be here and working to ensure nothing links the duque to Tiago's death. I would hate it if you were to meet a similar fate.'

'Thank you.' The prince's concern genuinely touched Herculano. 'I assume you have no choice but to go to Sintra?'

'I can't have my uncle making decisions about the kingdom without me, even if I am powerless to do anything about his hold on the council at the moment.'

Odete stared out of her bedroom window and watched as the sky went from a dusty orange to deep violet and the first stars started twinkling in the steadily darkening sky. Usually such a sight would calm her, but not today.

Mafalda had been nearly in tears again over the move to Sintra. She was convinced her father was trying to prevent her from discovering what had happened to Tiago. Odete suspected the same, but felt it best not to do more than give her charge soothing, noncommittal murmurs of sympathy.

'Well?' Odete said, and swung round the moment her maid arrived back in the room.

'He said he'll see you tomorrow morning,' Maria said, clasping her hands together like she was at prayer.

'He said he'd see me tomorrow?' Odete was more annoyed by this news than she was by her maid's excessive excitement over what she apparently thought was a blossoming love affair. 'Did you give him the note?'

'I handed it to his valet, and he gave it to the gentleman.'

'So you didn't see him read the note?'

In it, Odete had stressed the importance of meeting today and it annoyed her that Herculano hadn't responded appropriately.

'I'm afraid not. His valet relayed the message,' Maria said, gazing up at her anxiously.

She was a skinny woman with the bedraggled look of a scarecrow. Odete hadn't really wanted her as a maid, but knew her mother would dismiss her once she left home, so she'd brought the young woman with her. Now she was irritated by her even though it wasn't her fault that Herculano had responded in the way he had.

'He has no idea of how busy we'll be tomorrow?' she snapped, more to provide relief to herself than in the expectation of a reply from Maria. 'We have all our own clothes to pack and Lady Mafalda's things, plus any other items to provide entertainment, such as books and embroidery and cards and – well, you know as well as I do what a lot of work it is. I won't have a minute to myself and certainly not enough time to speak to him.'

'And no privacy at all,' Maria said. 'What with all the staff carrying the luggage down to the coaches.'

'Exactly.' Odete had never been in greater agreement with Maria. 'No, tomorrow simply won't do. I'll have to go and see him myself, right now.'

'Oh, but I think he was with somebody,' Maria said, back to looking anxious.

'Who was he with?'

'I don't know for certain, but I thought it was the prince.'

'Ah.'

Much as Odete might want to, she couldn't crash into Herculano's room and demand he speak to her, if the prince was there. When she'd first arrived at the palace, the prince had intimidated her. Then she'd warmed to him because of his open personality and started to wish and pray for more. Now, he was back to being a stranger and left her feeling uncomfortable.

'Then I suppose I'll have to try and talk to him at dinner.'

But dinner came to nothing. Try as she might, Odete couldn't catch Herculano's attention. No, it was more than that. He was ignoring her, because he never once glanced in her direction. He was always beside the prince with a bevy of men between them and he somehow managed to leave the dining hall earlier than her and Lady Mafalda.

Odete was so infuriated by this behaviour that she'd only just got back to her room when she left it again, determined to force Herculano to speak to her. She was stomping down the corridor to his room, her fists clenched, when she spotted him stepping out.

She was about to call to him when she realised he was dressed in his drabbest outfit and carrying a plain brown cloak. That could mean only one thing. He was on his way out!

Considering he'd flat out refused to allow her to go out with him at night, she bit back her call, spun round and ran to her room.

'Quick, Maria, get me a plain dress and my cloak, hurry!'

Fortunately, Maria rose to the challenge and had Odete out of her evening gown and into her plain walking dress in a flash. Odete flung her black cape over the lot, pulled up her hood and ran for the door.

'My lady, should I not go with you?' Maria called after her.

Odete didn't bother to slow her headlong dash to respond. She ran down the stairs and through the emptying corridors, praying she could catch up with Herculano. She had no idea where he was going, but she was determined to find out.

Odete nearly tripped in her haste as she barrelled out of the palace and looked left and right, gasping for breath. Herculano was making his way down the road towards the docks. As she watched, he shook out his cloak and hung it on his shoulders. It swayed and flapped about in the wind, echoing his gait.

Odete followed, relieved she'd found him. She firmly suppressed the thought that if he was heading for the docks, she shouldn't go along. He was close enough that she could call to him if she got into difficulties and, in the meantime, she'd be able to see exactly what he was up to and report back to Mafalda.

The docks were very different at night. Instead of the bright sun and hordes of orderly, hard-working sailors and porters, now the docklands were a maze of pitch-black alleyways punctuated by lanterns that lit the entrances to bars and brothels.

It was no less empty than during the day, though. Clusters of men spilled out of open doorways and stood about under the lanterns, speaking excitedly to each other, drinking from brown pottery tankards and almost all smoking long-stemmed white clay pipes.

The occasional shout or raucous laugh punctuated the general hubbub. Odete jumped when someone she was passing let out a shrill whistle. She swung round, terrified that the man wanted to draw her attention, but thankfully his eyes were fixed on a young woman who had pulled her left sleeve down so far she had exposed a more than tantalising glimpse of one pert breast. Odete pulled her cape more tightly around her, dragging her hood downward to make sure her face was completely in shadow and turned back to following Herculano.

Only he wasn't there! The street was filled with sailors, but the tall brown cloak she had been following had vanished. Odete's heart thumped with fright, and she contemplated turning around and going home.

She chided herself over her loss of courage and hurried onwards. She could catch up with Herculano and it would be fine. Odete pushed her way between two sailors who both had their backs to her, chatting to their friends. One man turned round to complain and then his eyes widened in surprise as he took in Odete's face.

'What have we here?' he said, and grabbed Odete's wrist.

His hand was as rough as the ropes he worked with and his grip was so strong Odete winced as she tried to pull away from him.

'Let go!' she said softly, reluctant to draw attention to herself.

'Let go?' The man laughed. 'If you don't want to be grabbed, girlie, you shouldn't be out here on your own.'

'I'm not on my own,' Odete said, and shouted, 'Herculano! Herculano, help!'

The sailor cocked his head as if considering and waited a few moments to see whether Odete's call might bring down an avenging protector. In the meantime, Odete's cry had drawn the attention of the other sailor she'd pushed past who also turned around to see what was going on.

'Isn't she a pretty one?' a second sailor said, as he pulled Odete's hood down.

'Leave me alone!'

Odete was surrounded by a sea of sailors, all watching her with increasing interest. She tried again to get free of the first sailor's vice-like grip and stepped backwards, which just made her bump into a third man. He blew a stream of pipe smoke into her face as he swung round, leering at her and revealing that he had a gold tooth.

'She can't be up to any good, a woman all alone out here at night,' the first sailor said, as he swung her back to face him by twisting her wrist.

'Herculano!' Odete screamed. 'Help!'

'There's no help coming, my lovely,' the second sailor said, and pulled Odete's cape off her and flung it into the watching crowd.

They all had a gleam of anticipation in their eyes that terrified Odete more than all the rest.

'My, what a pretty figure she's got,' sailor number two said with a hoarse laugh.

'Let go!' Odete said, as she made another desperate attempt to break free of the sailor who'd not once lost his grip on her. 'Let go!' Odete shouted, and kicked him hard on the shin.

'Ouch!'

As the sailor's grip loosened, Odete pulled away from him and ran. She made it all of two steps when sailor number three wrapped his arm around her waist and pulled her against him.

'There's no point in fighting us, dearie,' the man said, as he slipped his free hand down her leg and pulled her skirt upward.

'God, save me!' Odete cried as she kicked out at the man and simultaneously tried to bite his arm.

'That's enough!' a loud voice shrieked and a heavy black cane landed a solid blow on the sailor's head.

The sailor let go of Odete and staggered backwards, swearing. Odete leaped away from him and towards the being who had wielded the cane. This turned out to be an astonishing-looking woman, dressed in a revealing, low-cut, black lace dress with a matching black lace mantilla that enhanced her already impressive height.

'Come here, my dear,' she said, as she placed one black-gloved hand on Odete's shoulder and drew her closer.

'Oh, come on, Contessa,' the first sailor said. 'You can't have us believe she's one of your lot. She's a girl for certain and ripe for the picking.'

'You disgraceful lot deserve a flogging,' the Contessa said, as she waved her walking cane at the gathered mob.

A detached part of Odete realised that the silver handle of the cane was fashioned into a rather provocative nude.

'All the same, admit it, she's not one of yours.'

'You'd have to pay me to get a peek up her skirts to confirm it,' the Contessa snapped, 'and none of you degenerates can afford that.'

There was a murmur of curses and a couple of men spat on the ground. But they backed away enough for the Contessa to guide Odete between the parting mass of muttering men. She led her up to a discreet but very solid door and into a surprisingly comfortable sitting room.

An impressive chandelier and several candelabras made the room far brighter than the streets outside. Gold-framed pictures hung on the walls, gilt chairs upholstered in blue velvet were dotted tastefully about and a number of women, sporting frilly underwear and not much else, stood or lounged about. Three well-dressed men, one who'd removed his coat and unbuttoned his shirt, had their hands all over the half-dressed women. No, Odete realised with a shock, not women.

'Oh!' she gasped, and turned to look up at the Contessa.

In the brighter light of the room, Odete could see the woman's thick black kohl-lined eyes, the white powder of her face and the astonishing red rouged cheeks and the even redder lips. Her eyebrows were plucked to elegant but still thick black lines, her lids were heavy and hooded, and her nose and mouth were just a little too large and angular to be properly feminine.

'Oh!' Odete said again.

'Close your eyes, my dear,' the Contessa said, as she took a firm grasp of Odete's shoulder and guided her towards another door at the far end of the room. 'This is not the sort of place you should be familiar with. Lourdes, bring us some tea.'

Odete doubted the wisdom of going deeper into this den of iniquity, but whatever it was, it felt safer than the streets outside. She didn't close her eyes, though. She was embarrassed and intrigued in equal measure. Her mother would have been shocked at her wanton behaviour, but she couldn't help herself.

As she passed through the door, she caught sight of one of the paintings. It depicted a half-dressed woman, breasts in full view, with a grinning man pushing his rough tanned hands up her milky white thighs. Odete shuddered. The painting reminded her rather too forcefully of her recent encounter with the sailors.

'Sit,' the Contessa said, as she waved Odete towards a black velvet chaise longue that had a tasselled black fringe.

This room appeared to have been decorated for the Contessa because it matched her black dress and contained an elegant, black wood desk, but also a similar collection of paintings on the walls that made Odete blush.

The Contessa pulled the chair out from behind the desk, placed it opposite Odete and sat bolt upright, her ankles crossed elegantly over each other.

'Now, what brings a well-brought-up young lady like you to the docks, all alone at night?'

'Well... that's rather a long story.'

'I assume it has to do with a man. That Herculano you were crying for.'

'Not really.'

Odete searched the Contessa's face. It was disconcerting to see a man dressed in this way and behaving so much like a woman that he'd even altered the pitch of his voice. She should have been revolted, but the Contessa had come so spectacularly to her rescue that her gratitude was greater than her shock at what she was being confronted by.

'Tea,' announced another one of these strange amalgamations, as she placed a tray with an elegant silver teapot and two fine china cups down on the Contessa's desk.

She was half dressed. Her skirt was an attractive pink embroidered with roses, reminiscent of Mafalda's grand ball dress, but she only had a plain white bodice covering her obviously flat but hairless chest.

'Thank you, Lourdes.' The Contessa poured two glasses of what looked like a lemon peel infusion and handed a cup on a saucer to Odete. 'So you say it isn't about this man?'

Odete had serious reservations about telling the Contessa anything. Then again, she felt like she could trust this person and she realised she also had an opportunity. To grab that, she had to be willing to do a certain amount of sharing of her own. She balanced her cup and saucer on her knees and watched the rising vapour as she considered.

'Did you hear that there was a body found at the docks a couple of days ago?'

The Contessa laughed.

'You're going to have to be more specific. There are murders and muggings practically every day around here. It's one reason you shouldn't have ventured in.'

'They found this man stuffed into a wine barrel.'

'Ah, I have heard about that, actually. It happened in the Escovar warehouse, not so? That's right next door.'

The fact that the warehouse was next door was news to Odete. It was funny how the docklands looked so different at night.

'Yes, the Escovar warehouse,' she said, and took a tiny sip of the lemon tea. It was still scaldingly hot.

'So, the dead man was something to you?'

'He meant a lot to someone I am close to. I am trying to find out who killed him.'

The Contessa laughed again.

'Finding murderers in the docklands would be an impossible task at the best of times. But believe me, if your killer doesn't want to be found, then leaving the body here is his best bet. Nobody cares what happens to people here.'

'Or what they do,' Odete said, looking the Contessa up and down meaningfully.

'That is also true,' she said with an amused grin.

'Which was another reason I'm here. I suspect... there is someone who is involved with... your sort,' Odete said, finding it tremendously difficult to come out and say what was so patently obvious.

'Oh no, my dear, don't try to blame it on us. I have enough with jilted lovers, priests and the Inquisition snatching my girls off the streets. I have no wish to be fitted up for a murder, too.'

Odete didn't want to offend the Contessa. She really couldn't afford to. 'I'm sorry. I didn't mean to upset you.'

The Contessa gave an eloquent shrug that implied it would take more than an insult from a girl to upset her, and took a sip of her tea.

'What was the name of the murdered man?' she asked, without looking up from her cup.

'Lord Tiago Andrade.'

'Ah, a lord, no wonder people are out looking. I've heard there were a number of men about yesterday and today combing the docks to discover what had happened to him. They left us alone, however. No lord would believe his son capable of falling in love with us, even if they themselves might visit us.'

And here was her opportunity.

'Is Lord Onofre Paiva someone who visits you?'

The Contessa paused for a fraction of a second too long before she said, 'I've never heard of him. When did your young man get murdered?'

'He went missing on Tuesday night.'

Odete wished she could push the Contessa harder on the matter of Lord Paiva, but she'd changed the subject so quickly that Odete doubted she'd be able to bring it back.

'Tuesday?' The Contessa's face twisted into a wry smile that made her look far more masculine. 'That was the night Almira vanished. She was snatched from her bed and hasn't been seen since, no matter where we search. But you can guarantee that nobody gives a damn about her.'

'I'm sorry.'

Odete was grappling with what to ask next when Lourdes reappeared.

'There's a big strapping man outside asking for information. He says his name is Herculano Escovar, and he's got a sketch you might want to see.'

Odete's heart skipped a beat with fright. What would Herculano say when he found her here?

'*The* Herculano Escovar?' the Contessa said as she surged to her feet.

'I think so,' Lourdes said.

'I'd best see him outside. It wouldn't do for him to discover our guest.'

For a second, Odete was tempted to go along with this plan so that Herculano never found out about how she'd fallen into this predicament. But at the same time, she'd been worrying about how to get home, and here was one very easy route.

'It's alright,' Odete said, aware that she was blushing. 'I know him.'

'*He* was the Herculano you were shouting for?'

'I'm afraid so.'

'So he's come in search of you?' the Contessa asked, tilting her head thoughtfully.

'I doubt it.'

For a moment it looked like the Contessa was going to interrogate her further, then she gave a shrug.

'Well, we'll find out soon enough. Show him in, Lourdes.'

'Lady Odete!' Herculano gasped, as he stepped into the room halfway through removing his cloak.

'Hello,' Odete said, as she rose, shamefaced, to greet him.

'What the devil are you doing here?'

'I followed you,' Odete muttered, gazing at her toes and feeling very much like a naughty child.

'Of all the stupid, nonsensical and downright dangerous things to do. I told you I'd see you tomorrow.'

'Tomorrow will be too late!'

'Much as I hate to intrude on what is turning into quite an amusing argument,' the Contessa said, 'might I ask what brings you to our modest little house, Your Excellency?'

Herculano looked the Contessa up and down and gave her his usual slight nod that was as much of a bow as he gave anyone.

'Forgive my intrusion, madam. I wanted to know whether you recognised either of two men.'

'Ah, so you and she are working on the same thing,' the Contessa said, tapping her index fingers together. 'But as I have already explained to her, I know nothing about Lord Onofre Paiva.'

'Don't you?'

Odete was impressed by how Herculano reflected neither dismay nor much interest in the Contessa's denial. Instead, he reached into his coat pocket and pulled out a drawing of Tiago Andrade and held it out for her inspection. 'So you don't know Lord Paiva?'

'No, that's not–' The Contessa stopped, aware of the trap she'd fallen into. 'I don't know that young man.'

'He has never been here?'

'I can't tell you that with absolute certainty. But in my business, we have to be careful about who we let in, so I pay attention to names and faces. I don't think that boy ever came here.'

'But Lord Paiva is a different matter?' Herculano said, as he pulled out the lord's image from his other pocket and held it out for inspection.

'I don't know him,' the Contessa said, her lips set stubbornly.

'We both know that isn't true,' Herculano said with a slight, humourless smile. 'But perhaps you'd allow me to speak to the person he visited most regularly.'

'I will do no such thing.' The Contessa closed the gap between her and Herculano and towered over him. 'You can't come into my house and make demands like this.'

'Do you know, I believe I can.'

Herculano's calm impressed Odete. She would have been flustered if she'd had to face down someone like the Contessa.

'What makes you so sure of that?' the Contessa hissed.

'Because, much to my surprise, when I looked into it today, I own this building,' Herculano said, tapping his heel on the floor.

'Are you threatening us with eviction?'

'Only if you persist in withholding information.'

'Alright!'

The Contessa threw up her hands in defeat, went back to her chair and slumped into it.

'So will you allow me to speak to Lord Paiva's regular?'

'I can't,' the Contessa said, apparently reviving as she sat bolt upright again. She returned to her now lukewarm tea and downed it in a single gulp. 'She's vanished.'

'Oh!' Odete gasped. 'She isn't the one... Almira, that you mentioned before, is she?'

The Contessa gave a grudging half nod, half shrug.

'She's gone missing?' Herculano said.

'On Tuesday night,' Odete said, giving him a meaningful look.

'By all the saints.'

'I haven't seen Lord Paiva since either,' the Contessa said, 'although that isn't entirely surprising. He only drops in when he can and that varies.'

'He'll be heading to Sintra tomorrow, so you won't see him for a while. Well, I suppose that wraps that up,' Herculano said, and held out his hand to Odete. 'Come on, miss, we'd best get you home.'

Odete contemplated a put down by pointing out she was a lady, not a miss, followed by another rebellious thought that she should tell him she could find her own way back. In the end, she did neither but meekly took his hand and allowed him to help her to her feet.

'Thank you,' Odete said, giving the Contessa a curtsy. 'I won't forget that you saved my life.'

This drew a sharp look from Herculano but, thankfully, no comment.

'You'd best get your cape. You don't want the hordes outside to see too much of you.'

'I can't,' Odete whispered, feeling increasingly foolish. 'I lost it.'

Herculano's eyebrow flickered upwards, but all he did was hand her his cape. 'Wrap yourself in this then.' And with a nod of farewell to the Contessa, he ushered Odete out of the Molly House.

13

A n unfamiliar racket in the corridors outside his room
woke Herculano. He groaned as he pushed back his
sheets and swung his legs out of bed.

'Good morning, sir,' Arriscado said, popping his head
around the bedroom door. 'I take it the noise woke you.'

'It's damned early,' Herculano said, as he rubbed his face
energetically. 'I assume this is to do with the trip to Sintra?'

'The journey will take all day, so the party always needs to
be up early. It won't disrupt the palace's ability to provide
you with breakfast, though.'

Breakfast was the least of his worries. Herculano was more
concerned about Lady Odete. She'd maintained a frosty
silence all the way back to the palace last night but had still
conveyed, via dagger glances, that she blamed Herculano for
the predicament she'd fallen into.

What that was, he dreaded to think. He only prayed
that the Contessa, an extraordinary being if ever he'd seen
one, had intervened before anything truly catastrophic had
occurred.

Herculano wondered what experience he'd actually had with
women. Since he could remember none of it, he wasn't sure

how, or even whether, he should broach the subject with Lady Odete.

His uncertainty bothered him but didn't stop him from rushing through his ablutions and dressing. In less than half an hour, he was on his way out of the palace. Hordes of servants hampered his journey through the halls and corridors, either carrying things out or rushing back to fetch more.

What they were loading was a mystery because everything was either in trunks or wrapped in sheets of cream canvas that was securely tied with thick rope. Whatever it was, it looked like most of the contents of the palace were going with the royal party.

Herculano followed the orderly procession of porters out via the main double doors that opened onto the Commercial Square. The part of the square closest to the palace had been cleared of the usual traders and their stalls. A line of soldiers in the royal livery of red, white and gold kept the crowd of interested onlookers at bay.

Inside the cleared area were at least a hundred plain carts being filled with goods. Closest to the door stood a row of extremely grand coaches. The middle one was presumably the prince's as it stood taller than the rest due to a gigantic golden crown that formed its roof, while its carved and scalloped exterior sparkled with gold. The royal crest was painted on the door, but that hardly seemed necessary as an indicator of the royal occupant.

There was no sign of the nobility that would be riding all the way to Sintra. Herculano assumed they were still in bed nibbling on their breakfasts. It appeared that, so far, only the servants were hard at work.

Just as he'd decided he was wasting his time and had turned to go back to his quarters, Odete emerged from the palace, a sheet of paper clutched in her left hand, a pencil in her right and a preoccupied expression on her face.

'Lady Odete.' Herculano projected his voice so that she would hear him over the racket of early morning traders, jostling servants packing the carts and higher-ranking servants shouting orders. 'Lady Odete!' Herculano shouted, as she gave no sign of having heard him.

At the same time, he pushed his way through a single file of porters. This time Odete did look up, but she looked less than pleased to see him.

'What can I do for you, Your Excellency?'

Her formal tone surprised Herculano. It checked what he was going to say. Was she still angry with him? If so, did that indicate that whatever had happened in the docks was serious?

'Are you alright?'

'Why wouldn't I be?'

'Well...' Herculano looked around. With all the people about he was reluctant to say anything that might be overheard and gossiped about later. 'Last night's events,' he said, and attempted to convey more by flicking his eyebrows meaningfully.

'I told you last night, I'm fine,' Odete said, and looked down at the paper she was holding.

It appeared to be a list and Herculano realised that Odete had followed one of the heavily-laden servants out and was now checking off what he dropped into a cart.

'Careful!' she snapped at the sweaty, red-faced man. 'Her ladyship's favourite tea set is inside that box.'

The porter muttered an apology then wheeled away, heading back into the palace. Odete followed him and Herculano had no choice but to do the same.

'You said last night you wanted to speak to me, yet now we have our chance and you're giving me the cold shoulder.'

'Yes, precisely, I needed to see you last night because I knew I wouldn't have any time today. Only you decided, without consulting me, that you didn't have time for me yesterday.'

She sounded tired and exasperated, so Herculano kept his tone as neutral as possible, although he was feeling more than a little hard-done-by to be so roundly blamed.

'How was I to know you'd be this busy?'

'You could have asked!' Odete said, as she swung around.

Herculano nearly walked slap bang into her and came to a stop that was far too close for comfort, looking straight down at Odete's head.

She pushed him away with all her strength and said, 'So I went out after you and... and...'

Herculano was astonished and dismayed to see that Odete looked to be on the verge of angry tears.

'I'm sorry,' he said, and bowed his head contritely. 'I should have shown more consideration. Now, please, are you really alright?'

'I'm fine,' Odete said, taking a deep breath. 'It's just the upheaval of the move that's wrung my nerves. Please forgive me. It's always this hectic and the other ladies-in-waiting are useless at organising. They're currently hiding in our room for fear that I'll make them help. Actually, it's the last thing I'd want,' Odete said, as she glanced down at her list again.

It apparently reminded her of all she still had to do, and she set off again at speed. Herculano assumed she was heading back to Lady Mafalda's quarters and followed along behind. She was right about one thing: it would be difficult to have a proper conversation when she was so distracted.

'What did you want to talk about yesterday, anyway?'

Odete shrugged and said, 'I suppose it doesn't really matter anymore. The deed has already been done.'

'What deed?'

'Bringing Lady Mafalda more fully into the investigation.'

'She was already in the investigation.' Herculano ducked just in time to prevent getting swiped by a long and heavy-looking canvas-wrapped article being lugged past the two of them. Lady

Odete was so short, it passed harmlessly over her head. 'She was the one who asked you to find Tiago, after all.'

'This feels different,' Odete said, and stopped again, this time halfway up the stairs. 'More dangerous.'

Herculano could hardly disagree. He worried the prince had pushed the duque too far by embroiling his daughter in the quest to find her lover's killer.

'Could you have stopped her?'

'Probably not, but that's different to the prince–' Odete stopped abruptly.

Herculano nodded.

'It is a dangerous game all around. I wish neither of you women were involved.'

Odete shrugged and resumed climbing the stairs.

'Was that all you had to say to me last night?' Herculano asked, and instantly regretted it because he got another fierce look from Odete.

'I also wanted to discuss what we do next, since we will no longer be in Lisbon.'

'You can leave that to me. I'm staying behind.'

'You are?' Odete asked, and might have stopped again but Herculano placed a hand against her back and kept her in motion with a gentle application of pressure.

'As I said to the prince, I have nothing I can usefully do in Sintra.'

'What do you intend to do here?'

'I'm not entirely sure. Everything has happened so quickly that I haven't had a chance to come up with a plan. And I doubt I've ever carried out this kind of investigation before, so I'm working in the dark.'

'You doubt you've ever done such a thing? Surely you know?'

Herculano paused. They were back on the top floor, and now all the doors to the various suites, aside from his own, were open, with porters and servants steaming back and forth.

'I lost my memory,' Herculano muttered under his breath, leaning close to Odete's ear.

She blinked in surprise at him, possibly because of the over-familiar gesture and probably also because of the information he'd just imparted. Herculano wondered why the devil he'd said anything at all. Why was he sharing this secret, one that had only been relayed to his senior staff and otherwise known only to the prince and Dr Zuniga?

'You lost your memory?' Odete mouthed.

Herculano was relieved she was also being quiet.

'When? How? Oh, this is nonsense, and I have too much to do to be distracted by this. No, actually, tell me.'

'Last Tuesday night,' Herculano said. 'I don't know how.'

'Last Tuesday?'

Odete looked so horrified that Herculano hurried to clarify. He leaned down and hissed into her ear, 'I know it sounds suspicious, but honestly, I had nothing to do with Tiago's death.'

'How would you know, if you've lost your memory?'

'Because I've been told so by two witnesses who said I was with them all of Tuesday night.'

'But they don't know what happened to you either?'

Herculano double-checked that none of those toiling about them was paying them any attention and tried to come up with something plausible to say. Losing his memory was one thing; telling Odete about the body swap was out of the question.

'They found me when I was already unconscious and kept watch over me for the entire night, so you see, it can't possibly be me.'

'That's assuming what these two witnesses told you is true. Who are they?'

Herculano just blinked at Odete. He hadn't considered that Arriscado and Dr Zuniga could have been lying to him and the prince. The possibility that either he or the prince might have had something to do with Tiago's death took hold for a second, then he dismissed it, annoyed with himself. They had no reason to kill Tiago. All the same, he would check with Dr Zuniga.

'I'm afraid I can't tell you at the moment,' Herculano said, brought back to the bustling palace by a sharp poke from Odete's finger.

'Then we have nothing more to say to each other,' Odete said, as she spun around and hurried back to her quarters, her attention already reclaimed by her list.

Odete ensured she had one of the forward-facing seats in the coach, beside Lady Mafalda, by pointing out that as she did all the work she had earned the more comfortable position. Pia and Maria da Luz guiltily accepted their fate and sat with their backs to the driver.

The coach had a wide body that ensured they were not pressed against each other, which was just as well as it was hot and stuffy with the sun beating down on them. The interior was panelled in a light-coloured knotted walnut and the seats were a deep red leather. Cushions that she and the ladies had embroidered over the years provided additional comfort.

Red velvet curtains shielded the ladies from curious eyes, but Odete had a reasonable view through a crack where the curtains met. Outside, a pushing, heaving throng peered at them as they leaned over the barricade made by the royal guards and shouted excitedly to each other.

'Here we go,' Maria da Luz said, as a trumpet sounded and, with a lurch, the coach bumped into motion. 'We're off and I can't wait until we're finally in Sintra with the cool mountain air and the breeze. It will be a welcome respite from the dust and the suffocating heat. I only wish we could open the curtains immediately.'

'You know we can't,' Mafalda said, and gave Maria da Luz a meaningful glare. 'Not till we've got away from the gawping crowds of Lisbon.'

Maria da Luz correctly interpreted the glare as a warning to keep quiet, and dropped her gaze to study her gloved hands. Odete wondered how long the silence would last. However long, it wouldn't be long enough. Maria da Luz simply couldn't help herself.

Odete's eyes were dry and tired after a restless night brought on by her close call in the docklands and the need to rise at dawn to supervise the packing. She was about to close them when a shadow drew her attention and she peeked through the gap between the curtains again.

It was the prince. He was riding his speckled white stallion and dressed in a blue satin riding outfit with a broad-brimmed hat trimmed with matching blue ostrich feathers that danced lazily with each bounce from his horse. Odete had never seen him looking as colourful. It suited him, but it felt wrong - how could he have changed so much?

Then another rider pulled into her narrow view. It was Herculano! He was dressed in a simple brown suit and riding a bay. He'd said he wasn't going to Sintra, so why was he riding beside the prince?

Why had he told such a pointless lie? Didn't he know he'd be found out immediately? Odete wanted to fling aside the curtain and demand an explanation, only decorum prevented it.

Besides, over the rumble of coach wheels on cobbles, the drum of horses' hooves, the tramp of accompanying soldiers and the crowds gathered along the road shouting to each other, there was such a cacophony it was hard to hear the women in the carriage, let alone make herself heard to somebody high above her on a horse.

To even get his attention would require her to lean out of the coach in a most unladylike manner and shriek at him. It would be uncouth, draw everybody's ire, and in no way give her a chance to give Herculano a piece of her mind.

So she sat back against her seat, closed her eyes resolutely and wondered why she even cared. Why did Herculano bother her so much? Why had she been so angry with him last night that she'd foolishly gone out on her own into the docklands?

She could tell herself that she'd taken precautions, but she'd never been more frightened in her life than when the sailors grabbed her. She'd also been more relieved than she'd admit to Herculano that he'd accompanied her home. It was a sign of consideration from him that he hadn't roundly condemned her behaviour and consigned her to the list of wanton women other people would have accused her of being under the same circumstances.

Then again, he'd dismissed her request to meet and now he was accompanying the prince when he'd said he'd be staying in Lisbon. What did she make of that? It seemed at odds with the view she had been developing of his personality.

She'd slowly decided he was a solid and trustworthy man. Probably a fairly tolerant one too. After all, he'd gone with her to all the hospitals and taken her to the docks to check Tiago's body. He'd even showed consideration towards her when he'd made sure she didn't have to tell Mafalda about Tiago.

Weighed against that was their first encounter. He'd clearly been listening at Dr Zuniga's door. Why do that if you were a confidant of the prince?

Trying to resolve all those questions gave her a headache, which was augmented when Maria da Luz started up again.

'We're nearly out of Lisbon,' she said, as she hauled herself upright and put her face to the gap Odete had been gazing out of. 'I can even see the Belém Tower in the distance, thank goodness. Any minute now, we'll be able to open the windows and the curtains.'

She sat back in her seat with a broad, satisfied smile. Odete ignored her, along with everyone else, but it didn't dampen

Maria da Luz's enthusiasm or still her tongue. Odete leaned her head back against the cushions and closed her eyes, gave a deep sigh and drifted off to sleep.

A sparkle of light turned the dark interior of her vision to bright orange and made Odete open her eyes again. She was surprised to discover, even though it felt like no time had passed, that they were abreast of the Belém Tower now. It was a massive stone structure jutting out into the broad river mouth. Its crenellated towers and battlements bristled with cannon that would decimate any ship that came to attack the city.

'There, that's better,' Maria da Luz said, in the process of pushing back the curtains.

It was that which had so dazzled Odete, because now the carriage was filled with light.

'And next I'll do the windows. The sea breeze will be most welcome.'

Odete glanced at Mafalda. She always took the seat with the view of the river that would shortly open out to the sea. But she wasn't taking in the view or even noticing Maria da Luz's chatter.

The poor thing looked pale and unhappy. Odete decided it was better to leave her to her introspection. She wouldn't want to talk yet, and certainly not in front of Pia and Maria da Luz.

Odete felt rather detached herself. Naps did that to her. She was only half awake and unable to think clearly. Since the journey would take all day, there was no need to worry about waking up, so she leaned back again and gazed at the dancing points of light reflecting off the small choppy waves.

Odete always enjoyed trips to the seaside. She had spent hours as a girl standing on the edge of a sandy beach, the waves washing about her ankles as she sank into the wet sand, mesmerised by the light dancing over the turquoise and blue waves. She felt as if she was standing on the edge of reality, gazing out into creation.

The Bible said that in the beginning God created the heaven and the earth. Odete had always wondered about that moment

and what had come before it. In her mind, it must all have
started with water: a rolling, heaving, swirling, restless darkness
that filled eternity.

Then a spark, the first light the water had ever seen,
flashed into existence and danced from wave tip to wave tip,
multiplying each time it landed until it filled the void with
sparkles that dazzled the Creator, who could finally look upon
His dominion.

Was it then that He created His first island? Sufficient only for
a single being to stand on, just a flat stretch of sand interrupting
the flow of the endless ocean.

Odete thought she'd make a lazy God. She might have
stopped there and sat down, cross-legged, to take in the
astonishing beauty of that first day.

'It will be lunch soon,' Maria da Luz said, breaking the spell
of Odete's rather pleasant daydream.

She wished she could go back to it, but lunch was indeed
imminent. The coaches had slowed and those ahead were
drawing into a loose circle. The royal guard was spreading out,
pushing any curious bystanders back.

The royal party always stopped in the same place each year.
While the king and, later, the duque allowed the people to line
the roads and watch the royal cavalcade go past, they drew the
line at being ogled while they ate their lunch. So they cleared a
wide area of all spectators before the royal party arrived.

Odete was relieved to leave the confines of the coach and
stretch her legs. They'd had the windows open for a while now,
but the air felt fresher outside. Thankfully, Odete didn't have
to do any organising here besides helping Mafalda out of the
coach.

This was the halfway point of their journey and where
they stopped following the road that hugged the coastline and
headed inland into the forest-clad hills filled with pines, oaks
and sweet chestnuts. The picnic area was a level clearing that
had been selected for the view. It looked down the mountain to

a broad beach. To the left was the road back to Lisbon. It was little more than a sandy, rock-strewn track at this point. To the right were the sea cliffs and more mountains.

Odete followed Mafalda as they headed towards the long trestle tables covered in white damask tablecloths that had been set up under the royal pavilion. This had all been sent ahead the night before to ensure it was ready for the royal party when they arrived.

'I don't think I'll ever tire of this view,' Odete said, as she watched Mafalda taking her seat.

'No, I suppose not,' Mafalda said, without bothering to look around.

'You poor thing, you must be very tired,' Pia said, as she settled beside Mafalda and took her hand.

Maria da Luz made similar soothing noises as she sat on the other side of Mafalda. So now Odete was at liberty to slip away unnoticed. She couldn't bear to sit down again so soon.

Usually, she took this opportunity to go for a walk along the edge of the wood that surrounded their picnic space. Today she was determined to confront Herculano. So she scanned the increasingly crowded space, looking for her quarry.

He was easy to spot because all she had to do was look for the prince and his entourage, who were leading his fine horse away to be brushed and fed. Herculano was standing beside the prince, having such a serious discussion that they seemed unaware of their surroundings.

Odete couldn't insert herself into the conversation, so she decided she'd go for her walk after all. She made for something that was little more than a track used by animals that skirted the area. As she did so, she spotted the treasurer, Lord Paiva. He was talking to a priest and had such a stricken expression that Odete stopped to watch.

From her distance, she couldn't hear what the priest said, but Lord Paiva's whole body trembled when he replied. The priest nodded apparent acceptance to whatever it was the treasurer had said, handed him a letter with a contemptuous look, and walked off. Odete was torn between following the priest to figure out who he was, and following Lord Paiva, who hurried away into the thicket Odete had intended to explore.

Since Herculano had asked her to look into him, finding out what Lord Paiva was up to seemed more important. So Odete did her best to look like she was merely on her usual meandering walk and followed the man.

There was only one path into this fragment of forest and one couldn't wander too deeply in because of the cordon of guards set up to protect the royal party. So Odete was certain she'd have no difficulty finding Lord Paiva.

She kept to the track, which led to an outcrop of granite boulders that ranged in size from something like a pumpkin all the way to that of a carriage. The rocky pile looked like it had been heaved up from the ground during the Creation and was now slowly being swallowed by scratchy climbing brambles.

Lord Paiva was sitting on one of the boulders at the bottom of the mound, clutching the letter. His hands were shaking so violently that he was having difficulty getting it open. He was, thankfully, so absorbed in his task that Odete decided it was safe to get closer. She flattened herself against a boulder and cautiously peered around it just as Lord Paiva opened a single sheet of paper. His gasp was so loud it made Odete jump.

Inside the folded sheet was a thick lock of blonde hair tied together with a pink ribbon. Lord Paiva stared at it for a moment, then held it to his nose and took a sniff.

'Her perfume! No, please, dear God, not this!'

Then he burst into tears and great sobs wracked his body.

Odete leaned forward to try and see what was written on the page, and discovered that it was blank. Apparently, the blonde lock conveyed the entire message, and what a terrible message it had to be.

Odete felt bad for Lord Paiva, rocking back and forth in anguish as the tears flowed unchecked down his face. But there was nothing she could do. He'd be angry to see her and would never reveal the meaning of the lock of hair.

Odete, though, thought she had a notion of who the hair belonged to. Maybe it was a good thing Herculano had come after all, she thought, as she slipped out of the forest and into the main clearing where the servants had started laying out the food.

As always, Odete looked first for the prince. It was a hard habit to break. Herculano was still beside him, but he was saying his farewells and turned to walk away, so Odete hurried to intercept him.

'I thought you said you weren't going to Sintra, Your Excellency,' Odete said, as she stepped out in front of Herculano.

'Lady Odete!' Herculano stopped and gave her a slight nod of acknowledgement. 'I am not going to Sintra. I came part of the way, but now I am heading back.'

'Without having lunch?' Odete was vexed to discover she was sorry Herculano wouldn't be in Sintra after all.

'There isn't time for it.'

Herculano spoke in a distracted way, his eyes flicking over Odete's head. She resisted turning around to see what was more interesting than speaking to her and suppressed the secondary urge of giving him another ticking off. Instead, she took a deep breath and fixed him with what she hoped was her most compelling stare.

'I have something very important to tell you.'

'Do you?' Herculano said, looking surprised. 'I don't suppose it can wait?'

'Not if you're going back to Lisbon, it can't.'

Herculano pulled his eyes off whatever was preoccupying him with considerable difficulty, seemed to regret his abruptness and said in an apologetic tone, 'What is it, my lady?'

Odete wondered at his change of tone, and whether it should please her that he'd made an effort to pay her attention, even if his gaze did flick for a moment back to whatever had attracted his attention.

'I've just seen Lord Paiva crying over a lock of golden hair. It was given to him in a letter from a priest.'

'A priest!' Herculano exclaimed so loudly that it made Odete jump.

'Why is that so surprising?'

'No reason. What else?'

'That's all.' Odete grabbed Herculano's sleeve because he'd nodded acceptance and started to walk away. 'I just thought you should check with the Contessa, about the... girl, the one that went missing.'

'The contessa?' Herculano was back to being distracted and impatient as he pulled his arm free and took another step down the path. 'Which contessa?'

Since the royal party was filled with dukes, counts and their respective families, Odete supposed his confusion made sense. But it annoyed her as she was trying to be discreet.

'*The Contessa*,' she said with emphasis, 'in the docklands.'

'Ah! Yes, of course. Now I really must be going,' Herculano said, and ran full tilt for his horse.

Herculano pelted down the path, exasperated by Lady Odete and sorry at the same time that he'd left her so abruptly. It was just that he had someone to follow. At the start of the journey, he'd seen the duque deep in conversation with a priest. Given the duque's open disdain for religion, it had struck him as odd.

For that reason, as he'd ridden with the prince and the two of them tried to work out what to do next, Herculano kept a discreet watch on the priest. He'd retired to ride amongst the lesser servants following the royal party. He didn't stand out because he was much the same as about a dozen or so other priests that were also travelling to Sintra to support the various noble households they worked for. The royal priest rode in a carriage, but the lesser gentlemen were riding, walking, or hitching a ride on a cart, depending on the wealth of their benefactors.

Herculano had lost sight of the priest when they arrived at the picnic place. He now suspected that was because he'd made sure not to be spotted when he was handing over his note to Lord Paiva. It had to be the same priest, didn't it?

Now, unlike everyone else, he was riding back to Lisbon. That was what had made Herculano impatient and why he'd tried to keep the priest in sight as he spoke to Odete, despite her exasperation. But now the man had vanished around a bend in the road.

There wasn't a moment to lose, even if he had been looking forward to the fabulous spread of the royal picnic. Herculano shouted for the man who was tending to the prince's horse, to bring him his and be quick about it. Herculano leaped into the saddle, kicking the horse's side to get him into motion. The horse swung its head back with a snort, annoyed to be wrenched away from his feedbag, but, finally, he accepted Herculano's urging and broke into a trot.

It was odd that the priest had come all this way only to return. Had he really just come to hand a note to Lord Paiva? Or had he, like Herculano with the prince, been needed by the duque for something else? Time would tell.

As Herculano made his way down the hill, he noted that the crowds that had gathered to watch the royal party had already dispersed. He supposed that the spectacle of the royal carriage with its golden crown, the rest of the fancy coaches, the liveried staff and gloriously clothed nobility, was a rare and exciting event for a people who spent the rest of their days in their little villages, fishing and farming and otherwise scratching out a tenuous living. But once the cavalcade had passed, there was no reason to hang about. Now, aside from some women gossiping outside their whitewashed cottages, a few men tending the small fields and, once he got down to the sea road again, a fisherman knotting his nets beside a beached boat, there were precious few people in sight.

Finally, Herculano spotted the black square hat of the priest in the distance, his pompom bobbing about. Herculano pushed his horse forward till he could see all of the priest and his mount. It looked to be a mule. They were solid, reliable animals but tended to obstinacy and a lack of interest in going anywhere at speed. It didn't look like the priest was in a hurry, anyway.

So Herculano slowed his own horse down and considered what to do next. Should he join the man and pretend that he was merely a traveller on the road looking for a bit of companionship and safety in numbers? Or did he keep his distance and hope he wasn't spotted?

Since he was following a possible agent of the duque, Herculano decided it was best not to reveal himself. He resigned himself to a slow ride back to Lisbon, which he supposed had the advantage that it gave him a chance to think.

The blue sky was dusted with clouds that blazed orange in the sunset by the time Herculano and his quarry arrived in Lisbon. Herculano pushed his mount to close the gap between himself and the priest. He couldn't afford to lose him now, not when he was so close to finding out who the man was.

The streets were filled with the inhabitants of Lisbon closing up shop as the light faded. One man threw slops out into the middle of the road, a pack of dogs descending to forage whatever was worth eating. Herculano's horse shied away from the dogs and he had to go wide to avoid them as well as a man dragging a cart filled with wine barrels. The problem with all these people was that it would be far easier to get distracted and have the priest vanish.

Fortunately, the man didn't go far. He rode up a curving, cobbled street that opened out into a moderate square dominated by an old stone church with a plain pitched roof covered in terracotta tiles.

The priest rode up to a side door that presumably led to the sacristy, dismounted and rapped against the iron-studded wood. Herculano pulled his horse to a stand just outside the patio, hooked his bridle to a handy iron ring protruding from a house wall and crept forward.

Light spilled out of the church as an old man opened the side door, holding up a lantern.

'Who's there?' he said in a trembling voice.

'It's only me,' the other priest said.

'Ah, Father Lopez,' the priest said. 'Where have you been? I expected you to give the Mass this morning.'

'I had urgent business to take care of,' Lopez said, and stepped inside. 'Get the servants to sort out my mule.'

'Of course,' the elderly priest said.

Herculano waited till they had led the mule away to the stables before going to take a look at the front of the church. The door was unlocked, so he slipped inside.

There was a table filled with votive candles that flickered in the gloom and two fat candles standing at the altar that were also lit, but other than that, it was nearly pitch-black inside. The floor, however, was occupied by a mass of the poor. Most were sitting in the gloom, not tired enough to sleep. Some, though, had already curled up, wrapped in what little they had. One man by Herculano's feet was snoring gently.

Herculano wondered whether he or any of his family had been forced to take refuge in a church when he was a boy. It was one of the safest places to be if you were destitute. He wondered how he knew that. Maybe it was a memory, vague as it could be, but knowledge of the past, all the same.

Herculano spotted a man leaning against the back wall of the church who looked quite awake, so he crossed the church, dropped to his haunches in front of the man and gave him a nod.

'Forgive me this intrusion, but may I ask you a question?'

'Ask, stranger,' the man said in a rasping voice, 'and I'll see if I can provide an answer.' His face was grotesque even in the dim flickering light because somebody had sliced his nose clean off.

'What is the name of this church?'

'You must not be from around these parts. This is the Church of the Baby Jesus.'

'I see, and...' Herculano paused, unsure how best to phrase this question. 'Is it a safe place to be?'

'Safer than the streets. But not by much.'

Herculano nodded and ventured a vague, 'The Inquisition?'

'Father Lopez was one of their staunchest investigators. He's firm but fair.'

'And the other one?' Herculano asked. There was always more than one priest, and he didn't want to look like he was only after information on one man.

'Father Jesus is harmless,' the man said, and swirled a finger around his ear in the universal sign that the man wasn't all there.

'I see, thank you.'

Herculano pressed a golden real into the man's hand and hurried away. He took a deep breath the moment he was outside; the stench inside the church from both the living and the dead was hard to stomach. Then he got back on his horse and headed for the docks.

His original plan was just to go home and get some proper sleep. It had been in short supply ever since he'd woken up with no memory. Since then he'd been catapulted into an investigation, the only bright aspect of which was that he got to go about with Lady Odete. Only now Lady Odete was annoyed with him and far away in Sintra.

She'd provided him with a line that was worth investigating, though: the question of the blonde lock of hair. Since it was night now, and he was close to the docks, Herculano decided he might as well head to the brothel and get that question resolved.

A short ride later, he was handing his horse to the watchman at his warehouse and then walking up to the Molly House. He got a wary greeting from the two thugs at the door and assumed that the madam of the house had told them to be on the lookout for him. They had evidently also alerted the Contessa, who sailed into the parlour and gave him an imperious curtsy, before waving her fan in the direction of her study.

'Sit,' the Contessa said, the moment Herculano stepped through the door. 'What brings our landlord to visit?'

Being the landlord to a brothel didn't thrill Herculano. It might be an idea to divest himself of the property as soon as possible. Then again, the money it brought in was impressive, and now that the Inquisition's wings were clipped, it wasn't such a dangerous thing to own. Unless, of course, he got on the wrong side of the duque.

'I have a question for you about your... young woman who vanished,' Herculano said, and his stomach grumbled hungrily as he noticed the half-eaten plate of a sausage and bean stew the Contessa was in the middle of.

'You have a question about Almira?' the Contessa said, sounding very surprised.

'Yes. Look, you don't happen to have more of that food, do you? I'm willing to pay a king's ransom for some.'

The Contessa looked momentarily taken aback, then burst into a shrill laugh and leaped to her feet.

'That I can arrange,' she said, and relayed a shouted order to whoever was on the other side of the door.

Within moments, a scantily-clad Moll arrived bearing a deep platter filled to overflowing with stew and a generous hunk of bread. Herculano gave a satisfied sigh and pulled the chair they had shown him to closer to the small side table where the food sat. He skewered a piece of sausage with the tip of his knife and chewed enthusiastically.

The Contessa filled a goblet etched with nymphs dancing around its rim with wine from an earthenware jug that had kept it nice and cool and handed it to Herculano before she tucked back into her own dinner.

'Thank you,' Herculano said, and gulped the wine down. 'I've had nothing to eat or drink all day and I've just realised how hungry I am.'

'So what was your question about Almira?'

'What was the colour of her hair?' Herculano asked, without bothering to look up from the food.

It was a really excellent stew, made even more delicious by the sharp edge of hunger.

'She's a blonde. She had Flemish grandparents. Why do you ask?'

'I can't tell you that right now.'

'Can you at least tell me whether you are looking for her?'

'I wasn't, but it turns out there may be some connection between the murder that took place outside my warehouse and the disappearance of your... Almira.'

'A connection?' An expression of alarm crossed the Contessa's face. 'Do you think she saw the murderer? Was she taken because of that?'

Herculano shrugged. He didn't know the Contessa well enough to tell her anything about the dangerous business he was involved in.

'If she merely saw the murder, I think they would just kill her to shut her up. Who would wonder about finding the body of one more dead prostitute?'

'That is sadly true.' The Contessa finished the last of her stew and dabbed carefully at her rouged lips with the edge of one black frilly handkerchief. 'But now you have come to my house to enquire about the colour of Almira's hair and that fills me with foreboding.'

Herculano felt he owed the Contessa at least a small piece of information for looking after Odete.

'I think she's still alive but being kept hostage for a reason I haven't worked out yet. More than that, I can't tell you.'

'So there may still be some hope?' the Contessa asked, as she took a long-stemmed white clay pipe out of her pocket and proceeded to fill it with tobacco.

Herculano wondered whether he'd been a smoker before. It seemed to be a popular pastime amongst the merchants, yet he felt no urge to join the Contessa as she lit up and took a deep, satisfied puff.

'There may be. Either way, I'll return your Almira to you if I find her.'

14

Odete woke to nothing but the sound of bird calls. This was such a refreshing change to the racket of Lisbon that she gave a deep sigh of contentment. She pushed herself upright in bed and looked over at Pia and Maria da Luz. They were both still fast asleep in the beds opposite hers. Their room here was smaller than in Lisbon. There wasn't much space to fit more than their three simple beds plus a couple of chests for their belongings and clothes.

What was different, though, was that they had windows on two sides that opened out onto shallow balconies. Odete slipped out of bed and walked barefoot across the cool, terracotta-tiled floor to one of the half-shuttered windows and peeped outside.

A grey fog restricted her view so that all she could see was a verdant green forest that dropped away into the valley below. Sintra, high on its mountain, was often swathed in clouds. It was one reason it was so much cooler than Lisbon.

Odete pulled her shawl more tightly around her shoulders and settled on the seat that had been built into the thick palace walls so that she could continue admiring the view. This quiet wasn't going to last, so she had to enjoy it while she could.

Breakfast would be brought up to them too, so that they wouldn't be bothered by the crush of servants setting the palace in order and making it comfortable for a royal stay. Even now, fires were being lit in the palace's impressive kitchens.

The kitchens were two adjoining rooms directly below a pair of massive beehive-shaped chimneys. The chimneys were so huge and distinctive that they dominated the palace and drew the eye. Fifteen years ago, before the earthquake, there had been three chimneys. But the earthquake had toppled one and the duque had decided to make the kitchens smaller and turn the third kitchen into a state bedroom.

The prince usually used it when he came to Sintra for official occasions. It had the grandest bed Odete had ever seen, set upon a raised stage. It was more for show than for being slept in. For sleeping, the prince retired to his bedroom on the floor above. Odete often wondered how comfortable the state bed actually was.

Maria da Luz mumbled in her sleep and Odete peered over at her, trying to guess whether she was about to wake up. Of all of them, she'd prefer that Maria da Luz slept the longest. Actually, she wanted to speak to Mafalda.

Mafalda, unusually, had been called away by her father just as the ladies were settling down to dine on the finger supper that had been brought up to their rooms. It was a selection of pies, cheeses, bread and wine, sufficient to make up for the fact that the kitchen wasn't up and running yet. To issue this summons at such an inconvenient time was unusual behaviour from the duque, and it immediately piqued Odete's curiosity.

What was stranger still was that Mafalda stayed away for hours and Odete had finally given up and succumbed to the sleep she so desperately needed. Now she was on the edge of her seat, wishing Mafalda would wake up before the other two ladies-in-waiting and tell her what her father had said. This was by no means a given. Mafalda had a healthy respect for her father and would usually follow the few commands he gave her.

'Odete?' Mafalda whispered as she poked her head around her bedroom door.

The timing couldn't be better. Odete jumped up and hurried over, whispering, 'What is it, my lady?'

'Come inside,' Mafalda said, and withdrew back into her room.

Mafalda's bedroom was about the same size as her ladies-in-waiting's room, but it only had the one, large, four-poster bed. It also had a rather splendid balcony with elegant twisted columns that held up a roof that was inspired by Moorish architecture.

'Should we talk outside?' Mafalda said, as she pulled on her shawl.

Odete felt a tingle of fear pass through her at the suggestion. Clearly, Mafalda didn't want to be overheard either.

'If you wish it. Although it is rather chilly still and I think Pia and Maria da Luz will be asleep for a couple of hours yet.'

'Then we can talk in bed.'

Mafalda slipped back under her covers and leaned against the ornate, black carved headboard. Odete climbed onto the foot of the bed and sat with her knees pulled up to herself and her arms wrapped around them.

'What is it?'

'I wanted to ask you something,' Mafalda said, and pulled absently on the fringe of her blanket. 'It was something my father told me last night.'

'You were with him for a long time,' Odete said.

'My father asked me about the prince. The last time we spoke, I mentioned that he seemed different. My father told me last night that he'd noticed the same. He wanted to find out from me what exactly I thought had changed. Have you noticed any differences?'

Odete took a deep, thoughtful breath and wondered how much she should reveal.

'I suppose I have seen a change too, yes.'

'The worst is...' Mafalda stopped and now she looked truly distressed. 'The worst is that my father said the prince changed on the night that Tiago vanished. Not only that, but that merchant you keep going out with appeared the very next day.'

'Yes.'

Odete had worried about the same things.

'On top of it all, Tiago's body was found on a property owned by the merchant.'

'That is also true.'

Odete felt a growing sense of foreboding. Was the duque building a case against Herculano?

'But not only that,' Mafalda said, gripping the edge of the blanket even tighter. 'My father said it's as though the prince and the merchant have switched bodies.'

For a moment, the thought was so preposterous that Odete laughed. Then she cut it off abruptly, partly because of the mournful look Mafalda was giving her and, horrifyingly, because the more she thought about it, the more it had a ring of truth to it.

'That's absurd. How could such a thing even happen?'

'No... think about it. The prince used to always wear black, now he's wearing colours, but the merchant is always sombrely dressed.'

'Merchants are a sombre class. I'm sure Herculano has always dressed that way.'

'Well, what about the prince's change of heart about you?' Mafalda asked, showing that she'd been far more aware of the situation than Odete had realised. 'The prince used to like you. He'd always smile at you but not at me. Now he hardly notices you and he's nice to me. I mean, he used to really hate me. And now that Herculano fellow is always smiling at you, but he scowls at me.'

'No, he doesn't, don't be silly,' Odete said, but she was starting to feel breathless. 'It's impossible.'

'Not if Dr Zuniga is involved,' Mafalda said. 'The prince and him have always conspired.'

'Well, there you go then. If Dr Zuniga is the prince's ally, why would he swap him with another man?'

'I don't know. But my father will work it out,' Mafalda said, with chilling certainty.

Odete was now on the verge of panic. Whether the duque was right about the prince and Herculano hardly mattered. If he could make the case to the council, he could oust the prince altogether.

Odete had to get word to Herculano immediately about what was going on. The moment she had that thought, she stopped herself. Would she be playing into the duque's hands by running straight to the person he was trying to set up?

Why, after all, had the duque discussed any of this with his daughter? He'd never done that before. The only reason Odete could think of was because he was certain that what he told his daughter would get back to the prince.

Odete had worried about getting Mafalda too involved. She'd suspected the prince of using Mafalda to get at the duque. Now it looked like the duque had decided that two could play at that game.

Herculano woke to find Arriscado seated beside his bed, staring down at him.

'For the love of God, must you do that?'

'I am just happy to see you getting a good night's sleep for once,' Arriscado said, as he eased himself to his feet, his corset creaking.

Herculano was glad to get some uninterrupted sleep too. It felt like he'd been running at full tilt ever since he'd swapped bodies.

'Although I must ask why we are at the palace and not your home, right now,' Arriscado asked.

The question brought Herculano up short. Why had he come straight back to the palace without even considering the other house?

'Probably because this feels more like home.'

'You need to look after your own property and your own people now, sir.'

At least there was a note of sympathy in Arriscado's voice even if it was a gentle telling off.

'Not yet, not until everything is resolved.'

His words reminded Herculano of the question Odete had asked and that had been nagging away at him ever since. How did he know that Dr Zuniga and Arriscado had told the truth about that fateful Tuesday night?

'Am I right in assuming that Dr Zuniga didn't go to Sintra with the rest of the royal entourage?' Herculano asked, as he stretched to his full length and gave a mighty yawn.

'The doctor seldom leaves his laboratory. It would be a massive and dangerous task to dismantle and transport all his equipment, so he remains in Lisbon throughout the summer,' Arriscado said, while he riffled through the wardrobe and picked out a moderately sombre suit in a dark green.

'I really must get more clothes made for me,' Herculano said, as he headed over to the washstand. 'Do you think Dr Zuniga will see me this morning?'

Arriscado laid the suit across the bed and lovingly straightened out the creases.

'He will always make time for you.'

'Why would he do that?'

'Because of the role you played in saving the prince's life.'

Herculano splashed water over his face. It was lukewarm, but still quite refreshing.

'I thought the prince was the only one he cared about.'

'His first duty is, and will always be, towards the prince. But you were the prince for fifteen years, and he was your mentor. I believe he grew fond of you.'

Herculano gave a dismissive tut and said, 'He nurtured the prince's body.'

'True, he saw a different face then. But as with me, he is realising that it was your character, that part of your soul that never changes, that he grew close to. Not your face.'

'Do you think a woman might feel the same way?'

Herculano was thinking of Odete. Time spent in her company had made him feel even more fondness towards her than when he'd first met, or rather, become reacquainted with her.

'While it might be somebody's appearance that first attracts two people to each other, it is their nature that bonds and keeps them together. If what Lady Odete liked was your straightforwardness and your habit of acting with alacrity, I have no doubt her liking for you will grow.'

'My habit of acting first and considering the consequences afterwards, you mean?'

'The prince is more deliberative.'

'Maybe that is why he will succeed where I failed,' Herculano said, while drying himself off. 'The duque was always able to see me coming. The prince is a more devious opponent.'

'Hopefully that difference will work to both your advantages,' Arriscado said, as he helped Herculano get dressed.

From there it was just a short walk, through a considerably quieter palace, to Dr Zuniga's rooms.

'Come in, come in,' Dr Zuniga said, and hoisted a pile of papers off a green velvet chair with a gold fringe so that Herculano could sit. 'I was beginning to wonder whether I would ever see you again. It feels like you have been avoiding me.'

'Well...' Herculano looked about himself and noticed that the suspended crocodile was facing towards him, its mouth wide open as if preparing to swallow him whole. 'I haven't really had much free time, what with the death of Tiago Andrade and all.'

'He has been serving the prince,' Arriscado said, beaming at Herculano like he was a prize student.

Arriscado headed to the back of the laboratory and picked out a dusty bottle and three beakers from the shelf that held all the pickled body parts. He waggled the bottle suggestively at Dr Zuniga, and the alchemist gave an accepting nod, so Arriscado happily poured each man a generous measure of a dark golden liquid.

'Port wine,' he murmured, as he handed a beaker to Herculano.

It was a stronger drink than Herculano was used to for breakfast, but the two older men tucked in with gusto.

'So what brings you to see me now?' Dr Zuniga asked.

Herculano swirled his port around the edge of the beaker and watched the thin film of alcohol run down its edges.

'Somebody I respect asked me yesterday whether I believe the story the two of you have spun me. Tiago Andrade died on a Tuesday night, the same night as you claim you carried out the body swap. You are therefore witnesses to the fact that I am not the one who killed Tiago, only I don't know how reliable you are.'

'An interesting dilemma,' Dr Zuniga said, as he sat down on one of his high lab bench stools. He crossed one thin stockinged leg over the other and then took a meditative sip of his port. 'I can give you no proof, except that I give you my word as a gentleman. I would also hope that you accept I had nothing to gain from the death of Tiago Andrade.'

'In fact,' Herculano said, 'Tiago's death has upset all the work that the prince put into discovering the hold the duque has on his council, unmasking him and breaking his control. It is only then that the prince will be able to ascend the throne and become king. I know that, I keep telling myself that, but nowadays, with my lost memory, I have difficulties working out who to trust.'

'You have my sympathy.'

'I would prefer your support.'

'I will do everything within my power. My sole aim is to ensure that Prince Juliano becomes king.'

Herculano scrutinised the alchemist's face. It looked serene and gave nothing away.

'What are you doing to make that happen?'

'Returning him to his rightful body was my first step. Making you his trustworthy companion was my second. I will also continue to watch the duque and all those who serve him in an attempt to gain power.'

'So you are familiar with the people around the duque, are you?' Herculano asked. Maybe the alchemist could be of use after all.

'I would say I am familiar with those who bow the knee openly, as well as the men who visit him in secret.'

'What do you know of a certain Father Lopez?'

'Father Lopez? Mmm, so he's come slithering into the light, has he?'

'You know him then?'

The alchemist's look of concern fed Herculano's disquiet.

'Balthasar Lopez was one of the Inquisition's most dedicated investigators. While others may have consigned a few hundred to the pyres of the auto-da-fé, Baltasar Lopez was responsible for the deaths of thousands. They praised him for his dedication to rooting out heretics, but it's no such thing. He is evil to the core and revels in causing pain and death.

'The duque has used his bloodthirstiness for his own purposes. Usually, the duque likes to make a show of killing his enemies. He'll put them on trial and hold a public execution. It helps to keep everybody else in line.

'But occasionally he needs to do away with somebody quietly. That's when he uses Baltasar Lopez. Do you think he assassinated Tiago Andrade because he came too close to a secret?'

'Possibly,' Herculano said, and the mystery he'd been turning around in his mind ever since he'd been on the road following the priest back to Lisbon now felt like it had an explanation. 'But not in the way you might be thinking.'

'Not a straight assassination, then?' Dr Zuniga said, as he downed the last of his drink and reached across the lab bench to replenish his glass.

'On the night of the murder,' Herculano said, thinking things through and trying to get everything into an order that would make sense, 'a prostitute vanished from a Molly House right beside the warehouse where we found Tiago's body. This prostitute was blonde. Then yesterday, this Father Lopez handed Lord Paiva, a man known to have a fondness for cross-dressing prostitutes, an envelope containing a lock of blonde hair.'

'Ah, I see,' Dr Zuniga said, rubbing his chin over the rim of his beaker. 'So you think Tiago, who was spying on the duque's henchman, happened to see a kidnapping and hence was done away with?'

'It looks that way.'

Herculano was glad that the alchemist had come to the same conclusion as he had.

'You should waste no time in letting the prince know about this.'

Herculano shrugged and said, 'I would like to see if I can find the prostitute first.'

15

Odete settled into her saddle and took a satisfied look around. It had been a while since she'd been out riding. It was one of the joys of Sintra that the ladies had considerably more freedom. This was because the village itself was tiny, with only a small collection of shops and houses ringing the square around the palace and with a few palacetes dotted amongst the trees on the side of the mountain. One belonged to Odete's family and someday soon she'd have to pay her mother a visit. Thankfully, it wouldn't be today.

The day trippers gathered in a little group of riders on the cobbled square at the front of the palace: the prince, his royal guard and accompanying servants, and the ladies Mafalda, Odete, and Pia. Maria da Luz was an awkward horsewoman who was only comfortable in a coach. As they intended to take a steep track up to the Moorish castle, she declared herself unfit to go along.

'I'll stay and assist the staff with getting the palace in order,' she had said the night before, when the outing was proposed.

'There's nothing left to get in order,' Mafalda said. 'They did it all today.'

The last thing Odete wanted was to have to support Maria da Luz on any ride, and perhaps it was her dismayed expression that reminded Mafalda of how awkward it would be to have Maria da Luz tag along.

'I'm sure you are right,' Mafalda said, changing tack altogether, as was her prerogative. 'No doubt the servants will be glad to have your aid tomorrow.'

They were also being accompanied by Lord Xavier Alardo. He was one of the duque's council members and no friend of the prince. Now though, he and the prince were currently chatting with all the appearance of getting along, while the horses stamped and fidgeted beneath them. They were fresh and ready for their ride.

Odete hoped Pia would keep Lord Alardo occupied or, at the very least, distract him for long enough that Odete could speak to the prince. Odete had been aware for a while that Lady Pia had developed feelings for a man Odete found insufferably haughty. She suspected the feelings were mutual and that the lord liked Lady Pia too. She could see no other reason for him to join them.

'Shall we go?' Juliano said to the party.

'We will follow your lead, Your Highness,' Lord Alardo said, bowing low over his saddle.

Pompous twit, Odete thought as she flicked her horse's reins and they set off at a sedate walk. They quickly arrived at a narrow lane with massive trees that met overhead, providing a pleasant, deeply shaded ride. The journey up the hill would take all day, but Odete was anxious to speak to the prince.

She worried about what the duque had told his daughter and whether she should divulge it to the prince. It sounded so far-fetched as to be laughable, but it was better that he knew, even if the duque might have laid a trap by telling his daughter. Mafalda was bound to tell the prince anyway and it would be better if Odete could deliver the information along with a warning, and this would be her best opportunity.

At least when Herculano was around she could send him messages and, if he ignored her, she could pay him a visit. It would overreach what she was allowed to do to make a similar approach to the prince.

So the moment Lord Alardo dropped back to chat to Lady Pia and Lady Mafalda, Odete urged her horse forward.

'Lady Odete,' Juliano said, as he bowed his head in greeting.

Even his smile and his way of greeting her seemed different these days.

'Do you know what the duque has been saying about you?' she hissed as she got close enough.

'Whatever it is, refrain from looking quite so conspiratorial,' Juliano said, with the same lazy, speculative smile.

'He said you and Herculano Escovar may have swapped bodies.'

That wiped the smile off the prince's face.

'He said what?'

'He told Lady Mafalda that you changed on the night Tiago Andrade was murdered.'

Fortunately, the clatter of a dozen horses' hooves, plus the cacophony of birds in the surrounding trees, provided a decent cover for what Odete was saying.

'What a preposterous notion,' Juliano said, his eyes narrowing. 'Have you ever heard of such a thing?'

'Just because I've never heard of it doesn't mean it isn't so. I know little of the power of magic. And you know, better than anyone, that the duque doesn't even need it to be true.'

'He just needs to set rumours running. In that you are correct, and I see he is using his daughter to do so.'

'I'm afraid so. You should summon Herculano. He needs to know about this new threat.'

'Would you like that?'

'No! I just mean he should know.'

She was saved from having to say more by Mafalda, who rode up and pushed her horse between theirs. She had the expression of one who was determined to be involved in whatever they had been plotting.

'Did Odete tell you of my father's suspicions?' Mafalda asked.

'She was just doing so,' Juliano said, and glanced back at Lord Alardo, who was chatting away to Lady Pia and apparently oblivious to anything else.

'They would make a handsome couple, wouldn't they? What with both of them being fair.'

Odete wondered how much Mafalda actually knew of the battle for power that raged between the prince and her father. How would she feel if she found out that Tiago, her lover, had been working with the prince to unseat the duque? Would she feel betrayed by her lover or by her father? If it was by Tiago, how would she then react to the prince?

Odete, never having met her own father, wondered whether the ties of blood were stronger. They might be an especially tight bond if there were only the two, father and daughter. The duque might not speak much to his daughter, but Odete suspected that the frightening man had considerable affection for Mafalda. The duque, after all, could have remarried and had more children. Instead, he'd invested all his future ambitions in his daughter. He would not easily give her up, even if he was willing to use her to forward his aims. Odete shuddered at that thought.

'Are you cold?' Mafalda asked. 'I told you to wear a thicker riding jacket. It will be colder still when we reach the top of the hill.'

'Oh no, I'm fine. I will readjust to this cooler weather in no time.'

Mafalda gave Odete a dubious look, but that was as far as her concern extended for her lady-in-waiting. She was about to go back to her conversation with the prince when Lord Alardo and Lady Pia took the opportunity of the road widening to join them. After that, the group was too close together to have a private conversation.

It frustrated Odete and, for the hundredth time, she wished Herculano was around. She'd grown to rely upon Herculano, and felt like the whole situation would improve if he was there. As it was, she had to listen to Lord Alardo holding forth on the strategic significance of the fort they were riding up to see, and all the work the occupying Moors had done in the area to make the fort impregnable.

'Of course,' he said in his most condescending tone, 'the Moors are a cowardly race and, therefore, they also built a myriad of escape routes. This mountain is riddled with tunnels they could flee through like rats.'

'They couldn't have been that cowardly,' Odete said. 'How could a cowardly race conquer most of Iberia, North Africa and all the land up to India?'

Lord Alardo gave Odete the astonished look of a man who wasn't expecting a riposte and most certainly not one from a woman. Odete couldn't help but compare his reaction to Herculano who had never talked down to her nor been surprised to discover that she had opinions of her own.

'Aside from that,' Odete carried on, since she was probably already seen as an ill-disciplined and inappropriately opinionated woman, 'I doubt there's a fort or palace in all of Portugal that doesn't have a secret escape route. Does that mean that we are also all cowards?'

Out of curiosity, she glanced at the prince and noted that he was looking amused. His face went back to studied indifference as Lord Alardo turned to him.

'I hardly think this is an appropriate conversation for a lady, or an appropriate tone.'

Odete was ready to stand up to this man but realised it was best not to. He was getting angry and that would just make the day uncomfortable for everyone.

So she bottled up her ire and said, 'I beg your pardon. You are the military expert. I think I should leave the gentlemen to discuss such matters between them.' And with that, she allowed her horse to fall back.

Her capitulation had the effect of appeasing Lord Alardo who happily continued holding forth on the military significance of the fort.

Mafalda dropped back to ride with Odete and said, 'He is a great bore, isn't he? I don't know what Pia sees in him.'

Odete nodded agreement. Pia was still gazing adoringly up at Lord Alardo and hanging on his every word.

'My father told me that one of the tunnels through this mountain goes all the way to the sea,' Mafalda continued.

'I've heard one goes all the way to Lisbon.'

'Do you think that's true?'

'I have no idea. We have a tunnel that opens out into the stables at my home. We children were forbidden from ever going into it. Apparently, several servants had ventured in over the years, never to be found again.'

The hill became ever steeper as they climbed, and the path narrower and stonier. In places, all the gravel had washed away so that the horses' hooves slipped and sparked on the bare rock. Then the trees opened out and the little group arrived at the top of the mountain where only low scrub surrounded an impressive defensive structure made from neatly-shaped granite blocks.

'Finally!' Mafalda said. 'I'm hungry enough to eat lunch right away.'

'It will take the servants a while to set up the picnic,' the prince said, as he dismounted then went over to Mafalda's horse and held out his arms to help her down.

Everybody stopped what they were doing to stare at him in astonishment. The prince had never behaved in such a familiar way towards Mafalda before.

'I say, the duque is right about you,' Lord Alardo exclaimed, as he also dismounted.

'What do you mean?' Juliano said, giving Lord Alardo a bland, enquiring stare as he lowered Mafalda to the ground.

He carried on waiting as Mafalda straightened her skirts and Lord Alardo spluttered, 'Well... helping Lady Mafalda off her horse, for one. I've never even seen you speak to her before.'

'But then, you have spent very little time with me in general.'

'Well... that is... the duque keeps us very busy.'

'Perhaps that is true for now, but it may not always be the case.'

Juliano spoke in a calm, level way. In the past, he'd have snapped at Alardo, called him a fool and then stomped away. It was clearly unnerving his lordship to have the prince merely watch him in vague amusement.

With a chill, Odete realised it was a very similar expression to what she frequently saw from the duque when he was browbeating people into submission. It shouldn't have been strange to see it from the prince. After all, he and the duque were uncle and nephew and the prince had grown up in the palace. Yet, he'd never behaved like this before.

It was the most shocking confirmation of the duque's suspicion that the prince and Herculano had somehow been swapped. Because, Odete was realising, Herculano did behave in exactly the straightforward manner she used to admire in the prince.

The prince, however, merely smiled at Lord Alardo's surprise.

'If I remember correctly, an entrance to a secret tunnel out of this fort is fairly close by. Shall we go find it while the servants set everything up for lunch?'

'What a splendid idea!' Mafalda said, clapping her hands together.

Lord Alardo apparently decided it was best to go along with the prince and took the opportunity to help Lady Pia down from her horse. This left the group of servants who were supposed to help the ladies with only one person to support, so they all converged upon Odete.

⁂

Herculano decided that his best bet for finding out what the priest Baltasar Lopez was up to was to keep watch on him. So he found a beggar outside the palace and made a deal to swap clothes. Then, dressed in his stinking disguise of filthy rags, he headed for the Church of Baby Jesus.

The doors to the church stood wide open. Several beggars were clustered about the entrance, hands outstretched for alms from every person going into the church to pray, or on their way out after having made their observances. There wasn't a church in Lisbon that didn't have a similar collection of beggars. Ever since the earthquake, the number of homeless in the city had increased, as well as the number of people who could no longer work due to injury or disfigurement.

In the group by the church door was a man missing a leg, another with a dent in his skull the size of a fist, a woman with a missing arm, and another who appeared to be paralysed from the waist down and who lay on the ground, waving her arms in supplication. She was accompanied by a boy whose face was badly burned.

They ignored Herculano as he stomped into the church. There would be no pickings from a fellow beggar. The inside of the church was free of all beggars. Apparently, the leniency that allowed them to gather inside at night didn't extend to daylight hours.

This was confirmed as a deacon who'd been waving a thurible billowing incense-filled smoke, put it down the moment Herculano arrived, and hurried over.

'No begging inside the church,' he said in a high-pitched, officious voice.

'Where's Father Lopez?' Herculano asked.

A straightforward attack always worked best and the deacon looked disconcerted for a moment.

'Do you run errands for him?'

'Errands, yes, that's right,' Herculano said, playing along.

'He's not here right now. You can wait in the corner till he gets back. But I warn you, if I see you begging inside the church, I will have you expelled.'

Herculano nodded, settled in the dark corner as ordered, and prepared to wait. In the meantime, he took a better look around. As he'd noted the first time, it was a small and simple church with plain whitewashed walls and small, high-set windows. It left the place rather gloomy, but cooler than the Lisbon streets.

The only additional lights were the candles set on the main altar and a table to the right of the nave, upon which sat the votive candles. Herculano was so bored he counted the flickering flames and came to fourteen. Fourteen desperate prayers sent up to heaven.

Herculano wished he hadn't gone with quite such a dreadful disguise. The clothes reeked of urine and sweat and the smell grew stronger the longer he sat. He also felt a sharp itch between his shoulder blades, not the first such prick, and set to scratching. His clothes were swarming with fleas and lice.

It was with considerable relief that after several hours, during which time he valiantly resisted the urge to scratch himself, Father Lopez emerged from the sacristy. Herculano held his breath, hoping that the deacon hadn't mentioned him.

Thankfully, the man merely went up to the altar and spent some time fixing the candles. Then he made his way to the two small side chapels to the right and left of the nave and lit the thick candles on those altars. Given the size of the church, those small flames hardly provided any light to dispel the gloom. Then the priest returned to the sacristy.

Herculano decided it would be safe to get closer to the front of the church as the deacon, having fumigated what he could, had also vanished. He flitted from shadow to shadow until he was close enough to the door to hear the murmur of voices in the sacristy. There, he found another shadowy alcove and settled down to wait again.

It was approaching sunset when the priest reappeared. This time, he was carrying a plate of food and a mug, and he looked more furtive. He examined the church, apparently decided that the couple of women kneeling in prayer were paying him no attention, and crossed the chancel, walking surprisingly quietly.

On the other side of the nave, Father Lopez vanished into a small side chapel. Herculano heard the jangle of keys, a door being unlocked, a creak as it swung open and then a click as it shut again.

While he was alone, Herculano hurriedly skirted the edge of the church, keeping to the shadows that were growing in the gathering gloom of dusk. He made it to the edge of the little chapel just as Father Lopez reappeared, minus the food. Herculano froze and prayed he wasn't spotted. Father Lopez was so focused on not being noticed by the people in full sight in the church that he didn't appear to notice Herculano either as he returned to the sacristy.

Herculano slipped into the side chapel and took a look around. He couldn't see the door the priest must have gone through. So he made his way around, tapping at the walls. Right at the back of the chapel, behind the little altar, the sound of his knocking changed.

He felt his way along the shadowy depths of the wall. It all looked the same: the wall and the door, a white base, followed by a curved and textured central relief painted to resemble red marble, and the top half of the wall that had been painted to imitate some sort of jade green stone. But now, as his fingers ran along the edges of a very slight line, he came to a keyhole, hidden in the bulge of the red relief.

He pushed against the door, but it didn't budge. Herculano swore under his breath. What if the priest kept the key with him?

He turned to survey the chapel. A portrait of the Madonna hung on the left wall, a painting of a lion and a lamb hung to his right. Nothing else adorned the walls. The altar was also a simple one with a pair of candles and a runner embroidered in silver thread with thick tassels that hung over the edge of the altar to the right and left.

Herculano leaned forward, resting his hands palm down on the altar as he considered. There was a door, there was definitely somebody behind the door. But how did he find out who it was, short of ambushing the priest and forcing a confession out of him?

Would he have the keys on him? Herculano couldn't see why he'd have all the keys to the doors of this church. Then again, if it was a prison, he might be more careful.

Herculano decided he was wasting his time looking. His best bet was to wait till the priest came back and follow him in. Herculano pushed himself back to fully upright. As he did so his leg brushed the side of the altar and he heard a faint jingle.

'Holy little cherubs,' he muttered, and felt along the underside of the altar with his fingertips.

And there it was, an iron hook embedded in the marble. And a set of keys. Herculano wrapped his fist around the keys so that they wouldn't jangle as he lifted them out. There were five keys in all. One was slightly larger than the others, so Herculano tried it first on the door.

It opened with a loud click, just as it had done for the priest. Herculano cursed under his breath and listened. Nobody seemed to notice, so he eased the door open. It creaked and Herculano stopped immediately.

He peered through the gap but it was pitch-black inside. He'd need light if he was to go further in. He looked about and his eye fell upon the votive candles.

It felt sacrilegious to do it, but he stole one. Then he slipped through the gap into the dark space and closed the door behind him. A creak was preferable to giving himself away with a flickering light.

With the door safely shut, Herculano looked about himself. He was standing in a short tunnel, more like an alcove. Directly ahead of him stood a wooden door with a small square of iron bars at head height. Herculano held the candle up to the square and peered inside.

At first he thought the tiny room he illuminated was empty, then a pile of what he'd mistaken for rags moved.

'You there,' Herculano hissed. 'Can you hear me?'

A figure sat up, dressed in a white nightdress with lace trim. It was a blonde woman with thin, lanky hair, who kept her back to Herculano. As she turned around, Herculano smothered another curse.

The woman's face was gaunt and pale. White powder that had presumably covered the face was now streaked and caked into the creases. Stubble from several days without shaving sprouted over the chin and top lip. Black smudges surrounded the eyes from kohl liner, and there was a similar red smudge around the mouth where the lipstick had bled and then been smeared.

'Are you Almira?' Herculano asked.

The being stared at him with a frightened expression before he said in a high-pitched voice, 'Who are you?'

'My name hardly matters right now. But if it reassures you, I know the Contessa.'

'Did she send you?' Almira asked, as he scrambled to his feet. 'Not as such.'

Herculano was trying to work out what to do next. Should he leave Almira here, then go and fetch a disguise and horses so that he could then get the prostitute to the prince? Or would it be better to get him out straight away and then make haste to Sintra?

To buy himself some time he said, 'Is there anybody else here?'

'I don't think so,' Almira said, hurried to the door and clung to the bars with both hands. He was a short, slim man which, Herculano decided, suited him to his job. 'Please don't leave me here. I can't stand it in this dark and there are rats everywhere.'

That decided Herculano. He tried the first key. It wasn't the right one, nor was the second. By the third, Herculano was practically jumping out of his skin with the noise from the lock. This one worked. The bolt clicked back and Almira came rushing towards him.

'Wait,' Herculano said, holding out his hand. 'You need to disguise yourself before we go anywhere.' He pulled off his threadbare shirt and handed it to Almira. 'Put this on, and clean your face. You are most likely to escape detection looking like a man.'

'Holy Mary, Mother of God,' Almira muttered, as his lips curled up in distaste. 'That stinks.'

Then, possibly because Herculano looked like he might leave, he whipped the nightdress off, to reveal a skinny, white body and an extraordinarily frilly pair of drawers.

Herculano puffed out a daunted sigh.

'I have no idea how we hide those and I really don't want them sticking in people's minds.'

Almira, in the meantime, was rubbing his face vigorously with the nightdress. Once he was done, he tore it in half and handed it to Herculano.

'Here, use this as a shirt in exchange for yours. At least mine doesn't smell half as bad.'

Herculano examined the overly-feminine garment and weighed up the pros and cons of going out shirtless, which wouldn't be unheard of amongst the beggars. He decided he looked too well fed and his torso wasn't sun browned which would make him stand out. So he pulled the nightshirt on. It ripped around the shoulders and was ridiculously tight about his arms, but it would do.

Almira, in the meantime, was tearing the frills off the drawers, so in the end he looked like he was wearing a pair of grubby, white culottes.

'We must hurry. The priest always comes back to torment me when he collects my plate.'

'Why didn't you say something sooner?' Herculano snapped. 'Come on.'

He hurried back to the main door and cursed as the small votive candle burned nearly all the way to the base and spilled hot wax over his fingers. He twisted it to use the last remnants of light to find the keyhole and unlock it. Then he dropped the remnants of the fast-dwindling candle onto the floor and stamped on the flickering flame.

'Careful now,' Herculano said, as he held his finger up for silence and eased the door open.

It was darker now and the church had started to fill with beggars using it as their nighttime refuge. Herculano hoped that would help as he slipped out into the chapel. Almira followed and Herculano locked the door behind him and put the key back under the altar before he headed for the shadows and skirted around the edge of the church. They reached the front door and Herculano thought they might be home free when Father Lopez stepped out of the sacristy, took a look around and locked eyes with Herculano.

'Merde!' Herculano pushed Almira out of the church and, holding tight on to his skinny arm, said, 'Run!'

16

'It would have been good of you to tell us you were going out, Your Highness,' Viriato said from his position at the head of the stairs when the prince wandered into the palace near sunset.

Juliano was telling a joke which the ladies of the party, Viriato's daughter included, appeared to find wildly amusing. The only one in the group who didn't look impressed was Lord Alardo. Then again, the duque doubted that the young lord had a sense of humour.

Juliano, on the other hand, didn't lose his smile even when he had to realise he was being told off. It was that same annoying change in him. In the past, he'd have roared at Viriato that he could do as he damn well pleased.

Instead, the prince said, 'I beg your pardon. What exactly was it you had planned?'

What he planned was to blame someone for Tiago Andrade's murder, but he certainly wouldn't say that.

'I've called an emergency council meeting. Just because the court has moved to Sintra doesn't mean there aren't important matters to attend to.'

'You are quite right,' Juliano said, disarming his uncle once more. 'When do you want to meet?'

Viriato was far more used to butting heads than gaining agreement from his nephew. He'd always wished it was otherwise and that his nephew could be more like him. Now that Juliano was behaving in this moderate way, he found it irritating.

'We can wait for you to get out of your riding clothes. Will an hour be sufficient?'

'That will be more than enough.'

Juliano gave his uncle a nod of farewell and strolled off into the palace. Viriato watched him with gathering unease. He thought he knew exactly which levers to pull to get the result he desired from his nephew, and now he had an entirely new person whom he barely understood at all.

Frustration was a familiar sensation to him, though. People dragged their heels about selling land, administrators took their time agreeing changes to the law, the treasurer kept telling him there were no funds, and powerful families who wanted to stake claims to the rebuilt Lisbon jockeyed for position. He had dealt with all of them. He would deal with his nephew as well.

He shrugged away his irritation and headed to the throne room. The walls here were covered in blue tiles, each with an armillary sphere bulging out of the centre, representing the voyages of discovery undertaken by Portugal's adventurers. It was a shame they didn't bring more riches to the kingdom, the duque thought, as he made his way to the foot of a long table set in the centre of the room. It was most often used for dining when dignitaries were in attendance. Today the council would use it.

At the head of the table stood the throne on a raised dais. It was too far away for anyone actually sitting on the throne to comfortably take part in any conversation at the table. Viriato had enjoyed tormenting his brother-in-law by insisting he sat there during meetings, which had been an effective way of sidelining him.

The prince had never shown any interest in occupying the throne. He had merely pulled one of the other chairs around the table, set it at the head and sat down with a pugnacious expression, as if waiting to be ordered onto the throne.

Viriato had said nothing about it and merely started the meeting. He wondered now what the prince had made of that. At least he'd had the sense not to make a fuss about it and had merely joined in the meeting.

A pair of servants walked into the room, one carrying a lighting stick and the other a lit candelabra plus a stick. As they spotted the duque, they froze.

'I beg your pardon, Your Grace,' the man with the candelabra stuttered, looking appropriately rattled. 'I can come back.'

'Do you expect me to work in the dark then? Go ahead and do what you came to do.'

'Yes, Your Grace, thank you, Your Grace.'

The servant set the candelabra on the table and then, both men glancing anxiously at the duque at regular intervals, they set to lighting the gigantic candelabra that hung over the dining room table. First they lit their sticks from the flames of the candles on the candelabra, then touched that flame to the candles high above them. The candelabra itself was at least the height of a man, with two tiers: a smaller upper tier and a wider lower tier that ended with an elegant crystal ball dangling at the bottom. The cups holding the candles were shaped like cut glass pineapples and the curving branches that held them up were festooned with crystals.

The duque estimated that the cost of the chandelier could feed a noble family for a year. It was only right. It was important to reflect power in everything the king did, even when it was merely to provide light.

Lord Andrade was the second person to arrive, announced by the footman at the door. Viriato noted that he looked like he'd aged ten years since they'd found his son's body. Viriato could understand that. He'd lost his two young sons to the earthquake and the memory of that loss was a constant ache in his heart. To make matters worse, Tiago Andrade was the only son of the family.

'Thank you for coming,' Viriato said, and half rose from his chair.

Andrade gave him a look half mixed with pain and half with dislike as he gave the duque a nod of acknowledgement.

'Why do you need me at this meeting, Your Grace?'

'Because we have to speak of your son's death. I fear it was more than a mere mugging.'

The direct attack was always best, especially when dealing with an intelligent man like Lord Andrade, who must suspect him of being involved.

'I have no doubt it was more than a mugging,' Andrade said, his hard eyes holding the duque's gaze.

'Well, at least we are in agreement about that.' Viriato said, as the rest of the council arrived.

They were the usual: Lord Paiva the treasurer, the fat Lord Carvalho, the far more intelligent Lord Ledo, Lord Alardo, decked out in his military uniform, and the red-robed Cardinal da Gama.

Viriato wondered whether the prince intended to make him wait as he had for their last meeting and was contemplating locking the doors as punishment when Juliano strolled into the chamber.

'Gentlemen,' he said, giving them all an elegant bow. 'Please forgive my tardiness, but I couldn't resist a ride today. It's so seldom I get to do it when I'm in Lisbon.'

There was a chorus of men telling him not to worry, which he ignored. Viriato was pleased to note that Juliano looked surprised by Lord Andrade's presence and possibly a little regretful that he'd been out enjoying himself so soon after the death of his best friend.

'Lord Andrade,' Juliano said, 'I wasn't aware you'd be here today.'

'Evidently not,' the count said, dryly.

Things couldn't be going better, Viriato thought, as he held out his hands in a gesture of welcome.

'Gentlemen, please be seated.'

'Isn't it a bit late to be having a meeting now?' Lord Carvalho asked, as he pulled out a fan and started flapping it about energetically.

It did nothing for the sweat dripping down his face.

'I wouldn't have asked you to gather if the matter wasn't of the gravest importance,' Viriato said, taking the time to look each man in the eye before he continued. 'As you are aware, young Tiago Andrade was murdered recently.'

There was a sympathetic murmur and Lord Ledo, seated next to Lord Andrade, squeezed his shoulder.

'I have no wish to cause Lord Andrade any further pain, but I need to remind you that his son's body was found hidden inside a wine barrel on the Lisbon docks.'

'He was mugged, wasn't he?' Lord Carvalho said, looking confused. 'Why does that warrant a meeting?'

'Because I believe something more sinister is afoot,' Viriato said, as he looked across the table at the prince at its head.

Juliano arched an eyebrow but said nothing. His expression had hardened though, and his lips were pressed tightly shut.

'Observe,' Viriato said, waving his right hand negligently towards his nephew, 'how quiet the prince is. Do you not find that strange?'

'I thought we were here to talk about Tiago Andrade,' Lord Paiva said, nervously.

Ever since Viriato had ferreted out his weakness, the man had been completely in check and far more careful of what he said to the duque than he'd ever been before.

'It's one and the same,' Viriato said, holding his nephew's gaze. 'There is too much change in the palace and in the prince. It has fuelled my curiosity. On the day after Tiago Andrade was murdered, the prince introduced a wholly unknown person into his entourage.'

'You are speaking of the merchant Herculano Escovar, are you not?' Lord Ledo said, and his eyes narrowed thoughtfully.

'Are you aware that Tiago Andrade was found in a wine barrel on Escovar's property?'

A murmur rose from the assembled men.

'That is hardly surprising,' Juliano said. 'Herculano Escovar owns the largest warehouse on the docks and that is only one of three that belong to him.'

'But how did you come to meet him, Your Highness? And so soon after Tiago's death. Not to mention the marked change in you.'

Viriato was pleased to see that his last comment had surprised the prince. He'd obviously not been expecting such a direct attack.

'Dr Zuniga introduced Herculano Escovar to me. I thought it was important to improve my understanding of trade and Escovar was recommended as he's the richest merchant in Lisbon.'

'You could have asked me to recommend somebody if you wanted to learn more about trade.'

'Why would I?' A slight smile quivered on Juliano's lips and was hastily suppressed. 'When have I ever asked you for anything?'

'You see, gentlemen,' Viriato purred, 'when I said the prince has changed here we have a prime example. Let me ask you, Lord Ledo, how the prince would have acted only last week if I offered to introduce a merchant to him.'

Nicanor Ledo's eyes narrowed and he rubbed his hand thoughtfully over his chin.

'He would have flung the offer back into your face with a shout, and most likely have stormed out of the palace.'

'Quite. And how would he have reacted to the death of his closest friend and constant companion?'

'He would have been heartbroken. I doubt he could have remained this calm and collected and he wouldn't have gone out riding. Maybe for a gallop on his own, but not a picnic.'

Viriato noted the glance the prince threw at Lord Andrade. He had clearly realised the trap he'd fallen into.

Lord Andrade said, 'It's true, I would have expected more of a show of emotion from the prince. There has been a change and, I venture to say, not a good one. But I fail to see that there is sufficient evidence to blame the merchant, Herculano Escovar, for the murder of my son. I also fail to see the relevance of the change in the prince. One might even say that grief has a strange effect on people and that could explain all you have brought up, Your Grace. If that is all you have to say, then I believe I am wasting my time here.'

'I have more.' It did not surprise Viriato that Lord Andrade wasn't taking his side in this matter. But he was the least important person to convince. 'I believe there is devilry afoot. I believe the prince and Herculano Escovar have been switched, one with the other. I believe they did this so that the merchant could take over the kingdom, but in the process of the switch, young Tiago Andrade found out what was happening and he was done away with.'

'Preposterous!' Juliano cried, and leapt to his feet. 'I have heard some far-fetched, overly-ambitious flights of fancy from you in the past, uncle, but this really is too much. Why, if I had switched places with the prince, would he be trailing along happily beside me? Why wouldn't he be making a fuss? Why would he be expending all his energies to find Tiago and, once he was found, to bring whoever killed him to justice?'

'He would do all of that because you hold his fate in your hands,' Viriato said, with a tight, cynical smile. It was what he would do, after all. 'He is now a mere merchant and you could have him put to death whenever you wished.'

'But, is such a thing even possible?' Lord Carvalho said, blurting it out like a man who'd just shaken himself awake from a particularly deep sleep.

'Who knows what kind of devilry Dr Zuniga might be capable of?' Cardinal da Gama said, coming unexpectedly to Viriato's aid. 'It would also explain why the prince, or whoever you are, was introduced to the merchant by the doctor. There must surely be a better way to get to know a merchant.'

'I have never heard a more absurd tale in my life,' Juliano said. 'It is far more likely that my uncle was involved in Tiago's death and is now trying to shift the blame to somebody else while making a grab for the throne himself.'

Viriato only just managed to prevent himself from rubbing his hands together with glee. The prince might have gained self-control overnight, but he'd just made a tactical mistake.

'I have never wanted the kingdom for myself. That is why you are still alive, Your Highness, and why I am encouraging you to marry my daughter.'

'So that you may control me from the shadows? Well, it won't work, uncle. I will prove to you that I really am the prince and that you are responsible for Tiago's death.'

'I very much doubt that. But I am willing to put it to the council with a show of hands. Who is in agreement that we need proof that the prince is who he says he is?'

'How would we even do that?' Lord Alardo asked.

'We will get Dr Zuniga to do a test of his blood. As you all know, if the prince is a true royal, his blood will be blue.'

Viriato was rather pleased to note that the prince looked surprised and discomforted for a second at his proposal. Then his face set back into grim neutrality.

'We all know you will win this vote,' Juliano said.

'You'd do better to worry about the outcome of Dr Zuniga's investigation,' Viriato said. 'For if you are discovered to be an imposter you will be executed. And whoever is found to have killed Lord Tiago Andrade will follow you to the pyre.'

17

Herculano pelted down a narrow, cobbled street dragging Almira with him. He made sure that the man couldn't break free of his tight grip. He had to get him to the prince, but Almira was sure to have other ideas.

'Where are you taking me?' Almira gasped, as he struggled to keep up.

'Away from the priest. He saw us, he'll be coming after us.'

'Surely it would be better to split up,' Almira said, and tried to pull free.

'Then where would you go, huh?' Herculano said, each word forced out of him as his feet slammed into the cobbles. 'Back to the brothel where you were snatched?'

Herculano was pretty sure that somebody like Almira had precious few options. His silence seemed to confirm that.

'Still... where are we going?'

'To Sintra, to see the prince.'

Herculano skidded around a tight corner, crashed into the wall opposite, bounced off it and kept going, grimly pleased that his grip on Almira hadn't loosened one iota.

'The prince? Are you a madman? Why would you take me to the prince? Who are you?' Almira said, and increased his struggles to break free.

'Enough questions!' Herculano came to an abrupt halt and pulled Almira up close so he could see his eyes. 'You're involved in something much bigger than you realise. You would never have left that prison alive if it wasn't for me. Now it's time to play your part. After that, you can return to your old life if that is what you want.'

'For the love of God, what is going on?' Almira panted.

'No time to explain,' Herculano said, as he picked up the sharp sound of hoofs clattering down the cobbled street and set off again at full tilt.

Thank goodness he'd left his horse outside the palace, ready to be used again in a hurry. He'd also paid the palace guard handsomely to make sure the horse was still waiting for him when he got back. Even so, he was relieved to see the animal tied to the railings when they arrived.

'Thanks,' Herculano shouted, as he tossed a coin to the guard. 'There's a priest coming after us. If you can slow him down, I'll give you a bonus.'

'Gladly,' the guard said, with a broad grin.

Herculano threw Almira over the horse's neck like a sack of grain and leaped up after him, unhitching the rein and kicking the horse into motion.

'What are you doing?' Almira gasped, flailing about and trying to turn around.

'Stay still will you,' Herculano said, and urged the horse into a trot.

Unlike the pursuing priest, he had no intention of wearing his horse out, nor of injuring it with a slip on the cobbled streets. It didn't help that the horse was also having to carry the weight of two men.

'I can hardly breathe,' Almira said. His words were bumped out of him with the movement of the horse.

'It will be uncomfortable for a while. Once we're further away, I'll stop so you can get into a better position. We don't have time now.'

They had just turned off the road that led to the palace side door when Herculano heard the pursuing horse come to a halt and a loud argument start up. It seemed the guard was determined to earn his bonus, but it was unlikely to delay the priest for long. Herculano urged his horse into a faster trot, aware that the sharp clack of its hooves was easy to follow in the much quieter nighttime streets.

He was relieved when the cobbles ended and they were on the dry earth tracks out of the city. The grand buildings around the palace had gradually turned into the warehouses of the docks and then the greater shanty town that ringed the city where the makeshift houses of the poor and the dispossessed created a warren that was dangerous to venture into after dark.

That thinned out after a while and Herculano realised they were passing the Belém Tower. A permanent contingent of soldiers was based there, guarding the river entrance into Lisbon. They ensured no seaborne invasion would get through to the capital.

Herculano contemplated stopping there to ask for help, or at least an extra horse. But dressed as he and Almira were, he was more likely to be arrested and executed as a horse thief. He also had no idea whether the soldiers were more loyal to the duque or the prince, so it was best to keep going.

'Can I please sit up now?' Almira said, faintly.

'Alright,' Herculano said, and pulled the horse to a halt.

It would probably be better for the animal too, since Almira had been rocking about, making things difficult.

'Help, help!' Almira screamed the moment he slid off the horse, and took off, running towards the Belém Tower.

'Damn it,' Herculano said, as he dashed after him.

He reached forward at full stretch, got a handful of Almira's long blond hair, yanked him back and delivered a powerful slap to the hysterically sobbing man.

'I am your best bet for staying alive, you fool.'

'But I don't know what you want me for,' Almira cried, and fell to his knees. 'Please. I'll do anything you want. Just let me go.'

'The prince will want to know why you were taken by somebody working for the duque,' Herculano said, aware that it was a poor explanation.

'The duque? But I don't know any duques. Which duque?' Almira said, vaguely.

'Which duque do you think?' Herculano said, as he dragged Almira, still on his knees, back to the horse.

'For the love of God, no!' Almira gasped, as he realised what he'd got into. 'I know nothing, I swear.'

'You know Lord Paiva, don't you?' Herculano said, as he hoisted Almira onto his feet and pushed him back to the horse. 'And you are being used against him. That is what the prince needs to hear from you. Although, at this point, he would be better off if he could work out who was behind the death of Tiago Andrade.'

'Well, I don't know any Tiago Andrade.'

Herculano took it as tacit acknowledgement that Almira did know Lord Paiva and hoisted Almira up so he could mount the horse.

'He died on the same night as they kidnapped you, at my warehouse.'

'Oh!' Almira said. 'That man.'

'What?'

Herculano stopped mid-hoist.

'It was during the storm. I was being dragged out of my window, screaming for help. But nobody could hear me over the thunder and the lightning. Then, all of a sudden, this young lord comes running up, sword at the ready, to attack the priest.'

'The priest who was holding you hostage?' Herculano said, just to be sure.

'They had quite the fight. I thought I was rescued because the man was so young and strong. But the priest is fast like a snake and he stabbed the man. It took us both by surprise, I can tell you.'

'Holy Mary, Mother of God!' Herculano breathed, and then realised he could hear the sound of a horse coming down the road. 'Come on, we've got to get out of here. That priest will do whatever it takes to make sure you never tell this tale.'

His words finally convinced Almira, who swung up onto the front of the horse and said, 'Come on then, we have to get away.'

Herculano muttered a couple of profanities as he swung himself back into the saddle behind Almira and urged the horse into a trot. It wasn't keen, especially now when it was so late and it was probably dreaming of a nice warm stable and plenty of feed. Still, after a bit of forceful urging, it set off back into the night.

Herculano knew how it felt, but Almira's news had given him the jolt he needed to keep going. He'd had no idea how important Almira was, but his information could finish the duque. The only thing they still needed was a link between the priest and the duque.

Herculano didn't have time to work out how they got that. For now, he just had to keep Almira out of the priest's grasp. He'd worry about the rest once Almira was safe. He had to suppress a laugh, wondering what Almira would think of his own importance.

A couple of hours later, they were only at the start of the climb into the Sintra hills when the horse dropped out of its trot. Herculano had been aware of its laboured breathing and the sweat on its flanks for a while. But he was equally aware of the shadowy rider trailing after them. If the priest was still using his mule, he'd be slower than them. But there were two of them on the horse and mules had greater stamina.

It looked like he wasn't going to get Almira to Sintra ahead of the priest. Their only option was to fight.

'Almira,' Herculano murmured.

Almira's head jerked up. For the last couple of hours, Almira had looked like he was struggling not to drop off.

'Huh? What?'

'We're going to have to tackle the priest. We can't outrun him.'

'You can't fight him. He may not look like much, but he's deadly.'

'We'll ambush him. As soon as we round this bend, I'm going to pull up.'

Herculano had been thinking about what to do for a while and the curve in the road would not only hide them, but the boulders the road snaked around would give him a high point from which he could drop onto the enemy.

'You're mad,' Almira said, as Herculano hastily explained his plan.

'I'm not asking you to do anything but hide and wait.'

As they rounded the bend, Herculano dismounted and pulled the horse into the bushes.

'Well, I'm not going to fight him at any rate,' Almira said.

'Just promise me you won't run off. The fate of the kingdom is in your hands now.'

'Darling,' Almira said, visibly brightening to hear such a thing, 'where do you think I can go in this wilderness?'

He had a point. Not even a spot of light brightened the dark of the wooded hill.

'I'm trusting you.'

Herculano ducked to prevent being spotted and scaled the pile of boulders that overhung the path. The one thing Herculano had kept when he'd swapped clothes with the beggar was his dagger. It wasn't particularly long, but it was the only weapon he had.

He hoped he'd learned how to use it as effectively as he'd learned to shoot. Beating the prince at that had come as a surprise. He wanted to surprise the priest in the same way.

Herculano didn't have long to wait before the priest came into view. He was riding the same mule he'd used before and was keeping it to a steady trot. His pace suggested that he had no expectation of an ambush.

Keeping low, the dagger gripped in his right hand, Herculano offered up a hasty prayer that this would work. He waited till the priest was abreast of him before he leaped down onto him. They collided with a solid thump that knocked Father Lopez out of his saddle, and the two men landed hard on the ground.

The priest was thinner and more wiry than Herculano had expected, and as fast as Almira had warned. He rolled out from under Herculano and leaped to his feet with a hiss as he pulled a dagger from his robes.

Herculano contemplated telling him to surrender as the two men circled each other, but decided it would be a waste of breath. The priest lunged and Herculano only just managed to sidestep as he, too, lunged. His dagger got caught up in the priest's robes and the man grabbed his wrist with an iron grip and stabbed.

Herculano twisted sideways and kicked as the priest's dagger sliced through his ragged shirt and his skin. His foot connected with the priest's thigh and the man fell back, trying to drag Herculano's dagger out of his hand as he went. But Herculano wasn't about to let go and tried to stab through the enveloping black robe.

This time he hit something solid - the shoulder he suspected - and pushed the dagger as deep as he could. The priest grunted, pulled away and let go of Herculano's wrist as they went back to circling each other. Herculano could feel a trickle of blood slipping down his side from the cut the priest had inflicted.

He couldn't tell how badly the priest was injured because of his dark robes. He also needed to take the man in alive if he was going to get information out of him. But he wasn't sure how to do it.

'Give up, merchant,' Father Lopez hissed.

'You know me?' Herculano said, taken by surprise.

'If you escape now, know that I will hunt you down and kill you, no matter how far you run.'

'I have no intention of running.'

The malice of the man astonished Herculano. He spotted a gap and lunged towards the priest again and the man used his black cape to trap Herculano's dagger as he also lunged forward. Herculano was expecting that this time. He twisted out of the way of the dagger, grabbed on to the enveloping cape, yanked it towards himself and rammed his forehead into the priest's face. The man's dagger scraped his side again as the priest staggered backward, his face flung towards the sky, blood gushing from his nose.

He looked like he might regain his balance when Almira emerged from the shadows with a log. He swung wildly and it connected with the side of the priest's head with a solid thump. Father Lopez crumpled silently to the ground.

'Thank you,' Herculano said, gasping for breath despite the brevity of the battle.

'You're bleeding.'

Herculano glanced down at the two cuts to his side, one had sliced right down to his rib bone, the other was lower down but thankfully shallower.

'I'll live. Now let's get that priest tied up before he can do any more harm.'

18

It felt like somebody had been calling her name for an eternity when Odete realised she was asleep and she had to wake up.

'Lady Odete!' her maid whispered, while shaking her gently by the shoulder.

'What is it?' Odete opened her eyes, her maid's candle providing the only faint light. 'What's wrong? What's happened?'

'There's a beggar at the kitchen door. He paid one of the maids to give you this note.'

'A beggar who can write?'

Odete felt like she hadn't quite left all dreams behind.

'I don't think the note is from the beggar,' her maid whispered, as she pushed a crumpled sheet of paper into Odete's loose grasp. 'But he said it was urgent and really, my lady, it has to be, doesn't it? Otherwise, why would he give the kitchen maid a whole real to deliver this note?'

'A beggar gave money to the maid?'

Odete was certain she was still dreaming now. All the same, there was a letter, and she unfolded it and squinted at a very untidy scrawl that was hard to decipher by the flickering candle flame. There wasn't much to read, but what was written had her wide awake and sitting bolt upright in bed.

'Quick, Maria, fetch me some clothes. Anything dark will do. I must get dressed.'

'At this hour?'

'Of course, girl, what else what else would I do after receiving a note in the middle of the night? What time is it, actually?'

'I think it's nearly three.'

'Then there isn't a moment to lose. But be as quiet as possible. I don't want to wake anybody,' Odete said, as she flung aside her bed covers while keeping a wary eye on the other slumbering ladies-in-waiting.

'Of course.'

Maria scurried over to the wardrobe to find something suitable and returned with a deep olive green riding dress and boots. It was a good choice should Odete need to do any sneaking or running around.

As she dressed, she checked the note again. It was typically brief.

Lady Odete, I need your help. I'll be waiting at the kitchen gate. Yours etc. Herculano.

Considering the turmoil of the last couple of days and the duque's accusation made so boldly before the council that then spread like wildfire through the court, Herculano was right to be sneaking around. She had to tell him everything, for she doubted he'd already heard the news.

She was dressed in record time and only didn't run to the kitchen because of the noise her boots would make on the hard terracotta floors. The best she could do was a sort of tip-toe skitter along the dark corridors. She stopped each time she heard a noise or came near a patrolling servant, and dived for cover.

It was foolish really. She had every right to go to the kitchen at any hour, even as outlandish a time as this. But she didn't want people to know she was up, in case she was asked about it later.

The kitchen was surprisingly busy. The great fires were lit and preparations for breakfast appeared to be in full swing. Everyone was so preoccupied, Odete hoped they didn't notice her as she made a dash for the door that led outside.

It opened out into a courtyard, then a kitchen garden filled with ripening fruit and vegetables, that in turn led to a garden wall and the kitchen gate. A couple of men were ferrying bags of flour into the kitchen, so the door stood open. Odete lurked behind a pyramid of twining green beans till both men were looking the other way before she dashed outside.

It was dark and the narrow cobbled lane appeared to be empty. Odete looked left and right, cursing Herculano for vanishing when a low whistle caught her attention. At the end of the lane, a shadowy figure waved her over.

'Herculano?' Odete whispered.

'Yes,' he said, and stepped out into the faint moonlight.

'Good Lord!' Odete took a hasty step back. 'You reek. And what, in God's name, are you wearing?'

'It's a disguise.'

Herculano was grinning at her as if the whole situation was some great joke.

'A disguise?'

'Perfect for what I needed then, but impossible to gain entry into the palace dressed as I am.'

'It would be best if you don't come to the palace at all.'

'Why? What's happened?' Herculano asked, losing his smile. 'Is the prince...'

'He's fine, for now, but the duque has made an outrageous allegation and if you show up now, you're bound to be arrested.'

'What allegation?' Herculano asked.

'I'll tell you later,' Odete said because it was such a complication she didn't even know where to begin. Best to get everyone to safety first.

'What brought you to Sintra in such haste that you couldn't get out of that... that–'

'Disguise.'

Herculano crooked his finger for Odete to follow him. He walked down the lane, rounded a corner and pointed at a young, fair-haired man sitting on a horse, dressed half in rags and half in ladies' underwear, who gave her a self-conscious wave. Beside him was a mule with what looked like a long black sack slung over the saddle.

'You found the one the lock belonged to?' Odete said.

'I did.' Herculano beamed for all the world like a schoolboy who expected high praise for his efforts. 'And now I need somewhere to hide him and the priest before I speak to the prince. At least, that was my plan.'

'The priest?' Odete said blankly.

Herculano stepped up to the mule and its bundle and pulled what had looked like a part of the sack back to reveal a pale face. A gag was stuffed into his mouth and his nose was squashed and bloody.

'My God!' Odete whispered.

Herculano nodded as he pulled the hood back over the priest's head.

'Can you help?'

Odete started shaking her head, her mind a blank, then it came to her.

'My home!'

'Your what?'

'My family's house. You can hide the animals in the stable, and the people too, I suppose. And you'll be able to get clean and properly dressed at the same time.'

'I knew I could count on you, Lady Odete!' Herculano said.

Now it was Odete's moment to feel like a proud student.

'Follow me. It isn't far.'

The little party crossed the quiet, moonlit square and headed for a narrow cobbled lane that led uphill. Herculano walked just behind Odete, leading his two laden animals. Odete couldn't stop herself from continuously glancing back. First she always checked on Herculano. Next was the peculiar blond being, a man but with traces of women's makeup. Last was the motionless body of the priest.

It terrified her that Herculano had kidnapped a priest. But it was a reflection of how much she had grown to trust this man that she automatically assumed he had done what he had to do. Then she realised it was because she had all but accepted that he was the prince whom she had adored. Why he was disguised in this merchant's body she didn't know yet, but she was determined to find that out. But, if it was true, at least she no longer had to feel guilty about switching allegiances. What she had seen and fallen in love with in the prince, was exactly the same as what she'd warmed to in Herculano.

After about two hundred yards, Odete turned left into a canyon-like road with moss- and fern-encrusted walls rearing up on either side. They were the substantial walls that surrounded the palacetes of Sintra. She prayed they didn't meet anyone here because there was nowhere to hide.

Finally, after they'd walked for about half an hour, Odete came to a stop at a rusting wrought-iron gate draped with trailing plants. She reached up amongst the ivy and found a stirrup-shaped bell pull which she gave a good heave. She had to use all her strength because the rope that linked the bells to the chain was ancient and slack.

She heard the bell's faint clink coming from the kitchen where, unlike at the palace, she was certain the few remaining staff were still fast asleep. They wouldn't be for long because the bell had woken the household dogs who let out a warbling hunting bay. It still felt like an eternity before a flickering light appeared, followed by the kitchen door opening with an over-loud and eerie creak.

'Who is it?' a shaky, ancient voice called across the courtyard.

'Manuel, is that you?' Odete said, trying to keep her voice low to attract the least attention.

It didn't work. The dogs charged out of the kitchen, nearly knocking Manuel over, and washed up against the gate, yipping excitedly. Odete gave Herculano an apologetic grimace because her family's dogs had set the whole neighbourhood off and now there was a caterwaul of answering barks from the surrounding properties.

At least it had the virtue of getting Manuel to hurry to the gate. It also woke Pedro, who emerged from the stables, shouting at the dogs to be quiet.

'This is not as discreet as I was hoping,' Odete said.

Herculano nodded as he looked up and down the street.

'Let's hope most of the householders are merely cursing us for being inconsiderate, rather than suspecting an invasion of burglars.'

'Lady Odete?' Manuel said, as he held a lantern near her face.

'Yes, it's me, and a friend. Please hurry and let us in. He's had a long journey and could use a rest.'

'This is highly irregular.'

'I will explain everything once we're inside.'

To Odete's astonishment, Manuel actually looked like he might not open the gates. But finally, he reached into the pocket of his long-tailed black coat and pulled out a keyring stuffed with keys. While he flicked slowly through them, Pedro got the dogs under control.

'It's good to see you again, ma'am,' he said, hanging on to one particularly determined dog's collar.

'Don't go anywhere,' Odete said. 'As you can see, my friend has a couple of animals that will need to be looked after.'

'I'm not sure his lordship will be happy about that.'

'My brother is home?'

'He came when the royal household went to the palace,' Manuel said, as he fitted a chunky iron key into the gate's lock and twisted it with all his might.

'Of course, I should have realised he'd be home.'

'So the stable currently has his horse and the horse your mother uses for her carriage,' Pedro said.

'Well, it will have to fit another two,' Odete said, as she walked into the courtyard that was cobbled in large black stones.

Herculano followed her, leading his two animals and their loads. The family retainers examined the blond man in open astonishment.

'Beggars!' Manuel said. 'This I can't allow.'

'Since when do beggars have horses?' Odete said.

'And money,' Herculano said, and held his hand out, palm upward, to reveal a pile of golden reals. 'I will pay handsomely for your trouble, especially if you can provide my travelling companion and me with a bath and a change of clothes.'

'Ridiculous,' Manuel muttered.

Ancient family retainers could be so recalcitrant, Odete decided, especially if they viewed you in a paternalistic light. Fortunately, Pedro was swayed by the money and swept the offered coins out of Herculano's hand.

'Follow me.'

'Bring some clothes, a bathtub and some hot water to the stable,' Odete said, fixing Manuel with her most imperious glare. 'And some food and drink. They're probably in need of that, too.'

Then she hurried after Herculano. At least they'd crossed the first hurdle and were safely inside.

Pedro led them through a pair of arched double doors into a modest stable, now full of whining, curious dogs who wasted no time in giving the new arrivals a thorough sniffing. The two stalls were already occupied, one by a flashy black horse and the other by her mother's old grey. A modest coach was pulled up in the remaining gap. Straw covered the floor and a blanket was laid over a slightly deeper pile in one corner where, Odete assumed, Pedro slept.

Pedro lit the lanterns at the entrance and then turned to survey his suddenly very full stables.

'I'll help you unload,' he said, and made for the mule.

'That's alright,' Herculano said. 'I'll do that. But I'd appreciate if you could hurry the butler along with the bath.'

Pedro looked disconcerted and Odete realised why.

'Tell him I've given you permission to go into the house, or at least the kitchen.'

'Very good, m'lady,' Pedro said, and hurried off.

'Thank you,' Herculano said. 'It's best your family and servants don't find out about the priest.'

Odete nodded and said, 'You can hide him in the secret passage.'

'You have a secret passage? Really?'

'It's part of a network of passages and, rather conveniently, one of them opens out into our stable,' Odete said, and pointed at the back of the stables which were simply carved from the face of the mountain. There was a pile of tack, a few boxes and crates of feed, and a couple of shovels and brushes, all stacked against an almost hidden grey wooden door.

'Through there?'

'Yes.'

'Well, let's get the priest stashed while your stable lad is away.'

'Wouldn't it be better to wait a while? Pedro won't have forgotten so soon that you arrived with a load on the mule.'

'Hopefully he was more distracted by me,' Almira said, as he finally dismounted.

'Are you a pro... do you know the Contessa?' Odete asked, as she started putting pieces together.

'I was kidnapped from her house,' Almira said, glancing across at the black bundle.

'Ah, I see,' Odete said, as yet another piece fell into place. 'You have been busy, Herculano.'

'You have no idea. Almira, help me move all of this stuff.'

Odete had to acknowledge that it was true. Now that they had more light, she could see a pair of shoes sticking out at one end.

'What did you do to him?'

'We fought. I stabbed his shoulder and Almira bashed his head with a log. I have to admit, I'm worried that he hasn't regained consciousness yet.'

'Yes,' Odete said, and ran over to help the men clear the doorway.

Thankfully, the key was in the lock. It was rusted and resistant to turning, but Herculano gave it a solid thump with the side of his hand and then forced the key to turn until it gave a grinding clunk.

Herculano hurried back to the mule, pulled the priest's body over his shoulder and laid him down on the cool, damp floor of the tunnel. It went on for miles, Odete knew, but now, by the light of the stable lantern, she could barely see a couple of feet into its pitch-black depths.

Herculano lifted the priest's hood again and examined his face more closely.

'Well, at least he's still breathing. It would be damned inconvenient if he were to die.'

'You'd best wrap him in this horse blanket so he doesn't succumb to the cold. These passageways are surprisingly cool, even in midsummer,' Odete said, as she brought over a blanket that smelled strongly of horses.

'He doesn't deserve to be wrapped up,' Almira said, and spat on the unconscious man.

'Pedro's on his way back,' Odete hissed, as she caught the sound of voices and the bang of a metal bath bumping along the ground.

The trio hastily closed the door and pushed back everything that had been in front of it, just before Pedro arrived, trailing a couple of maids laden with piles of clothes, towels and soap.

'You'd best keep this,' Herculano said, slipping the passageway key into Odete's hand.

'No, you keep it,' Odete said, giving it back.

It was then, by the light of the lamps and a brightening dawn, that Odete realised Herculano looked rather pale. Worse was that his tattered white shirt had a rather gruesome bloodstain down one side.

'Were you injured?'

'It's nothing but a scratch,' Herculano said. 'I'll be fine.'

'Nonsense. I'll fetch some bandages and a healing salve. At the very least, it should be cleaned and bandaged.' Odete hurried to the kitchen, adding, 'Pedro, you set up the bath and tell the kitchen to be quick with the hot water!'

Herculano was exhausted and aching more than he was willing to admit to Odete, so it came as a relief to just lie in a warm bath for a while. Sadly, it wasn't long enough. He had to share the water with Almira and it would be unfair to force the man into cold water.

He heaved himself out of the bath and put on the smalls, stockings and breeches the ancient butler had grudgingly handed over. They had the virtue of all being black. But they were also too short, too wide about the waist, and hideously out of fashion.

Herculano suspected they were what remained of Odete's father's wardrobe after his sons had helped themselves to everything that was still wearable. All the same, he had little choice. It was far better than the beggar's rags at any rate. Those were now being torn apart by a pair of dogs who each had an end in their mouths and were growling and twisting as they tried to pull the other piece away from their fellow, while all around, other dogs bounced about and barked their approval.

'Are you ready?' Odete asked, her back turned towards him despite the screen they'd placed around the bath.

Herculano hesitated to step into view because he was embarrassed about appearing before Odete bare-chested. That had been on her order though. She was determined to treat his wounds.

He'd worried about the cuts himself while he'd been riding. The oozing blood had dripped down his side and onto his breeches. But by the time he got into the bath, the bleeding had stopped and a closer inspection confirmed that they weren't serious.

'I'm fine.'

'You still need to be treated.'

'You'd best do as she orders,' Almira said with a grin, as he hurried to the bath, stripping out of his clothes as he went.

Herculano saw a white bottom for a second before Almira plunged himself into the now-lukewarm, scummy water. Then Herculano steeled himself and stepped out into full view of Odete.

'Come to the door. I need proper light to see the injury.'

'Is that wise?'

It was morning now, and in the dawn light Herculano could see a moderate courtyard and a heavily ornamented palacete that was a confection of towers, balustrades, columns and balconies. At one time it had been painted sky blue but that was now faded and half obscured with vines.

'I'm afraid there is no hope at all of keeping your presence here a secret,' Odete said, as her fingers brushed gently over the edges of Herculano's wounds. 'The servants will talk and my mother will hear about it.'

'So we are hardly hiding.'

'Oh yes, you are. My mother is so ashamed of her impoverished state that she rarely leaves her house and the servants are forbidden from talking about what happens at home. So you are safe from the outside world, at least.'

'Well that is something. What about you? Will they miss you at the palace?'

'I left a note with my maid to give to Lady Mafalda. So I won't be expected back immediately.'

'Alright.' Herculano held his arms out away from his side so that Odete could wrap a bandage around his chest, now that she'd finished slathering on the salve. 'You'd best also tell me what happened lately that makes it dangerous for me to go to the palace.'

'Oh yes.'

It surprised Herculano that Odete looked around, apparently checking where everyone was. Since Almira was still in the bath and Pedro was occupied with brushing down the mule, they had some temporary privacy.

'Well...' Odete took a deep breath, then, like somebody plunging into cold water, she said hurriedly, 'the duque has made a very strange accusation that you and the prince have swapped bodies and that you are the prince, and the man currently on the throne is an imposter.'

'What!?'

Herculano was stunned into a moment of imbecility, blinking at Odete. That his secret had been guessed at was horrifying. To be confronted with this fact by Odete was worse.

His first instinct was to deny everything and laugh it off as ridiculous. He'd long since decided there was no point in revealing anything, since the past couldn't be changed. To suddenly be confronted by some approximation of the truth, left him reeling.

At times, though, he'd wanted to tell Lady Odete, because his feelings for her had strengthened and he didn't want to lie to her about anything, especially who he was.

'Is it true?' Odete asked, watching his face closely.

'It's preposterous.'

'Is it? I mean, we've all seen a change in the prince. And you... you seem so familiar, even though we've only known each other for a few days.'

'You didn't behave as though I was familiar when we first met.'

'No, but ever since then, and especially after the duque made his suspicions known, I've been thinking about how much you are like the prince. Or at least, like the old prince.'

Herculano shook his head and stepped back away from Odete and her probing.

'Please…' Odete said. 'I need to know, especially as the duque has sent for Dr Zuniga so that he may do some magic to divine the truth.'

That news, if anything, came as more of a shock. Things were going from bad to worse.

'The duque is mistaken,' Herculano said, frantically searching for the right words that would gain Odete's understanding and forgiveness. 'The swap that happened lately was to set everything to rights. The prince was returned to his rightful body and I to mine.'

'For the love of God, you're admitting it?' Odete gasped. 'But I don't understand.'

'Why would I hang around pretending to be a merchant if I was the prince? That's nonsensical.'

'You'd hang around so that you could get your body back,' Odete hissed, aware that both Pedro and Almira, who was now out of the bath, had cocked their heads to listen.

Herculano shook his head and went back to the screen to fetch the shirt and coat draped over it. He shrugged himself into the jacket that turned out to be too tight about the shoulders. Even the dogs had picked up on the tense atmosphere and sat, heads cocked.

Herculano took his time tucking in the shirt and doing up the jacket buttons before he returned to Odete, took a tight grip of her wrist and pulled her away from the stable and to a quiet part of the yard.

'I suppose I may as well explain everything. Otherwise you're just going to come up with more and more outlandish theories.'

And so he told Odete, as succinctly as he could, everything that he knew of the body swap.

'So you were just boys when this all happened?' Odete said, once Herculano had finished.

'And both victims of the earthquake.'

'But you can't remember anything?'

'Not a thing.'

'And the prince remembers everything you did growing up, but nothing of the life he lived?'

'That's about the sum of it,' Herculano said, and paused as the ancient Manuel emerged from the side door of the kitchen and headed towards them.

'Lady Odete,' Manuel said in the tone of a disapproving schoolmaster, 'your mother and his lordship would like to see you. They are in the drawing room.'

'This early?'

'The house is in an uproar, given the goings on,' Manuel said, with a disapproving look aimed at Herculano.

'Oh dear, well then, I'd better speak to them.'

'I'll go with you,' Herculano said, because he didn't want to let Odete out of his sight and not only because he was afraid of what she thought of him now.

'That may not be the best idea,' Odete said, looking him over dubiously.

'Maybe not, but I'm going anyway.'

Herculano was pleased that Odete just gave an exasperated sigh and headed towards the house. Manuel looked like he might try to object, but Herculano gave him a supercilious raised eyebrow that was sufficiently intimidating to make the old man back down. Herculano hurried across the courtyard to get ahead of Lady Odete so that he could open the doors for her as she stomped through the house.

'Lady Odete and His Excellency...' Manuel said and fizzled out.

'Herculano Escovar,' Herculano said, and gave the two people in the room a smart bow.

'Mama,' Odete said, as she curtsied and offered her mother an apologetic smile.

'Odete,' Lady Salema said in a thin, tired voice without rising from the chaise she was sprawled along. 'What outlandish scrape have you landed yourself in now?'

'I beg your pardon?'

'You know exactly what she means,' the young Lord Salema snapped as he stopped his pacing across a threadbare Arraiolos rug. 'You are forever getting into trouble.'

Herculano guessed he was being ignored because the mother and brother were fixated on telling off the youngest daughter of the house. Probably also because he looked to be down on his luck and forced to wear the borrowed clothes of their deceased family member.

'When have I ever got into trouble?' Odete gasped. 'You've scarcely seen me for the last three years and I've behaved without fault in the royal household. As you should know, Henrique.'

Herculano watched the young man. He was dark like his sister, with the same deep brown eyes, but while Odete had a determined, intelligent face, her brother tended towards the peevish. He was well dressed, in a neat brown suit with a modestly embroidered jacket. Everything about him proclaimed the civil servant, but he made Herculano wish he'd asked more about Odete's family before.

'What exactly is going on? Why have you let this... this...'

Words apparently failed Lady Salema as she waved her folded fan in Herculano's direction.

'Herculano Escovar,' Herculano said, giving her ladyship a bow and what he hoped was a winning smile. 'The prince introduced me to Lady Odete. Since then, we have grown closer. I deeply regret arriving at your home in such an outlandish fashion, but I am glad that I have had a chance to meet you.'

'You are?'

'I have some business that needs to be resolved, but as soon as I have dealt with it, I would be grateful if you will allow me to return. I have something I wish to discuss with you.'

'Now look here,' Lord Salema snapped. 'That sounds very much like you wish to make an offer for my sister, and that I won't allow.'

'Won't you?' Herculano rounded on the brother with one eyebrow arched. He was a taller, more powerfully built man and he used that to intimidate. 'I am sorry to hear that. In the meantime, Lady Odete and I need to return to the palace. We have urgent business with the prince.'

With that, Herculano took Odete firmly by the hand and pulled her out of the room. She looked so stunned that for once she was incapable of speech, which was just as well. Herculano was far too aware of the massive gamble he'd just taken and expected a telling off.

'What are you doing?' Odete said as soon as she'd gathered her wits sufficiently to pull her hand out of Herculano's powerful grip.

'I'm sorry,' Herculano said, giving her a rueful smile as he followed after her. 'I imagine that was a bit sudden.'

'A bit sudden?' Odete was getting angrier by the minute and so incensed that she ignored Manuel and the two maids who emerged to see what was going on. 'What is this talk of marriage?'

'Wouldn't you like it?' Herculano said as they stepped out of the house into the dazzling early morning sunshine.

'Have you completely lost your mind?'

'Not at all.' Herculano made a vain attempt to catch both of Odete's hands as he turned to face her. 'I know that wasn't the best way to tell you how I feel, but now that I have–'

'How you feel? You are possibly an imposter and at the very least in such grave danger that it may end your life. You turned up dressed like a tramp and,' Odete said, lowering her voice to a hiss that only Herculano could hear, 'with hostages. And you think now, now is an appropriate time to propose?'

'I didn't actually propose.'

'You didn't... Well!' Odete gasped, stunned by his brazen attitude.

'We need to find a way to speak to the prince. I think the best way is for you to tell him where I am.'

Odete wanted to slap Herculano for changing the subject, but her sensible side came to her rescue. Whatever she had to say to him, and it was a lot, would have to wait. As she'd already pointed out, his life was in danger. They had to resolve that before she could have it out with him over his inappropriate non-proposal.

It was with that thought uppermost in her mind that Odete hurried back to the palace accompanied, upon Herculano's insistence, by one of her mother's maids. Apparently, he wasn't going to allow her to wander around the village like a wanton woman. His parting words.

Under other circumstances, Odete might have been pleased that he was behaving in such a proprietary manner. But everything she'd learned about Herculano and the prince was too sudden and at such a bad time that it exasperated her and left no space to consider her own feelings beyond worrying about the danger they were all in.

Odete dismissed the maid at the palace door and hurried to the ladies-in-waiting's apartment.

She was ten paces from the door when a cool voice said from behind, 'Now what have you been up to, Lady Odete?'

Odete's breath caught in her chest. She knew that voice. She swung around to find herself not only facing the duque, but also a handful of soldiers.

'Your Grace,' Odete managed to say, although she didn't know how, for she was terrified and rooted to the spot.

'It appears you have been busy,' the duque said, coming closer.

Odete found her gaze fixed on the metallic sheen of his coppery satin jacket and its fern-like embroidery.

'I couldn't sleep so I went for a walk.'

Odete raised her voice. Her only hope was if other people heard her and came to investigate. Although it was so early most people were probably still in bed.

'You went for a walk?' The duque leaned down so close that she could see the powder he'd dusted over his freshly shaved face. 'On your own? To your mother's house?'

How on earth did he know that? Odete wondered and then realised she'd been followed.

'I haven't seen my mother in a while.'

'So you thought you'd head out to visit before the sun was even up and take along a couple of... I hesitate to call them gentlemen, callers,' the duque said, and his lips curled into a sardonic smile that terrified Odete.

'I don't know what you're talking about.'

Odete went back to speaking as loudly as she could while the soldiers that had accompanied the duque closed in around her so that she couldn't run even if she'd wanted to.

'I assume one of those gentlemen was the merchant Herculano Escovar, but I am very curious to know who the other one was.'

Odete realised that there was no point in pretending that she'd gone home alone. The duque was clearly fully informed about whom she'd met. She was only relieved that they didn't also know about the priest.

'I have nothing to say.'

'We'll see about that. Take her,' the duque said with a flick of his head as he turned to leave.

The soldiers moved in and Odete shouted, 'No, you can't do this!'

'My dear, I can do exactly as I please,' the duque said, rounding on her. 'You are a traitor to the court and I am doubly disappointed in you for betraying my daughter.'

'I did no such thing!'

'Lock her up,' the duque said to the captain of the guard.

'Leave her alone,' a quiet voice said.

Everyone swung around to find the prince newly emerged from his room, looking particularly regal in a marine blue suit.

'This woman has attempted to hide the man you swapped bodies with,' the duque snapped. 'He must be brought before the court so that we can get to the bottom of what is going on. As you are most likely not even the prince, your word carries no weight here.'

'I am the prince and until Dr Zuniga arrives to carry out his test, you will treat me with the respect due to me. You will also release Lady Odete, for she has done nothing wrong.'

'Papa?' Mafalda said.

Odete had never been happier to hear her voice and she strained against the hold of the guard and craned her neck to catch a glimpse of her. Mafalda, Pia and Maria da Luz were all clustered about the door, still in their nightclothes and swathed in frilly dressing gowns.

'Mafalda, this is no concern of yours,' the duque said.

'On the contrary,' Juliano said, as he strolled over to the ladies' door. 'This has a lot to do with her and, if I am not mistaken, also to do with Tiago Andrade.'

That was a good strategy, Odete thought, because if there was one thing that might turn Mafalda against her father, it was the urgent need to know what had happened to her lover.

The duque, however, was not one to give up easily.

'Lady Odete knows nothing about that. I will interrogate her to find out what she does know.'

'There is no reason whatsoever to interrogate a lady-in-waiting,' Juliano said. 'You would do better to hand her into the care of the other ladies. If you must bully somebody, speak to me.'

By now, more members of the royal court had emerged from their bedchambers and the hall was becoming over-full of nightdress-clad spectators. The duque was not one to back down, but apparently he decided against providing a scene for a very eager bunch of onlookers.

'Release Lady Odete, but place a guard at this door. She is not to be allowed out.'

The guard who had a tight and painful grip on Odete shoved her towards the waiting women, who parted to let Odete in and then hurriedly closed about her. Odete had only a moment to exchange a pleading look with the prince before the door slammed shut. Her greatest fear was that Herculano was betrayed, and the duque had already sent men after him.

19

Herculano kept his eye glued to the gap of the stable door and watched the gate. He was so tense after his night ride, the battle with the priest, and anticipation of what was to come that he didn't feel remotely like sleeping. On top of that, he'd gone and proposed. It was in the vaguest way possible, but it was a proposal nonetheless and he was kicking himself over it.

He'd been shocked to hear Odete's revelation that everyone apparently knew or suspected that he and the prince had swapped bodies. Strangely enough, it had come as a relief that Odete knew the truth, all of it. The rest might think it was the first time, but Odete knew it was the second.

He'd even confessed that he wasn't actually Herculano Escovar and that he'd started life as a pauper. Odete, knowing all of it, and apparently not being upset, had given him the confidence to consider marriage. It hadn't been his intention to say anything until they were out of their current mess, but he'd felt compelled to with Odete's mother.

Hopefully he hadn't entirely put Odete off by doing so. He had to admit, the one advantage of no longer being the prince was that he could propose to whomever he liked. Less advantageous was that the lady herself and her family were entirely able to turn him down.

'Must I wear this dreadful suit?' Almira said in a petulant voice.

Herculano turned to examine the man who looked ridiculous, swamped in an over-large, old-fashioned brown suit with saggy white stockings.

'Dressing like a man might be the best disguise possible for you. Has anyone seen you dressed in any way other than a woman?'

'Not since I was a boy,' Almira said, flicking his long blond locks back from his face.

'There you are then, and for God's sake, tie your hair back and keep your hat on. The less people see of your face, the better. Unless you want to be caught by the duque and tortured to death.'

Almira shuddered and hastily tied his hair into a ponytail with the black ribbon he'd been given, then rammed a floppy wide-brimmed brown hat over the lot.

'Happy?'

'You should probably avoid speaking too. You sound like a woman,' Herculano said, and thought that his effeminate features, now more visible after his shave, were also a problem. 'Do you have a male name?'

'Even if I did, I wouldn't tell you what it was.'

'I need something I can use. Almira is a bit obvious.'

'Am I really in so much danger?'

'Getting kidnapped by a priest wasn't enough for you?'

Herculano went back to watching the gate and also looking out for Pedro, who'd promised to return with wine. Herculano hoped the family and the servants weren't planning on handing him and Almira over. He was fairly confident none of the household had realised the package the mule had been carrying was missing.

A hint of motion caught his eye, then he spotted an arm on the other side of the gate, followed by a helmeted face peering cautiously through the ivy into the yard. It was hastily withdrawn.

'Merde!' Herculano swore and ran for Almira, grabbed him by the arm and pulled him to the back wall and the not-so-secret door. 'Soldiers, they've found us.'

'What?' Almira gasped. 'Lady Odete betrayed us?'

'Not her.' Herculano pushed all the tack and detritus away from the wall as he fished in his pocket for the key. 'Grab that lamp. We're going to need it.'

It was a good thing Odete had given him the key, after all. In the distance, Herculano heard the creak of the gates being opened. He unlocked the door to the secret passage, pulled Almira inside, who nearly dropped the lantern in the process, and shut the door as quietly as possible. He closed and locked the door, but left the key where it was, blocking the lock.

They stood in the tiny pool of light provided by the lantern and looked around. It was cool and the air was so moist Herculano could feel it on his tongue.

'What do we do with him?' Almira hissed and poked at the wrapped form of the priest.

'We take him with us.'

'Where?' Almira said, waving his hand into the darkness of the tunnels.

'I have no idea,' Herculano muttered as he hoisted the priest onto his shoulders.

The man weighed a ton and was so floppy that Herculano decided he must still be unconscious. If that was the case, the blow to his head was serious and might just carry him off. If it hadn't already.

'Let's go,' Herculano said, giving Almira a shove with his free hand.

'Do you think there are any sudden drops in this place?' Almira asked with a shudder as he set off in a cautious jog.

'Let's hope not.'

Herculano was more worried about the pursuing soldiers. It wouldn't take them long to see that the stables were empty and guess where they'd gone, especially if anyone from the house was with them. Their only hope was if there were multiple paths in this tunnel and they could lose their pursuers in the maze.

'Which way?' Almira said as he came to a stop at a fork in the path.

'Uphill. Let's always head uphill.'

'Isn't that a bit obvious?'

Herculano shrugged, which he realised Almira couldn't see.

'Just do that for now, and hurry,' Herculano said, as the sound of splintering wood came to his ears.

The two men ran up the right-hand path, given fresh energy by the sound of pursuit, and came to a second fork. Almira carried on running, taking the left fork, still heading uphill. Herculano was regretting his instruction. The priest felt heavier with each step they took.

'It's a door,' Almira said, as he came to yet another stop.

'Well, open it.'

Herculano prayed it wasn't locked. Almira tried the door and, with a bit of forcing, it opened with a rusty creak and Herculano hurried through. Despite the noise, he decided it was best to close the door. That way their pursuers wouldn't be able to see the faint light of their lantern.

'Just a minute, do something for me,' Herculano said. 'Check if this priest is still alive. There's no point in carrying him around if he's already dead.'

'Do we have time?'

'I can run faster without him,' Herculano said, catching his breath with this stop. 'But hurry.'

Herculano felt some fumbling behind him and then there was a moment that seemed to go on forever.

'Holy Mary, Mother of God,' Almira muttered and jumped backwards, crossing himself over and over again.

'What?' Herculano asked as he swung round.

'He just opened his eyes and glared at me.'

'Alright then, let's go,' Herculano said, and broke into a trot.

He was relieved the priest was still alive, but also sorry that he'd have to keep carrying him.

'Three possible paths,' Almira said, as they came to a crossroads.

'Uphill.'

Herculano didn't want to come to a stop because he was afraid if he did, he'd not be able to get going again.

'Do you hear that?' Almira whispered, his voice even more tense now.

Herculano did. The soldiers had apparently gone through the same creaking door and, by the sound of the footsteps, there were a lot of them.

'Hurry,' he said, and ran towards the most upward-looking slope before them.

'We should split up,' Almira said, coming up behind him. 'At least that way, one of us has a chance of getting away.'

'You'd like that would you, to just slip away from all of this?'

'And do what?' Almira gasped, the lantern shaking in his hands. 'You were right. I have nowhere to go and if that priest survives, he'll come for me for certain.'

'So what will you do?'

'If I tell the prince that I am Lord Paiva's... friend, will he protect me?'

'He would,' Herculano said, although he wasn't actually sure. When all was said and done, he didn't actually know the prince very well.

'Then I give you my word. I will do everything I can to avoid capture and get to the prince. If you give me your word you will do the same and put in a good word for me when I need it.'

'Alright, you have my word.'

Herculano doubted it would matter if either of them got caught, but if Almira was willing to play fair with him, he would do the same.

'Another door,' Almira said, 'and this side passage.'

'You take the door. I'll take the other path.'

'The lantern?'

'Keep it.' Herculano reached for the wall with his left hand. He could find his way as long as he kept his hand on the wall. 'If you get out of here, find Lord Tiago Andrade. It was his son you saw getting murdered. He's got the greatest interest in keeping the only witness to his son's death alive. He'll get you to the prince.'

'Alright, thank you.' The door creaked open and Almira hurried through it with a muttered, 'Good luck.'

Herculano was plunged into darkness as the door swung shut and set off at a much slower, staggering run. His legs were burning and shaky from his load and he wondered how much further he could carry the priest. He had a bad feeling that he wouldn't be able to keep it up for much longer. That initial spurt of energy from the start of the chase had already fizzled out.

'Here, I'm here!' a croaking voice rasped.

Herculano realised with a shock that it was the priest.

'Shut up!' Herculano hissed and flung the man to the ground.

'Here, you fools, hurry,' he said more strongly.

Herculano scrabbled through the dark, reaching for the wrapped bundle, trying to find the priest's mouth in the dark.

'You're the duque's man, aren't you?' he muttered, as his fingers felt along the coarse robe.

'Even if I was, I'd never tell you,' the priest said as loudly as possible and then went back to shouting for help.

Herculano reached a tapering end only to discover he'd gone the wrong way and his hands were frantically grasping a pair of shoes.

'Did he get you to kidnap the prostitute?' Herculano said, loudly enough to be heard over the man's shouts.

'I would have gone after that scum with or without an order.'

'But I saw you talking to the duque on the road to Sintra, so I already know you work for him,' Herculano said, working his way back up the priest's body.

'Much good it will do you,' the priest said, and Herculano could see his evil grin as the soldiers arrived and their lanterns banished the dark.

The only thing he could do was keep the priest quiet, so they didn't learn about Almira. He had only a moment to box the priest hard on the temple, knocking him out, before the soldiers fell upon him.

20

Odete stood on Mafalda's balcony, watching as a group of men brought in load after load of kindling that was placed beside a stake erected in the centre of the square.

'Is that for Herculano?'

Mafalda shrugged.

'It's for whoever turns out to be the imposter prince and the murderer.'

'Well, it isn't Herculano, as God is my witness.'

'How can you be so sure?'

'Because I have got to know Herculano and I know he isn't the prince,' Odete said, praying with all her might that Herculano wasn't currently being tortured in the dungeons.

She'd been devastated to hear of his capture the previous day and felt like she'd betrayed him. This had led to deeper questions about how she actually felt about him. The non-proposal had been a surprise, but, after she'd given it due consideration, not an unpleasant one. Even with the danger around her, she couldn't help falling deeper in love with a man she'd thought she'd never be able to get close to.

'Do you really know he isn't the prince?' Mafalda said, with a disbelieving attempt at a smile that turned into a sneer. 'Or are you only saying that to protect the man who murdered my Tiago?'

'Herculano didn't do that either, and neither did the prince. My lady, you need to look at the evidence and make up your own mind. Don't let anyone else tell you what to do,' Odete said, turning from the scene below to cast an imploring look at Mafalda.

'By which you mean I shouldn't obey my father.'

'I'm just saying you have a mind of your own. Weigh the evidence for yourself. Don't let anybody else tell you what to think.'

Odete had very little hope of convincing Mafalda. She was hurt and vengeful about losing her first love and she wanted somebody to pay. She didn't really care who that was.

'What evidence, precisely?' Mafalda asked. 'The evidence that Herculano owns the warehouse where they found Tiago's body? Or the evidence of the change in the prince so he scarcely cares that his best friend was murdered?'

'The prince did everything he could to find Tiago, even getting Herculano to help.'

'Which is also strange. Why did he bring in a man nobody has ever met at court?'

'Probably so that he could be impartial.'

Odete thought it best not to say anything about actual body swaps. She was determined to give the appearance of finding that whole story highly improbable.

Mafalda was about to reply, when her maid hurried out onto the balcony and said, 'My lady, Dr Zuniga is here to see you!'

'He's arrived from Lisbon already?' Mafalda said, looking up at the sun to ascertain that it was only late afternoon.

The two ladies exchanged a surprised glance and followed the maid back into the sitting room. Pia and Maria da Luz were balanced on the edge of their seats in awe-filled curiosity, watching their guest. Dr Zuniga was standing with his back to them, gazing out of the window at the view of the square below.

His hands were crossed behind his back, grasping his feathered hat.

Odete suppressed a shudder to see him. He'd always struck her as particularly intimidating. Not in the same way as the duque, who terrified people because of his raw power. Dr Zuniga's power was hard to explain and therefore more unnerving.

'Lady Mafalda,' Dr Zuniga said as he turned to give the ladies a sweeping bow, the feathers of his hat waving as his hand traced a figure eight in the air.

'Dr Zuniga, what brings you to see me? And so soon after your arrival.'

Sometimes Mafalda impressed Odete with her composure. Maybe she thought she was safe from the machinations of others because of her father.

'I came to ask you a question in private, if you please.'

'Just you and me?'

Dr Zuniga's hooded gaze settled on Odete and he said, 'Lady Odete may stay too, if you wish, but the rest must leave.'

The rest were a currently outraged-looking Pia and Maria da Luz, as well as their personal maids and a kitchen maid who'd brought up their afternoon coffee.

'Go,' Mafalda said, waving everyone away.

Odete waited to see whether she was expected to stay or go. Given their current strained relationship, she wasn't sure. Since Mafalda said nothing about her, she decided to stay.

'That's better,' Dr Zuniga said, once the room was emptied and the doors closed upon them.

'So why have you come?' Mafalda said in growing impatience.

'First of all, to offer my condolences. I understand you and young Tiago Andrade were close,' the alchemist said, watching Mafalda's face.

Her edge of anger was replaced with hurt, which she impatiently pushed aside.

'What else?'

'I thought it important to tell you something here, where I won't be interrupted or shouted down. I fear the trial tonight may be a rather boisterous affair.'

'Alright, so get on with it.'

'You need to know that I spent the evening with both the prince and Herculano Escovar on the night Lord Andrade was murdered.'

'So you're saying it couldn't be either of them? But it could have been an assassin sent by one of them.'

'But, I reiterate, it wasn't the two who are to be tried. And by your logic, it could be an assassination ordered by anyone, outside the court, or in.'

Odete held her breath, trying to guess the effect Dr Zuniga's words would have on Mafalda, because he had implied it could also be the duque.

'One also wonders what kind of fool would hide a body on his own property,' Dr Zuniga said. 'Then, when it is found, take the body to a church and notify the man's father. It rather goes against his own interests.'

'Maybe,' Mafalda said, but looked like she wasn't ready to concede.

'No matter. I have said what I came to say. Now I must speak to the duque. He is, after all, the one who summoned me.'

Dr Zuniga stood, gave the ladies a bow and, when he thought Mafalda wasn't looking, gave Odete a meaningful glance. In an instant, she was sure his visit had nothing to do with Mafalda and everything to do with her.

So she sprang to her feet and murmured, 'Let me show you to the door.'

'Thank you,' Dr Zuniga said, and shook her hand as he took his leave.

Odete was astonished to feel a piece of paper being pushed into her hand, and closed it tightly. The alchemist gave her an enigmatic smile and wandered away, looking for all the world like a man out for a pleasant walk.

'Excuse me for a minute,' Odete said, and, since she got no reaction from Mafalda, who was glaring after the retreating alchemist, left the room.

The only place she could think of where she wouldn't be disturbed was the water closet. So she all but ran there, locked the door behind herself, and sat down on the closed toilet lid before she had the courage to open her clenched fist and examine what she'd been handed.

Never in her wildest dreams had she expected to have a secret message slipped to her. To hold a message at a time when the life of the man she loved was at stake, was preposterous. It was so upsetting she was nearly in tears. She shook herself, determined to be brave, and opened the note.

It was, due to the size of the scrap of paper, brief.

Please provide, as a matter of urgency, a small vial of your blood. Deliver it to Arriscado, Herculano Escovar's manservant, before the court meets.

Odete stared blankly at the note, trying to understand it. Why on earth did he need her blood? No, wait, everyone knew why Dr Zuniga had been called. He was due to perform the one royal duty everyone took seriously: the test of royalty.

What did it mean that the alchemist needed her blood, which she knew would turn blue? Her mother was forever going on about her illustrious royal ancestor. So the alchemist needed blood that would turn blue and he already knew it wouldn't with the prince.

Had Herculano lied to her? Was he actually the prince? No, she decided, whatever else happened, she trusted Herculano. For his sake, she would do what she had to do.

So she felt in her skirt pocket for her seashell perfume bottle and flipped open the gold lid. Since she had already applied some perfume today, she feared using even more would be overwhelming. So she poured what remained in the bottle into her handkerchief, folded it tightly and put it back in her pocket.

She couldn't bring herself to pour her expensive perfume down the privy.

Then she reached into her hair and drew out a long pin that was currently holding up her ornate hairdo, augmented by a considerable wig of the same dark brown as her own hair. She hadn't really wanted to dress up for the trial, but the other ladies had insisted. Now she was glad she at least had the pin.

She took a deep breath, steeled herself and plunged the tip of the needle into her thumb. She gave a squeak of pain, then held the bottle up to her thumb, pressing against the flesh and gathered the deep red drops from her throbbing flesh.

Her perfume bottle was half full of blood when it stopped flowing. She hoped it was sufficient. Now her maid would have to get it to Arriscado and Dr Zuniga.

Herculano clanked through the palace, the chains about his ankles making it impossible to stride. Iron manacles also bound his hands before him. As if that were not bad enough, he was still wearing Odete's father's ill-fitting and now torn suit.

His hair was unbrushed and unkempt and, because he'd put up a fight in the tunnel, he was sporting a throbbing bruised cheekbone and a tender bloody lip that filled his mouth with the taste of iron.

That was the least of his worries. They'd kept him away from the prince so that they couldn't confer, and his two witnesses were gone. The priest had probably slipped away under the protection of the duque. Almira, if he'd found a way out of the tunnels, had most likely scampered back to Lisbon. Whatever was about to happen would be the final say on the matter. Dredging up a witness days later would be no help since he was destined for the pyre tonight.

Herculano suppressed a shudder. There was no point worrying about the future. Now he had to keep his wits about him and not go down without a fight.

Still, he slowed as they approached the throne room where the roar of excited onlookers could be heard through the closed doors. The guards flung the doors open as Herculano approached and the hubbub subsided as everyone turned to examine the prisoner.

'Move,' the guard said, and gave Herculano a shove.

Herculano staggered forward into the incredible heat from the press of hundreds of bodies and blazing chandeliers. Herculano's hair prickled to be watched by so many eyes.

They had removed the chairs to make more space for the spectators. Men, for that was all he could see, stood packed so tightly that if one were to faint, the bodies of everyone else would prevent him from falling.

'Bring him here,' the dry, familiar voice of the duque said.

Herculano turned towards the throne. He expected to see the duque sitting there, but it was empty. The man himself was standing to the left of the throne, resplendent in a severe black suit that made him look like a judge. No doubt that was intentional.

Prince Juliano stood to the right of the throne, dressed in a silver satin suit that made him look very regal indeed. Also deliberate. This was their final showdown. Herculano feared the prince would lose and never be able to fight against his uncle again. He regretted he was partially to blame for that.

Then a wave of rage washed over him. If the damned Dr Zuniga hadn't meddled in the first place, they wouldn't be in this predicament now. Then again, if the alchemist hadn't meddled, Herculano would have landed up as a pauper's corpse amongst the ruins of Lisbon. He supposed he should be thankful for the extra years he'd gained, even if he didn't remember them.

Then he spotted a huddle of women, protected from the surging crowd by a ring of guards. They were dressed for all the world as if they were going to a ball. Lady Mafalda, at the head of the group, was resplendent in a frothy blue gown covered in pink roses, but Herculano homed in on Odete who looked pale and frightened. Her hands were clutched to her chest, although she was putting on a brave face. He wished he wasn't causing her this pain.

The sound of a trumpet drew everyone's attention. Dr Zuniga left the group of councillors who were clustered to the left of the duque. He walked up the two shallow steps that led to the dais, stopped and bowed to the prince first and then to the duque.

'Dr Zuniga, you know why you are here,' the duque said in a flat, emotionless voice.

The alchemist gave the duque a cold, knowing smile and a bow.

'You wish for me to perform the ritual of royal blood. It is my duty and I will do what is required of me.'

'As will I,' Juliano said as he stepped up to Dr Zuniga and held out his hand.

A hush of anticipation fell over the crowd as everyone craned their necks and stood on tiptoes to see. The alchemist gave the prince's thumb a jab with a sharp little ceremonial dagger and collected the falling droplets on a matching silver salver.

Herculano held his breath. What would the people do when they saw the prince's strange blue and red marbled blood?

The alchemist did a dramatic chant and twirled his hand over the plate. A cascade of star-like sparks fell from his hands, bounced on the platter and overflowed onto the floor. It took Herculano by surprise as that hadn't happened when the alchemist had tested his blood before.

'Behold, the blue blood of the prince,' Dr Zuniga intoned as he held the plate out for inspection.

Herculano was amazed and relieved and checked the duque's face. He looked unperturbed by the result but turned to the bevy of religious people clustered at the front of the crowd. Cardinal Caio da Gama, Patriarch of Lisbon, resplendent in a voluminous red robe, stepped out of the group of men in black robes.

'This result was to be expected. We all know the prince's body hasn't changed. It is merely his soul that was switched. The blood would therefore remain the same.'

'Indeed,' the duque said. 'But we have more evidence.'

He nodded towards the guards who had a firm grip on Herculano. The trio shuffled forward and forced Herculano onto his knees before the duque.

'This man is the one we believe is now the vessel of the prince, and the prince,' the duque said, giving Juliano a slight nod, 'is actually inhabited by an imposter.'

A shout of dismay and disbelief rose from the watching crowd and Juliano smiled.

'It is a preposterous charge, is it not?'

Herculano was impressed by how calm he appeared. If they had swapped their positions, he'd have been roaring at the crowd not to be idiots. He hoped the observers did not miss his previous fiery temper that he was trying hard to control lest he lead to unnecessary speculation.

'My uncle has worked diligently to get me to crumple before him, accept his direction and become his puppet. You all know how hard I have resisted that.'

'Not you, him,' the duque said, pointing at Herculano. 'What is more, you have gone so far as to frame that man as a murderer of your best friend.'

'Why would I do that?' Juliano snapped, losing his vaguely amused expression.

'Because you wish to snatch the throne.'

Herculano wondered what the duque actually wanted from this meeting. Was he trying to get the prince proclaimed as an imposter and sent to the pyres?

'If you think I am the prince, why am I hauled into the chamber bound in iron like a criminal?' Herculano shouted.

A stunned, 'Ah!' rose from the crowd.

'Are you the prince?' the duque asked, giving him an enigmatic smile.

Herculano glared at him. If he said he was, he'd be saved, but be forever beholden to the duque.

'The very idea is absurd.'

'But I have been told you have lost your memories, so how would you know?' the duque purred.

Herculano's gaze flicked to the prince who looked shaken for a moment before his calm returned.

'This is a pointless debate,' Juliano said. 'We all know the intent is to undermine me so that the duque can strengthen his hold over the kingdom. But I won't allow it. This sideshow is beside the point. I will show you the full depths to which the duque has sunk and then you can all decide whom you are willing to support.'

The prince let his gaze drift slowly over the crowd in the throne room and then he looked towards the doors at the end of the hall. They swung open and the elder Lord Tiago Andrade walked in with a young blonde woman on his arm in an austere black dress. She waved and gave everyone a shaky attempt at a brave smile. With considerable pushing and shoving, the crowd parted to allow the pair to reach the dais.

Herculano realised with a jolt that the woman was Almira. He was surprisingly attractive and doing an excellent job of looking distraught.

'You all know Lord Andrade,' Juliano said. 'My friend, Herculano Escovar, recently released the lady from captivity. She was kidnapped and held as a pawn to be used against one of the duque's own council.'

Herculano was astonished by the gambit and by Almira's disguise, no doubt done to protect the treasurer. Although Lord Paiva clearly didn't know that and had turned as white as parchment.

'This woman?' the duque said, and stalked up to Almira, who took an involuntary step backwards. 'A woman? Really?'

'A witness,' Lord Andrade said. 'My son went to the aid of Miss Almira when she was dragged from her bed in the middle of the night. He was murdered as a result.'

'And so your narrative begins to crumble,' Juliano said to the duque, filling the surprised silence that had fallen over the watching crowd. 'I have a witness proving that I wasn't the murderer and neither was Herculano Escovar.'

'You expect me to accept the word of a floozy that you had nothing to do with the younger Lord Andrade's death?' the duque said, maintaining his composure.

Herculano looked around the room, gauging the reaction of the watchers who had so far switched back and forth in their allegiance like waves on the ocean. He reached the huddle of priests and was struck by the fact that one of the men had a wide-brimmed hat, rather than the four-cornered brimless hat that priests usually wore. His head was bowed so that most of it was in shadow, but his mouth was visible and it held a familiar sneer.

Herculano's guards were distracted by the alluring Almira and the drama between the prince and his uncle, so Herculano shook off his guards with a roar and charged the huddle of religious men. Because of the chains he took minute, girl-like steps, as he barrelled towards the priest.

He thumped into Father Lopez with all his weight and the two of them fell backwards into the crowd. Herculano pulled the man's hat off and threw it away.

'Almira, look,' he bellowed. 'Tell everyone who this is!'

Almira gasped and covered her mouth with her hand.

'It's him!' she said in a tremulous tone. 'That's the man who kidnapped me, killed Lord Andrade and then kept me locked up in a pitch-black prison.'

'Lies!' the priest snarled as he pushed Herculano away and scrambled to his feet.

'This is Father Lopez,' Herculano said, keeping a tight grip on the man's robes so he couldn't escape, and being dragged upright in the process. 'I saw him speaking to the duque when we were on our way to Sintra. I thought that was strange, so I followed him back to Lisbon and to his church. It was there that I found Almira. I can take the council to the prison in which she was being held.'

An astonished gasp filled the hall and Juliano turned to the duque.

'He is your man, and he is accused of killing my friend.'

'I have never met that priest in my life,' the duque hissed.

The priest's face twisted in disgust, but before he could say anything, Herculano pulled them both towards the prince.

'Then how is it that I had this priest as my prisoner when I was captured? And how is it that now he's standing amongst his fellow priests as an innocent while I was thrown into the dungeons?'

Juliano nodded his thanks to Herculano and stepped up close to the duque to whisper, 'It's over, uncle.'

'Never,' the man snarled.

'Accept it,' Juliano said, and turned back to the watching courtiers. 'You all know what an implacable man my uncle is. It can surprise none of you that he has been involved in a scheme to maintain power. Let me explain why he had Almira kidnapped.'

Herculano, still hanging on to the priest, glanced at Lord Paiva again and saw him stepping backwards, trying to hide behind his fellow councillors.

'This woman is the lover of one of the council. She was being used to blackmail him into submission. I have no doubt my uncle has other ways of controlling the rest of the men he assembled to make decisions for the kingdom. He has also used this band of men to keep me from the throne. Well, enough. My uncle's misdeeds have been exposed. It is time for him to step down.'

'I did what I have done for the kingdom and its people,' the duque said, and his voice was vibrant with anger. 'I am the one who rebuilt Lisbon after the earthquake.'

'And we are grateful to you for that. But now it's time to hand the throne over to me.' Juliano leaned so close to the duque that only he and Herculano heard him say, 'Take exile, uncle. It's your only way out. I'll make sure you live comfortably in the Azores. I also promise to look after Mafalda. I'll marry her and keep her safe.'

Herculano was shocked and wanted to tell the prince not to do it. It felt like too much of a capitulation.

'And if I don't?' the duque asked.

'Then Lord Andrade and I will make sure you stand trial for murder.'

The duque glared at Juliano and bit the inside of his cheek before he gave a slight nod.

'Tell them,' Juliano said, looking out at the waiting people.

The duque stiffened and surveyed the room. He had a powerful presence and silence rippled outwards as he examined first one face and then the next.

'The prince and I will resolve this matter in private. I am sure he is right. It is time for him to take the throne.'

A whoosh of surprise was forced out of the watching crowd but the duque didn't wait for the inevitable barrage of questions and recriminations. He gave the prince a stiff bow and swept out of the room.

'Release that man,' Juliano said, pointing at Herculano. 'The only thing he is guilty of is serving me. And put those restraints on the priest.'

'Thank you, Your Highness,' Herculano said, and gave the prince a deep bow as the chains and manacles were unlocked and put on Father Lopez who was dragged away.

'You did well.'

'I would be grateful if I may retire now.'

'Of course, go. I, on the other hand, will have a busy night calming and convincing everyone.'

Herculano suspected Juliano was right. Everyone was debating at full volume about what they were going to do next. Herculano was relieved that it was no longer his concern.

21

H erculano woke in an unfamiliar bed with Arriscado snoring away gently in the chair beside him. At least he recognised the old man, and today he was reassured to see him.

'Wake up, Arriscado,' Herculano said, poking the man's shoulder. 'I see I'm still stuck with you.'

Arriscado gave him a sleepy smile.

'I'm afraid we may be together for a while, sir.'

'Is that so?' Herculano gave a mighty stretch, ignoring the twinge in his sore muscles. 'I hope that isn't because the prince is still in a bind.'

He was worried about what might happen next and prayed that they were indeed out of the woods.

'Actually, I thought you might need my help when you return to your life as a merchant. What with having lost your memory.'

'So things are resolved at the palace, are they?' Herculano said, getting out of bed.

'As much as they can ever be. The duque is currently confined to his quarters, where he will remain until he is safely transported to the Azores.'

'Mmm,' Herculano murmured, rubbing the rough stubble on his chin. 'So the prince did it. I battled against the duque for years without getting anywhere and Juliano wrapped everything up in ten days. It appears he is indeed better suited to the role.'

'I would rather say things came to a head,' Arriscado said as he waved a hovering manservant away. 'Tiago Andrade went out on your orders and his murder provided the wedge with which to oust the duque.'

'I'm sorry it turned out that way,' Herculano said, feeling the pain of loss once more, even though he didn't remember his friend. 'What of Lady Mafalda? Is the prince really going to marry her?'

'I believe he will. He appears to have none of the antipathy towards her that you feel.'

'Perhaps because he never actually felt trapped by the situation.'

Herculano paused as the same manservant reappeared carrying an enamelled bathtub and followed by a bevy of maids with steaming buckets of water. He watched with pleasure as they poured out the second bath he was going to have within a week. It felt excessive, but considering the pummelling he'd taken from the guards sent to capture him, and the filth of the dungeon, it was a good idea.

'What of Lady Odete?' Herculano asked, once he was alone with Arriscado again.

'She will remain at the palace. I believe she is Lady Mafalda's most trusted lady-in-waiting.'

'She's the only sensible one,' Herculano said, as he stripped himself out of his nightshirt and slipped into the warm bathwater.

He was suddenly less interested in getting clean and far more anxious to see Lady Odete again. Arriscado must have realised the same because he made quick work of scrubbing his master and washing his hair.

Herculano had only just finished getting dressed when there was a knock at his door. It sounded hesitant and Herculano immediately thought of Odete. He raced Arriscado for the door, got to it first and wrenched it open.

'Oh,' Odete said and took a startled step backwards as the door was yanked open.

'Lady Odete,' Herculano said, grinning at her like a fool. 'I am very happy to see you.'

'Apparently so,' Odete murmured, but looked far less enthusiastic.

'Has something happened?' Herculano asked, ushering her inside and reluctantly admitting her accompanying maid.

Fortunately, Arriscado intercepted the maid and led her to the furthest end of the room. Herculano could at least speak to Odete without being overheard, even if they were being watched.

'Everything's fine,' Odete said as she settled on the sofa Herculano led her to.

He felt quite bold sitting down next to her, while being careful not to sit too close, for propriety's sake.

'I am very relieved to find you looking so well,' Odete continued, although she kept her eyes fixed on her hands folded in her lap.

'And I am relieved that you are also well and still at the palace. But has something happened? You seem distressed.'

'I am ashamed. I was followed by the duque. You must feel severely betrayed by me.'

'I can't say I was surprised. The duque has always been–' Herculano stopped abruptly. He didn't want to talk about such matters. 'Since the situation has been resolved and I understand the prince is now in command of the kingdom, we need not concern ourselves about it anymore.'

'Do you think so?'

'How is Lady Mafalda doing? I suspect she has been making a scene.'

'She's young and has suddenly been tipped into a new world. How would you take it?'

Herculano was pleased to see some of Odete's feistiness return as her eyes flashed in defence of a young woman that she surely found tiresome at times too.

'I'm sure she and Juliano will be fine once they're married.'

Finally, Odete looked up at him, examining his face thoughtfully.

'Which brings me to my next question,' Herculano said, gathering his courage. After all, his non-proposal hadn't gone down so well the first time.

'What is it?' Odete said, with a slightly arched brow, examining Herculano levelly.

'I am but a pauper who has been elevated to the rank of a merchant. I know that is probably unacceptable to your family.'

'Quite unacceptable. I'll have you know, we have royalty amongst our ancestors.'

'You do?' Herculano said, thrown by the response. He'd hoped Odete, at least, wouldn't be put off by his lack of status.

'Blue blood,' Odete said, holding up her thumb to reveal a red spot with a slight bruise.

'Good Lord! It was your blood?'

'What was wrong with the prince's?' Odete asked, double checking that they were out of earshot of the maid.

'Mine and his appear to be inextricably mingled. His blood has a marbled blue and red effect that would have been impossible to explain under last night's dangerous circumstances.'

'I see.'

Odete smiled happily at Herculano, apparently pleased to have that final mystery resolved. Her smile reassured Herculano.

'So, what of your family?'

'As for my family, as long as you dress in an excessively expensive suit and tell my mother that you are the wealthiest merchant in Lisbon, I suspect she will be willing to overlook everything else.'

Herculano took her hands in his with a delighted laugh and said, 'So you will marry me?'

'Prince or pauper, you are the man I will wed,' Odete said, smiling up at him.

Enjoyed this book? You can make a huge difference

If you are like me, you use reviews to decide whether you want to buy a book. So if you enjoyed the book please take a moment to let people know why. The review can be as short as you like.

Thank you very much!

Also By

MEDIEVAL HISTORICAL FICTION available ePub, paperback and hardback

Fraternity of Brothers, *Life of Galen, Book 1* – Cast out for a crime committed against him, his future looks bleak. Until an unexpected visitor gives him hope for justice. A fight for acceptance, absolution and friendship in Anglo-Saxon England.

Comfort of Home, *Life of Galen, Book 2* – Proven innocent, he's returned from exile. Can he recover all that he lost? A tale of friendship and return to a family he thought he'd lost, set in Anglo-Saxon England.

Kindness of Strangers, *Life of Galen, Book 3* – Trapped in a land plagued by vikings, can one small miracle be all they need to survive? A tale of miracles, betrayal and friendship while under viking siege.

The King's Hall, *Life of Galen, Book 4* – As if being commissioned to create a book to turn back the Apocalypse isn't enough, intrigue and romance threaten to destroy everything he's come to rely upon. Friendship, love and intrigue at the court of King Aethelred the Unready.

Restless Sea, *Life of Galen, Book 5* – Just when they thought they could go home, they're thrust into an adventure at sea. A journey that tests the bonds of friendship.

Friend of My Enemy, *Life of Galen, Book 6* – Captured by an implacable enemy, their future looks bleak. Will escape even be possible?

Road to Rome, *Life of Galen, Book 7* — A journey across a turbulent continent. Will Galen find the answers he seeks?

Eternal City, *Life of Galen, Book 8* — *Coming JUNE 2023*

AUDIOBOOKS with a human narrator

Fraternity of Brothers, *Life of Galen, Book 1* – Cast out for a crime committed against him, his future looks bleak. Until an unexpected visitor gives him hope for justice. A fight for acceptance, absolution and friendship in Anglo-Saxon England.

Comfort of Home, *Life of Galen, Book 2* – Proven innocent, he's returned from exile. Can he recover all that he lost? A tale of friendship and return to a family he thought he'd lost, set in Anglo-Saxon England.

Kindness of Strangers, *Life of Galen, Book 3* – Trapped in a land plagued by vikings, can one small miracle be all they need to survive? A tale of miracles, betrayal and friendship while under viking siege.

HISTORICAL ROMANCE: available ePub, paperback, hardback and audiobooks with AI narration
Sanctuary, *a sweet Medieval mystery* – He needs shelter. She wants a way out. Will his brave move to protect risk both their hearts? An optimistic tale of redemption with heart-warming characters and feel-good thrills.
The Duke's Heart, *a sweet Victorian romance* – His body may be weak, but his dreams know no bounds. Will she be the answer to his prayers? A disabled duke, a strong and determined woman and a slow-building relationship.
Duchess in Flight, *a swashbuckling romance* – She's on the run from a deadly enemy. He lives in the shadows of truth. When their lives merge, will their battle for survival lead to love? A reluctant hero, a woman and her children in distress, a chase to the death.
What the Pauper Did, *a body swap mystery romance* – How do you define yourself? Is it through your appearance, your memories or your soul? Intrigue, murder and romance in an alternate Lisbon of 1770.

CONTEMPORARY ROMANCE available ePub, paperback, hardback and audiobooks with AI narration
Scent of Love – Can two polar opposite perfumers be able to overcome their differences and create a unique blend all of their own? Love, intrigue and clashing values in the perfume houses of Lisbon.
Sky Therapy — A detective and the son of a serial killer. Is it safest to stay apart, or will they risk everything for love?

SCIENCE FICTION/ FANTASY available ePub and paperback
City of Night, *Eternal City, Book 1* – World-threatening danger, a female demonologist, an unwitting apprentice, a city in a single tower, a satisfying ending.

SHORT STORIES: available ePub, paperback, and AI narration
Living, Loving, Longing, Lisbon – A collection of short stories inspired by the city of Lisbon, written by people from around the world who live in, visited or love Lisbon.

FREEBIES: available ePub and AI narration
Shorties – My shortest works: futuristic, contemporary and historical.
White Rabbit of Lisbon – A whimsical short story. What will happen when a rabbit and a raven fall in love?
Scourge of Demons – How would you deal with your demons? A short story set in the world of the Life of Galen series.
The Greek Gift – A Christmas short story. At the gym he ignored her; will it be any different at the Christmas Eve party?
Christmas Fates – A Christmas short story. Aurora Dawn is about to learn the true meaning of Christmas and it has nothing to do with how many of the latest must-haves she can sell.

About Author

Marina Pacheco a binge writer of historical fiction, sweet romance, sci-fi and fantasy novels as well as short stories. She writes easy reading, feel-good novels that are perfect for a commute or to curl up with on a rainy day. She currently lives on the coast just outside Lisbon, after stints in London, Johannesburg, and Bangkok, which all sounds more glamorous than it actually was. Her ambition is to publish 100 books. This is taking considerably longer than she'd anticipated!

You can find out more about Marina Pacheco's work, and download several freebies, on her website:
https://marinapacheco.me
Website: https://marinapacheco.me
Patreon: https://www.patreon.com/marinapacheco
Facebook: https://bit.ly/marinas-books
email: hi@marinapacheco.me

Acknowledgments

Although writing is a solitary exercise, it is enhanced by the support and enthusiasm of friends and family. I may not have got to this point without their encouragement. I owe special thanks to:

My writing friends and my beta readers, who sent back constructive suggestions, and my advance copy team for their early reviews and comments. All of you have taught me so much over the years.

My editor, Katharine D'Souza of Katherine D'Sousa Editorial Services for her thoughtful and kind feedback that significantly improves all my work. http://www.katharinedsouza.co.uk

My meticulous proofreader, Candida Burrows. Any errors that remain in the book are purely my fault. cb0880921@gmail.com

My cover designers, for their fantastic cover. www.100covers

All I can say is thank you, and let's do it all again!